CFS
LIBRARY

Mr. Monk Helps Himself

The Monk Series

Mr. Monk Helps Himself

Mr. Monk Gets Even

Mr. Monk Is a Mess

Mr. Monk on Patrol

Mr. Monk on the Couch

Mr. Monk on the Road

Mr. Monk Is Cleaned Out

Mr. Monk in Trouble

Mr. Monk and the Dirty Cop

Mr. Monk Is Miserable

Mr. Monk Goes to Germany

Mr. Monk in Outer Space

Mr. Monk and the Two Assistants

Mr. Monk and the Blue Flu

Mr. Monk Goes to Hawaii

Mr. Monk Goes to the Firehouse

MR. MONK HELPS HIMSELF

A NOVEL BY

HY CONRAD

Based on the USA Network television series created by

ANDY BRECKMAN

AN OBSIDIAN MYSTERY

OBSIDIAN
Published by the Penguin Group
Penguin Group (USA) Inc., 375 Hudson Street,
New York, New York 10014, USA

USA | Canada | UK | Ireland | Australia | New Zealand | India | South Africa | China

Penguin Books Ltd., Registered Offices: 80 Strand, London WC2R 0RL, England
For more information about the Penguin Group visit penguin.com.

First published by Obsidian, an imprint of New American Library,
a division of Penguin Group (USA) Inc.

First Printing, June 2013

LIBRARY OF CONGRESS CATALOGING-IN-PUBLICATION DATA:
Conrad, Hy.
Mr. Monk helps himself/Hy Conrad.
p. cm.
ISBN 978-0-451-24093-4
1. Monk, Adrian (Fictitious character)—Fiction. 2. Private investigators—Fiction. 3. Eccentrics and eccentricities—Fiction. 4. Obsessive-compulsive disorder—Fiction. 5. Murder—Investigation—Fiction. 6. San Francisco (Calif.)—Fiction. 7. Mystery fiction. 8. Radio and television novels.
I. Breckman, Andy. II. Monk (Television program) III. Title.
PS3553.O5166M7 2013
813'.54—dc23 2013001049

Printed in the United States of America
10 9 8 7 6 5 4 3 2 1

Set in ITC New Baskerville

To Jeff, as always

AUTHOR'S NOTE AND ACKNOWLEDGMENTS

When it was announced I was taking over these novels, *Monk* fans started contacting me in droves, all asking the same question. Was I going to reboot the series, like a Batman or Spider-Man franchise, or just pick up where Lee Goldberg left off?

To be honest, I never thought of rebooting. To me, the *Monk* characters are real. On the TV show, the other writers and I took Monk and Natalie to a certain place in their lives. Meanwhile, in a parallel universe, Lee continued to expand them, smoothing out little bumps and creating new ones. I didn't want to mess with that reality.

In the new books, some things will naturally be different, because Lee and I are naturally different. For example, his Natalie knows a lot about architecture. Mine, not so much. His Monk is more obsessed with numbers and symmetry. Mine is a little more phobic.

In many ways, Lee strengthened the *Monk* franchise. For one thing, he knows San Francisco and the wonderful character of the town. We wrote the show in Summit, New Jersey, and, while we did have a San Francisco map, it was pinned on the far wall and no one wandered over there very often. I'll try to improve on our atmospheric quality; I promise.

The same goes for forensic accuracy. Lee had called on a cadre of experts to make sure his details were right. Despite our own police consultant, the *Monk* writers tried not to burden ourselves with too many facts. At one point, the production team called to tell us our formula for bomb making was ridiculous. We replied, "Do you really want us broadcasting how to make a bomb?" That shut them up.

The good news is that we were sticklers for logic. We may not have known bomb making, but we insisted that the logic of every story always worked.

The other good news is that I was with the show from beginning to end, for all eight years. I was the mystery guy, while everyone else had come from the world of comedy. Along the way, I think I had some influence on the way Monk talked and interacted. In other words, he wound up a little bit like me, which makes writing for him a pleasure.

When I first told Andy Breckman I was doing this, his response was "Great. You can use some of the Monk stories we never got to do."

Mr. Monk Helps Himself is one of those stories. I brought it into the writers' room during season six. We played around with the idea until it morphed into something totally different—"Mr. Monk Joins a Cult," guest starring Howie Mandel. That's how it happens in a roomful of writers. There are dozens of great plots, half thought through, buzzing around in our collective memory.

As for acknowledgments, first and foremost, there's Andy Breckman, the founder of the feast, the heart and soul of Monk.

I also want to thank Lee Goldberg for creating this parallel universe and for taking such great care in preserving the characters and sending them off in new, unexpected directions.

I know Monk doesn't like change. But I hope you can put up with a little. It's part of life, as Natalie keeps telling him.

If you would like to say hello, I would love to hear from you, either on my Facebook fan page or at my Web site at hyconrad.com.

Enjoy!

Mr. Monk
Helps
Himself

••••• CHAPTER ONE

Mr. Monk Takes the Temperature

My boss has gotten easier to handle since I realized he's a magpie.

I don't mean that literally. Literally, he's a consulting detective for the San Francisco PD, a man who has solved hundreds of impossible cases, usually with me at his side keeping him calm and handing him antiseptic wipes.

I mean that he's distracted by shiny objects—only in his case the objects are odd numbers and germs and dirt and a hundred major phobias. Exactly one hundred. There's a list in a binder, centered on the coffee table. Whenever a new phobia pops up, he has to either eliminate one of the old ones or, more often, combine a couple.

By the way, in case you're thinking that's not bad, he keeps an addendum in the back listing over three hundred secondary phobias that didn't make the cut.

Just last week, he was watching Animal Planet and discovered his horrific fear of aardvarks. I don't know why this didn't come up years ago, especially since it's probably the first fear in the alphabet. But, in order to accommodate aardvarks, he had to lump together spiders and insects, even though spiders are not technically insects. He now labels it his creepy-crawly phobia and it's number seven.

As you probably already know, my boss is Adrian Monk—a man who has put away so many bad guys the state of California was thinking of naming a cell block after him.

My name is Natalie Teeger, unlegendary, underpaid and overworked. I'm not saying overworked like a coal miner or a medieval peasant. But overworked like the assistant to a brilliant and very stubborn six-year-old.

For years I'd been Monk's sidekick, dealing with his quirks and phobias, but also helping him more and more on his cases. Then, through a long series of events—I won't go into them here, but they included a fire bombing and a very weird murder—I was hired as a police officer across the country in the beautifully upscale town of Summit, New Jersey.

I know that sounds odd. Who in her right mind would move away from her friends and family and start over as a rookie cop? Natalie Teeger, I guess. I just felt it was important, for my self-esteem, to prove that I could be a cop on my own.

Well, I did it. I proved it. And now I'm back in San Francisco with Monk. With one big change. He won't be my boss. We'll be partners—once I pass the California Private Investigator Exam.

Monk himself isn't a licensed PI. For one thing, he's horrible at tests. Not because of the questions, but because he has to sharpen and resharpen the pencil and then fill in every circle so that it's completely black and within the borders. So it's up to me to get the license and incorporate and make our business legit. Monk and Teeger, Consulting Detectives.

Back to the shiny object.

When I rolled out of bed that Friday morning, I knew I had to come up with a distraction, something that would keep Monk from figuring out the real reason I needed this upcoming weekend off.

I'd been planning this getaway for a long time. I needed it. And I'd paid for it, nonrefundable. The last thing I wanted was Monk coming up with some excuse why I couldn't go. Or, worse, coming with me. That would transform the weekend from "all about me" to "all about him," and I would need another weekend, right away, just to get over it.

Lucky for me the phone rang during my first cup of Peet's French Roast, and half an hour later, Monk was busy focusing on two home invasions, two assaults and a murder. Very shiny.

I know how callous that sounds, but the murder would have happened anyway. And the most distracting object you can put in front of Adrian Monk is a good old-fashioned crime scene.

The first home invasion was on Vernon Street in Ingleside Heights. When Monk and I ducked under the crime scene tape, we found ourselves inside a lovingly restored Craftsman bungalow. Captain Leland Stottlemeyer was there to greet us and hand us disposable gloves and those blue booties to fit over our shoes. "Morning," he said, with a bit of a growl. "Body in the kitchen."

Captain Stottlemeyer and Monk go way back. He had been watch commander when Monk joined the force. He'd also been the best man at Monk's wedding and the first person to try to console him when his wife, Trudy, was killed by a car bomb. He was the man who had had to fire Monk when his fear of life became too disabling, and the man who had hired him four years later as a consultant on the city's most puzzling cases.

The body, in this case, belonged to Barry Ebersol, midforties, a little soft through the middle, an account manager at an advertising agency. Now he was just a pudgy corpse with stab wounds in the back and hands and a meat thermometer sticking out of his chest.

He was lying on the beige granite tiles, a few feet from black marble countertops and a gorgeous fireclay farmhouse sink. It always makes me sad when people die right after remodeling. Seems such a waste. But I guess murder is always a waste.

"Is that a meat thermometer?" Monk asked, and followed up with a little shiver. "That's so wrong."

"Any murder weapon is wrong," the captain suggested.

"But that belongs in a rib roast, at worst a pork loin, not in a person. It's sick."

Stottlemeyer shrugged. "A carving knife belongs in a rib roast, too. And you've seen dozens of those used for murder. What's the difference?"

"I don't care what you say. It's wrong and sick." That was Adrian Monk for you. Anything out of his normal realm of experience made him uncomfortable, even if he couldn't explain why.

The CSIs had retreated into the dining room. The two of them stood in the doorway, gloved and bootied and with the smallest of smirks crinkling their mouths. "At least we know his body temperature," the taller one said, pointing to the thermometer.

Stottlemeyer brushed his bushy mustache, but I could tell he was smiling. "It was a break-in," he informed us, and pointed to a broken glass panel in the kitchen door, right above the lock.

"In broad daylight?" I asked, practicing for the day when I actually got my license. "That's risky."

"Ebersol's car is in the shop. The intruder must have seen the empty driveway and assumed he'd left for the day."

"So . . . ," I went on. "Ebersol catches the guy in his house. One of them grabs a meat thermometer from"—I looked around until I saw it—"from the pot of utensils by the window. They fight. And Ebersol gets stabbed."

"He put up quite a fight," Stottlemeyer agreed, glancing once more around the kitchen.

It was a mess all right. I had to keep my eye on Monk's hands. On more than one occasion, when his OCD was particularly bad, the captain and I had to forcibly keep him from straightening up. There had been one case where he came back after the CSIs left and scrubbed an entire crime scene apartment. The killer actually got her cleaning deposit back.

This time his hands didn't even twitch. "A home invasion gone bad," Monk said with a dismissive shrug. "Why call us in?"

"Because there's a nearly identical one five blocks away."

Soon we were standing in the kitchen of another bungalow. This one hadn't been renovated. In fact, the whole house could have used some work. On the plus side, the victim was alive.

Stottlemeyer had stayed behind at the first house. At this scene, our tour guide was Lieutenant Devlin. She's been Stottlemeyer's number two for a few years now, ever since Lieutenant Randy Disher decided to leave and become police chief in the aforementioned town of Summit. I'll bet you could live your whole life in Summit and never once see a meat thermometer used improperly.

It had taken me a while to get used to Amy Devlin. Before coming here, she'd been an undercover officer, a breed that seems to live on macho bravado. It couldn't have been easy for her to hold her own in that boys' club. When she came here, Devlin brought a lot of that swagger with her. But we don't swagger much in Captain Stottlemeyer's world. We're more like a family—a dysfunctional family that probably spends too much time together.

"This was the second attack," Devlin said, gnawing on a toothpick in the side of her mouth. She was slightly taller than me, with an incredible body and short black hair that looked like it had been coiffed by Edward Scissorhands.

Monk wasn't listening. He was staring down at an evidence bag in his hands. Inside was another bloody meat thermometer. "This is wronger than wrong. His voice was trembling. "Wronger than wronger than wrong."

"Maybe it's a coincidence." I'm glad Devlin said that, not me. But I was thinking it.

"Coincidence?" Monk shot back. "Over two decades in police work and I've never seen a meat thermometer used to kill. Now we have two in one day? Less than a day. How far apart were these attacks?"

Devlin checked her notes. "Twenty minutes. A neighbor heard the altercation at Ebersol's house around eight a.m. It was an elderly woman and she called it in without coming over to check. At around eight twenty, Ms. Phister called nine one one and reported the second attack."

The victim this time was Angela Phister, a twentysomething bartender with a closetful of T-shirts and a Harley parked on the front weed patch. She had been luckier or stronger or just angrier than Barry Ebersol. When the paramedics arrived, she was lying in a pool of blood, left for dead, clutching a deep hole in her side.

"She was being evacuated when I arrived," Devlin said. "I'm going over to San Fran General after this to see if she's strong enough to talk. All the evidence points to this being the same perp."

I know I've previously stated that Monk doesn't use sarcasm. I stand corrected. The look he threw her was pure sarcasm. "Really? You think? Don't jump to any conclusions."

He shook his head and put on a new pair of gloves. A second later and he was opening and closing drawers. He finally found what he was looking for. It was a bottom drawer filled with a few dozen cooking utensils. "This makes even less sense," he said.

"What do you mean?" Devlin asked.

Here's where I jumped in. I was almost a full partner, and I wanted to show that Monk and I were on the same page. "He means the first attack is reasonable."

"Barely reasonable," Monk interjected. "Reasonable anarchy."

I jumped in again. "Ebersol kept his meat thermometer in a pot on the counter. So it's reasonable that someone might have grabbed it to use as a weapon."

"Barely reasonable."

"But the second victim, Angela Phister, kept her utensils in a bottom drawer."

"No one grabbed a knife, even though they were right here." Monk pointed to the magnetic strip by the stove, covered with a row of cheap kitchen knives. "No, they opened a drawer—a bottom drawer—and rooted around and found the most disgusting, improbable weapon imaginable. Why?"

Devlin gave the room a few seconds of thoughtful silence. "Maybe it's not her thermometer. Maybe the attacker brought his own."

"Brought his own?" Monk gasped and blinked. "You mean instead of a gun or a knife? He started a crime spree with a handful of meat thermometers?"

"Maybe they mean something to him."

"Meat thermometers? Do you think our killer is a deranged chef who wants to make sure his victims are well done?"

"I don't know!" Devlin shouted. "Give me a theory, Mr. Genius. Any theory. Why do we have two such attacks five blocks apart within twenty minutes?"

"Well, it's not a coincidence," he shot back. "And it's not a new rage in weapons."

"Then what is it?"

I certainly didn't have an answer. But Monk did. I could see the light dawn in his eyes.

"There weren't two attacks. There was one."

"What do you mean?" At least she'd stopped shouting.

"Angela Phister is our bad guy," Monk said, thinking as he talked. "She and Ebersol fought in his kitchen. Don't ask me why. One of them grabs the meat thermometer. And both of them get stabbed, which serves them right for picking such a stupid weapon."

Devlin scrunched up her nose, like she was fighting off a nasty sneeze. "Then why would she go home and call the police?"

"She needed medical attention. And how else could she explain her wound? Any hospital would report a serious wound like that, and you guys would be on it in a minute."

"I suppose we would," Devlin said grudgingly.

"Of course," I added. "You're too smart to let that slip."

Devlin nodded and took the scenario from here. "So, she goes home, grabs the thermometer from her own kitchen, and makes up the story about being attacked by the same perp." Her mouth scrunched again. "But why kill Ebersol in the first place?"

"I told you not to ask me that."

"You asked for a theory," I reminded the lieutenant. "We gave you a theory. As far as I know, it's the only one that makes sense."

"That's fair," she had to admit. "All we have to do is comb through the evidence and see if it fits. Damn. Why do murders always come right before the weekend?"

"Oh, speaking of weekends . . ." This was my opportunity and I took it. "Mr. Monk, I won't be around this weekend. I'm spending some time with my girlfriends."

"What girlfriends?"

Devlin laughed. "C'mon, Monk. Every girl has girlfriends."

"Okay," he mumbled, then began to circle the kitchen. His hands were up now, framing the scene like a director on a movie set, his eyes focused on everything and nothing. "We'll manage without you. Have fun."

What did I tell you? A magpie.

CHAPTER TWO

Mr. Monk and the Cult

Of course I wasn't spending the weekend with girlfriends. Monk was right. I didn't have any, not in the Carrie Bradshaw, let's-go-to-Vegas sense. I had told my twenty-two-year-old daughter, Julie, that I was attending a weekend seminar, preparing for the upcoming California PI exam, which was also a lie. I didn't even bring along my study guide.

Lying usually bothers me, especially to loved ones. But this weekend was special. I didn't need their permission or curious questions. The very thought of explaining it to anyone seemed to diminish the whole experience. Look at me. I'm having a hard time just explaining it on paper.

It all began back in Summit, when Randy Disher first invited Monk and me to come and help him out. One of the people we met while in Summit was a blond, blue-eyed beauty named Ellen Morse. Monk was attracted to her immediately. The feeling was mutual. But it all ground to a halt when he found out what she did for a living.

Ellen had opened a store on the main drag in Summit called Poop. And, yes, that's what it sold: dinosaur poop fossils that were real works of art; poop stationery and inks; fireplace logs made from Scottish peat; even poopy bags for dogs. These were made from a special plastic mixed with ground, sanitized dog feces and sold mainly as a novelty item. "Pick up your dog poop with our dog poop."

I won't go into detail about Monk's on-again, off-again relationship with Ellen. After all, this weekend was about me, not him. But when Ellen impulsively decided to open up a Poop store in San Francisco, only part of her rationale was to get physically closer to my boss.

The other part was to be closer to the BPM Sanctuary at Half Moon Bay.

"I can't believe you never heard of it," she said one day as we lingered over a couple of chai lattes at the Starbucks directly across from her Summit store.

"I've heard of Half Moon Bay," I replied. It was a sleepy little town south of the city, with seaside cliffs and pristine beaches. The majority of tourists tend to ignore it for some reason, maybe because it's too close to San Francisco and all the flashier attractions of the city.

"But you never heard of Miranda Bigley?"

Of course I'd heard of Miranda Bigley. She was a national presence, a self-help guru, queen of the infomercials, right up there with Tony Robbins.

"It's not as tacky as it sounds," Ellen assured me. "In fact, it changed my life."

I knew that Ellen was obsessive-compulsive. It was one of the things that drew her to Monk and made her so understanding of his foibles. Her OCD symptoms were much less severe than his. But there had been a time, she told me, just a few years ago, when she had almost been paralyzed by her need for order and neatness.

Then one night she saw the infomercial for BPM—Best Possible Me.

"Sure, I was skeptical," she told me that afternoon. "We've seen these things a million times. But something spoke to me that night. Maybe it was Miranda herself. She seemed so genuine and understanding. It made me think I could have control over my life."

Our Starbucks chat ended with her lending me the CDs. For the next few weeks, whenever I was alone in the patrol car, or lying on the pull-out sofa in Randy Disher's living room late at night, I listened to Miranda's voice.

Her life plan, as she called it, was simple. It probably wasn't all that different from other self-help strategies. But Ellen was right. Something about Miranda spoke to me, too, telling me what to accept about myself and how to improve the rest. It was, in short, a revelation.

This introduction to BPM happened at a pivotal point in my life. I had persuaded Monk to move cross-country with me to accept temporary jobs with the Summit PD. When Randy Disher offered to make our positions permanent, I jumped at the chance, but Monk opted to move back to San Francisco. Of course, I would eventually change my mind and move back as well.

I may have made it sound easy when I wrote about all of this before. But it takes a toll on you. It has to. You question your judgments about life and you worry—worry so much—about your family and what you're putting them through.

Everyone had been wonderful, of course. Randy said he understood completely. But I knew I was leaving him and the town of Summit in the lurch, one officer short, even though he had done so much and bent so many rules to get me hired in the first place.

Miranda and the BPM CDs were just about the only thing that got me through the ordeal, helping me understand my decisions and realize that this is all part of my path to create a better me.

All right, enough of my personal mumbo-jumbo. Let's just say that as soon as I settled back into my cozy Victorian row house in San Francisco and unpacked my bags, I made my reservation for the BPM weekend retreat. It would be my necessary little gift to myself.

That Friday, after leaving Monk and Devlin to their meat thermometers, I drove less than an hour south to what was probably the highest point overlooking Half Moon Bay.

The BPM property was sprawling but modest. And absolutely perfect. The main building was a retro 1960s structure, all stacked stone and glass, like the James Mason house in *North by Northwest.* And like the James Mason house, it was cantilevered over a section of cliff.

The rest of the Sanctuary consisted of a small meditation center, more stacked stone and glass, surrounded by a collection of adorable shingled cottages, all situated on an emerald green lawn leading down to a different section of the same craggy cliff.

I checked in with the friendliest staff I'd ever met and had a light dinner with two dozen people, who were just as excited as I was to be there. After settling into my little one-room cottage, I listened to my favorite Miranda CD, then fell into bed. In five minutes I was serenaded to sleep by the pounding surf just fifty yards from my door.

The next morning, Miranda welcomed us and outlined the weekend. I'd come to know her well, or thought I had, from the infomercial and the CDs.

She was a slight woman, thin and fit and a few years older than me. Her hair was cut short at a few odd angles and dyed unapologetically red, almost crimson. But her best feature was her smile, wide and open, like Julia Roberts' before she started doing those more serious films.

For the rest of the morning, Miranda's husband, Damien, led us through an Actualization-Visualization session in the main building. It lasted almost three hours but felt like ten minutes.

I was having lunch afterward—a warm crabmeat salad over fresh greens from the Sanctuary garden. Delicious. I sat by myself at a table for two on the lawn, thinking how fulfilling it can be when you decide to own and celebrate your choices.

And that's when Monk walked in. He spotted me from across the lawn and headed straight my way.

"I knew you'd joined a cult," he said. Before I could stop him, he'd wiped down the other chair and joined me. "Am I going to have to kidnap you and do an intervention?"

"It's not a cult. How did you know I was here?"

" 'A,' you don't have any girlfriends, despite what the lieutenant says, and 'B,' I could tell you and Ellen had some sort of secret going. All it took was a simple two-hour phone call for me to worm it out of her."

Poor Ellen. I didn't blame her for buckling. Anyone would.

"How did you get here? You can barely drive. And you hate taxis, not to mention public transportation."

"I have my ways," he said with a twitch and an uncomfortable shrug. That's one thing I've learned about Adrian Monk. He may seem completely helpless, but he can do all sorts of things when he really wants to.

"How did the thermometer case work out?" I asked, hoping to distract him back to his shiny object. For a minute it worked.

"Ms. Phister's in stable condition," he reported. "And she's sticking to her story. She swears she interrupted a burglar who grabbed the thermometer from her drawer and attacked her."

"What about physical evidence?"

"The CS techs are concentrating on Barry Ebersol's kitchen. It's only a matter of time before they find a trace of her blood. Then it's a done deal."

"What about motive? Why'd she kill him?"

"Simple," he said with a dismissive wave. "Devlin kept trying to find some connection between the victim and Ms. Phister. I think Devlin's a romantic at heart. But then we found six bags of golf clubs in her garage, along with a lot of jewelry boxes. Nine to be precise. Plus eight iPads."

"So, Angela isn't a spurned lover. She's a break-in artist."

"Not an artist." Monk hated it when people tried to glorify crime. "She's a burglar. A thief."

"And she burgled houses in her own neighborhood?"

"Her own little crime spree. You know, over half of all crimes occur within half a kilometer of where the perpetrator lives. That's a fact. It was in the official newsletter."

"Burglars send out a newsletter?"

Monk smirked. "The Museum of Crime and Punishment

in Washington, DC. Very informative. Did you know that Jesse James was shot while he was standing on a chair, dusting the top of a picture frame?"

"You must have mixed feelings about that," I suggested.

He nodded vigorously. "I know. On the one hand, a cold-blooded killer was finally brought down. On the other hand . . . he was *dusting*!"

"Wasn't he also shot in the back?"

"Sure, but that's not the important part. The man was dusting. What kind of coward shoots a man when he's dusting?"

"I wonder if he finished the entire frame."

"My question exactly. I wrote a letter to the True West Historical Society but they never replied."

"Natalie, hello. Why don't you introduce me to your friend?"

I had been so busy distracting Monk that I never saw her coming. Miranda was standing right over us now, her Julia Roberts smile beaming down. Competing with her smile was a simple but stunning strand of natural pearls, perfectly matched. It was another one of her trademarks. She held out a hand toward Monk.

"Miranda." I was mortified. "This is my friend. Adrian Monk—Miranda Bigley. Miranda is the founder of the BPM Sanctuary." I was using my "don't embarrass me" voice, but it did no good.

Monk is usually a gentleman, except for things like opening doors and pulling out chairs. Germs, you know. This time he didn't even get up. "I would shake your hand," he said. "But 'A,' I don't shake hands, and 'B,' I don't shake hands with cult leaders."

"I appreciate your candor," Miranda said with an easy nod. "But you should leave yourself open to new ideas. That's the only way to maximize happiness."

"Happiness is overrated."

She smiled brilliantly. "You need to change your ratings system."

"No, thanks, Ms. Cult Leader." That was his idea of a snappy rejoinder.

"He's leaving," I blurted out. "I promise he'll be gone in two minutes."

"No problem. Enjoy your visit, Adrian." And she moved on to the guests at the next table.

"I guess I told her," Monk said, loud enough for everyone to hear.

"Mr. Monk, you have to go."

"I'm not leaving without you," he hissed. "Anyone who runs an infomercial is running a cult. It's a fact."

"What about cleaning products?" I countered. "They have infomercials. What about Billy Mays? Was he a cult leader? The man who brought us OxyClean and the Shamwow?"

Monk gasped, as if I'd just insulted the pope, a very, very clean pope. "Take that back. Billy Mays was a saint. How dare you say his name in the same sentence with this Jell-O-haired charlatan!"

"How do you know she's a charlatan?"

"Natalie, I know cults. I was in one."

That was, in fact, true. My boss had once gone undercover into the Siblings of the Sun, trying to find out if their leader had been involved in a brutal murder of a young woman at a highway rest stop. Within two days, we had had to kidnap

Monk back from the cult and deprogram him. It wasn't pretty.

"Cults are tough to resist," he said, looking as modest as he could. "I can just imagine what it must be like for someone who doesn't have my natural willpower."

"Natural willpower?"

We went back and forth like this for several minutes. I stopped paying attention.

My mouth kept moving. Clever words kept coming out. But I was focused over Monk's shoulder on Miranda, willing her to ignore us until I could force Monk—physically, if need be—to walk through the gates and off the grounds to whatever mode of transportation might take him home.

Miranda had moved on to the last table, a pair of couples who had traveled from Connecticut just for this weekend. I was afraid she might come back our way afterward. But she didn't.

Good, I thought, sending out whatever vibes I could. Keep going the other way.

And she did. Miranda slowly lifted her arms above her head in what resembled a yoga stretch. Then, with a steady, purposeful gait, she walked toward the sea and the sound of the surf against the jagged rocks. When she reached the edge, she barely hesitated.

Then she jumped off the cliff.

CHAPTER THREE

Mr. Monk's Kryptonite

People talk about things being surreal. Personally, I think the word is overused. But there's no other way for me to describe the situation.

At one moment, a smiling woman with everything to live for is walking among her fans, exchanging pleasantries and talking about a weekend full of self-improvement. The next moment, she's walking up to a cliff and jumping off.

Dozens of us saw it. And yet for the first few seconds, no one reacted. Again, surreal. It couldn't be real. People looked at one another, then back at the cliff, then at one another. Monk wasn't even aware anything was wrong, except that I was no longer even pretending to pay attention. Then someone screamed.

Damien Bigley was the first to move. "Miranda!" he shouted at the top of his lungs, and ran across the lawn. Then as if he'd just thrown a switch, the rest of us unfroze from our trance and followed him.

There was no barricade at the edge, just the end of the emerald green lawn, a few outcroppings of rock and a sheer drop. The tide was in—that was mentioned later in the sheriff's report—and the waves were crashing right up against the sandy cliffs. Miranda was nowhere in sight.

Monk and I had somehow wound up at the front. The pack of people pressed up against us, and for a second, I thought we might get pushed over the edge ourselves. Monk was in an especially dangerous position. He can't stand being touched, even under the best circumstances. And now, with a human horde behind him jostling for a better view, I could see him considering jumping, just to get away from them.

I grabbed his arm and he didn't pull away. "What happened?" he asked.

"Miranda Bigley jumped." I couldn't believe I was saying those words. But I guess they were true.

Everyone was gazing out over the Pacific now, listening through the surf for any sounds of life. Miranda had been wearing a bright yellow top, but there was no dot of yellow visible in the churning waves. One of the guests had taken out his phone and was filming the empty expanse of blue-green water.

Monk leaned into me, a very somber look in his eye. "Was it because of me?"

"What? No, Mr. Monk. Not everything is about you."

"Well, I was pretty brutal. I called the woman a cult leader. Some people can't take criticism."

"That's ridiculous," I shot back. "Miranda Bigley was a strong woman."

"And yet she killed herself right after talking to me."

"A lot of people feel that way. But there are no documented cases of Monk-related suicides. Believe me, I should know."

"Not until now. Cult leaders have very fragile egos."

The man with the camera phone pointed it off to a small red object bobbing in the foam, buffeted between a pair of black rocks. "Sandal," he shouted. "That's one of her sandals." Then he went back to filming.

Within half an hour, the San Mateo County Sheriff's Office had arrived, cordoning off the cliff with yellow tape and taking our statements. The helicopter arrived around the same time, making great sweeps up and down the shoreline. Within an hour of the jump, two coast guard boats were patrolling the waters in front of the Sanctuary. I could see several divers in scuba gear and wet suits waiting on deck.

The meditation center became the hub of the rescue operations. Monk and I sat in a corner, filling out statement cards. Actually, I filled out mine, then filled out Monk's for him. I find that this is faster, since he always takes so much time perfectly writing out each letter. More than once, people have mistaken his penmanship for a computer printout. In case you're interested, his chosen font is Times New Roman. For years and years, he did Helvetica, but then developed an issue with their lowercase "s."

"Do you think I should identify myself?" he asked, glancing across to a sheriff's deputy.

"You mean being a police consultant?" I looked up from his half-completed card. "I didn't mention it on mine. This isn't a crime scene."

"I mean as the person who drove her to suicide."

"You didn't drive her to"—I lowered my voice—"to anything. Don't flatter yourself."

"Can I borrow a pen?" The interruption came from a girl

in her midtwenties—tall and muscularly lean, with a reddish brown bob and bangs that accentuated her perfect jawline. I recognized her from the staff orientation. Teresa Garcia, the Sanctuary's massage therapist. When I'd arrived last night, I set up an appointment, but I didn't think either of us would be in the mood for it now.

"Sure," I said, and began to rummage through my bag.

"Have they found her yet?"

"Not that I know of." I handed her the pen. "Keep it."

"Thanks." She sighed. "It's so inexplicable. Miranda's whole business was self-fulfillment and happiness. She's talked people out of suicide. If she was having any troubles at all, there were a hundred people she could have turned to. Why, for heaven's sake?"

"Well, I did say something to her," Monk said. "About her cult—"

"Mr. Monk," I interrupted. "Teresa is a massage therapist here. Teresa, this is my friend Adrian Monk. He came for lunch."

I told you about my magpie strategy. This was another example. And it worked. The idea of talking to a woman who touches half-naked people for a living was too much. It would be like me learning that this woman was a snake handler or raised leaches for medical purposes. It was just enough to shut him up.

"Nice to meet you," Teresa said, and was slightly taken aback when Monk's hands flew into his pockets. "I'm sorry you had to visit us under such horrible circumstances."

I was prepared for the moment to get more awkward but was saved by the appearance of Damien Bigley, coming from the other side of the center. "Teresa, sorry to interrupt."

Damien was a George Clooney type. In fact, I wouldn't be surprised if he purposely modeled himself after the heartthrob actor. He was large but not heavy, well-dressed but not fussy. But it was a look that could easily turn disheveled—and at the moment, Damien was looking disheveled. He apologized to us as well, then turned back to Teresa.

"I have to get out of here for a while, to preserve my sanity."

"What about the press?" she asked gently. "There are at least two TV trucks outside the gates. You can see the antennas from here."

"They're going to be like vultures." He shook his head. "There's nothing they like more than irony. First the owner of the Segway company accidentally drives one off a cliff. Now a self-help guru commits suicide. They're going to reduce poor Miranda to a sick joke." His voice caught in his throat.

What he was saying was absolutely true. I remember the case of Jim Fixx. Back in my teenage years he'd been kind of a hero of mine, the man who practically invented jogging. I started doing it myself and lost a ton of weight, which did wonders for my popularity. But when Jim Fixx died of a heart attack while jogging, the late-night comics were all over it.

"Mr. Bigley," I said. "I'm so sorry. I don't know what else to say."

"Thank you. We'll get through this. Anyway, I need a little drive along the coast. Clear my head." He took out a set of keys. "The gardener's pickup is by the side gate. I'm pretty sure I can get away without being seen."

"I'll take care of things here," Teresa promised. She put a comforting arm on his shoulder and walked him out the door.

"I'm glad to see they're getting along," Monk said as they disappeared from view.

He expected me to understand. I didn't. "What do you mean, getting along?"

"They had a big fight. From the shade of the coagulated blood on his left earlobe, I'd say two hours ago. And there's the tiniest drop of blood on her collar. She hasn't noticed it yet, so I assume that's fairly recent, too. The most obvious theory is the two of them had a fight and she bit his ear."

Oh! I guess I'd seen the blood, too, now that I thought about it: a red spot at the very bottom of Damien's ear. And then the equally tiny stain on Teresa's top. I could have kicked myself for not putting the pieces together. But then Monk isn't perfect, either.

"Mr. Monk, I don't think that was from a fight."

"What else could it be?"

"Sex. In fact, I'm pretty sure of it."

If Adrian Monk was like a Superman of detectives, then sex would be his Kryptonite. He just didn't get it, which could be both charming and annoying.

"Sex!" His shoulders twitched twice, two involuntary spasms of revulsion. "Augh! People actually bite each other during coitus? I mean, I've read about it, but I thought it was just folklore."

"It's not folklore. Not that I've ever done it myself," I lied. What's a little love bite on the ear? But I knew he wasn't ready to hear that.

"Good. I don't want anyone I know biting each other like cannibals or preying mantises. What's this world coming to?"

I didn't know what it was coming to. I was too busy thinking about Miranda's husband and the tall Hispanic masseuse at his side. "So, Damien and Teresa are having an affair," I whispered.

"Or a fight," Monk said, then shrugged. "Okay, probably an affair. That would also explain him smelling of her perfume. You don't always get that from a fight."

"No, you don't," I agreed.

CHAPTER FOUR

Mr. Monk Goes Unanswered

I guess it didn't really hit me emotionally until the drive back.

We were barely onto the I-280, heading north when Monk brought up the obvious—insensitive but obvious. "Okay, maybe I didn't cause her suicide," he admitted. "It was her husband's affair. Ms. Cult Leader found out and couldn't handle it."

"That's not true," I protested. "Miranda helped hundreds of women deal with this exact situation. You didn't know her. You can't judge."

"It's not a judgment." He was tightly gripping his seat belt the way he always did when I drove. "In seventy-nine percent of suicides in which one or both partners are having an affair, the affair is the primary cause of the suicide. It's a well-known statistic."

"Well-known? I've never heard of it."

"That's because you don't read the annual report from the World Health Organization. It's in a footnote on page three forty-four."

"Statistics," I snorted, and kept my eyes locked on the

road. "Did you know that sixty-two point seven percent of all statistics are made up?"

"No. You're making that up."

"Exactly."

He winced. "I get it. Humor. Well, that doesn't change the facts. Your beloved cult leader—"

"Stop calling her that," I shouted into the windshield. "She has a name. It's Miranda and she was a wonderful human being. She was more giving and caring than you'll ever be. So don't pretend you know her, because you don't. You don't have a clue. Not a clue."

Looking back on those words, I can see how harsh they sound. But at the moment, they expressed exactly how I felt and I wasn't about to take them back.

For once, in a personal interaction, Monk said the right thing. Nothing. No protest, no statistic, no counterargument. It was probably the only way of stopping my rant, and somewhere inside, he knew it.

We sat for several minutes, until the merge onto 101 North. Then, calmer and sick of the silence, I punched the button on the radio. But instead of the comfort of the classic oldies on 89.3, I heard, "The drive for happiness is a modern phenomenon." It was her voice, soothing and self-assured. "No one asked the cave man if he was happy. Throughout most of history, it was only important that someone's God was made happy or the local lord or king. The life of man, according to an English philosopher, was 'solitary, poor, nasty, brutish, and short.' But we live in different times—wonderful times—with an almost limitless possibility for creating our own joy."

I had forgotten that I'd been listening to the CD on the drive down. I switched it off and the car fell once more into silence. Not quite silence. I found myself sobbing the rest of the way.

I dropped Monk off at his apartment on Pine Street, still crying (me, not him), then steered my middle-aged Subaru down Divisadero to a treelined street and my protective cocoon of a Victorian row house.

There was already a car in my driveway and I was so glad to see it. I parked on the street. By the time I made it to the front door, it was open. Ellen Morse appeared in the doorway, wearing my favorite white apron, her eyes wet with tears, holding open her arms. I fell right into them.

"I knew you taped a key under your mailbox," she said, shutting the door behind us. "I hope you don't mind. But I thought you shouldn't be alone." A familiar savory smell wafted in from the kitchen. "Meat loaf," she explained. "And mac and cheese. Comfort food was invented for moments like this."

This was so Ellen. She wasn't just being empathetic. Anyone can do that, except Monk. But to take it upon yourself to do something big, like buy groceries and break into my house and cook dinner. She even figured out where I kept the garlic press and how to work the temp on my rather temperamental oven.

It was just what I needed. After an early dinner and a bottle and a half of a Napa Valley merlot, we settled into the living room with the other half.

"I had the news on right before you showed up." She'd

obviously been saving this until I'd had my share of merlot. "They found a suicide note. In her bedroom. Her handwriting."

"What did it say?" I asked.

"That part hasn't been released. But I guess she planned it. It wasn't an accident or a spur-of-the-moment thing."

"I know it wasn't an accident. I just need to know why."

She knew what I meant. The system that Miranda invented, the Best Possible Me, had made such a difference for both of us. It was impossible to think that all those words were suddenly meaningless, that the woman who'd said them didn't believe in them enough to save her own life.

Ellen's phone was on the coffee table, and as we sat down with the remnants of the bottle, I could see it vibrating.

"Adrian," she explained, and watched as it went to voice mail. "I canceled on him tonight. He's been calling every ten minutes or so. Knowing him, I'm sure it's exactly every ten minutes."

"You're not going to answer?"

"What's the point? He'll whine and fixate on the fact that I canceled. Then we'll all feel bad and the whole reason for me being here will be defeated."

This made sense, but was also a little out of character. "Is everything all right?"

"Of course," she said in a tone that meant no. Then her tone turned philosophical. "I never needed to question my impulses. If I tend to give more than I get in my relationship with Adrian, that's been my choice."

"As long as it remains a choice," I added, echoing the Miranda Bigley point of view. "When you feel it becoming an obligation or a trap, then you have to reevaluate. Is that what you're doing? Reevaluating?"

This was a tough topic to bring up. I cared for Monk and Ellen both and wanted them each to be happy. Until now, I'd thought these goals were compatible, part of the same scenario. But maybe not.

"No, I love Adrian, quirks and all. I just wish sometimes he could be a little more supportive. For example, does he have to ridicule my career every time we get together? If he could cut the ridicule down to twice a week . . ."

"It was a big step for him, even to say the name of your store. I mean, 'Poop'?"

She shrugged. "Do you have any idea how hard it is running two stores twenty-five hundred miles apart? In this economy? And then to have a loved one constantly make insults . . ."

"He's capable of change."

"Maybe. But Adrian shouldn't have to change for me."

"Yes, he should. You're the best thing to happen to him in years. The only thing."

She chuckled and sighed. "This probably isn't the right time to discuss it, not on the same day our life coach jumped off a cliff."

"Good point." I gulped what was left of my wine and hunted around for the remote. "So . . . I think I have a few episodes of *Dancing with the Stars.*"

"Love that show," Ellen said with a lopsided grin. "Always makes me feel better."

"Does it really?"

"Sure. It's like hitting yourself over the head with a hammer. Makes you forget all about the pain in your foot."

I clicked and we were suddenly in the middle of the ABC local news. Two seconds later and the proverbial pain in the foot was back, throbbing more than ever.

Cindy Namaguci, the entertainment reporter for KGO, stood in front of the Belmont, the grand duchess of Union Square hotels. At her side, looking reluctant and a little trapped, was a familiar face. She had his Clooney-esque arm firmly grasped in her manicured claw.

"We were here this evening to do a segment on the opening night of the San Francisco Tech Expo, happening here in the Belmont ballroom. We'll be showing that later, on the eleven o'clock news."

The reporter's face was trying to strike a balance between tasteful sadness and the elation of a national scoop. "Right now, we've been lucky enough to come across Damien Bigley, chief operating officer of BPM Enterprises and husband of the self-help icon Miranda Bigley, who died today in an apparent suicide at their Half Moon Bay retreat. Mr. Bigley, your wife was beloved by millions of admirers. We're so sorry for your loss."

"Thank you, Cindy. I have no statement at this time." At the bottom of the screen, I could see the top of a rolling suitcase. "As you can imagine, I left the retreat in order to get a little privacy and to try to deal with this tragedy. If you'll excuse me . . ."

"Well, I guess there's no hiding from the press," she simpered.

"I guess not." Then he faced the camera. "My heart goes out to all of Miranda's followers. She was a phenomenal woman who gave so much to so many. Her legacy will go on."

"Can you give us an inkling what may have been behind her alleged suicide? I mean, apparent suicide."

"I don't know. If I'd had any idea at all that she'd been contemplating such a tragic act . . ."

"Who is that?" Ellen had stopped listening and was pointing to a figure in the background. It was a woman half hidden behind the trunk of a California date palm. I could barely make out a reddish brown bob. "Is that Teresa Garcia?"

Ellen had visited the Sanctuary several times during her trips to the West Coast and knew Teresa. Over dinner, I had told her about Monk's sexual deduction and we'd discussed it at length. She'd been as surprised as me.

"Yes," I confirmed, peering at the screen. From her body language, I could sense the athletically built therapist was not happy about her lover being caught on camera. She also had no idea that she was in the shot, looking furtive and impatient behind the trunk of a palm.

Within the next minute, Damien had extricated himself from the interview and pulled his rolling bag through the hotel entrance, leaving Cindy Namaguci to reluctantly go to a commercial. I turned off the set.

"It looks like they're going to be consoling each other

tonight," Ellen said, a tinge of anger in her voice. "I know Adrian is never wrong about his deductions. I just wish he'd been wrong this time."

"Damien and Miranda seemed like a perfect couple," I said, knowing how lame and clichéd that sounded.

"I'm surprised Damien could get a room, what with the Tech Expo in town."

Yes, that did seem odd.

I put the thought out of my mind. But it came back. Yes, it was odd. Every room in the city was usually booked during the three-day Tech Expo, especially a host hotel like the Belmont. And yet Damien and Teresa had gotten a room. Of course, they could have just lucked into a last-minute cancellation. But I had a different hunch.

I told Ellen of my suspicion and she was equally curious. "Is there any way we can find out?" she asked.

"You forget that I'm an ex-cop. Plus, I've had nine years' experience getting information with and without warrants, thanks to Monk." I glanced at the mantel clock. "We'll wait till they're checked in. Then I'll make a call."

We gave them a good ten minutes, during which Ellen opened a third bottle of wine. We promised ourselves, cross our hearts, we weren't going to finish it. Half a glass later, I dialed the front desk.

I had good instincts for how the Belmont's system worked, since I'd recently spent a night there. Normally, I would never dream of staying at such a big-bucks hotel, especially in my hometown. But six months ago my house had been broken into and a woman was killed in my bathtub, so I thought I'd treat myself.

"Hello? This is Teresa Garcia." I tried to make my voice sound young and perky. "We just checked in."

"Uh, yes, Miss Garcia." It was an eager young man with the hint of an Irish brogue. I could hear a few keystrokes on a computer. "Room 714. Can I help you?"

"I hope so," I said, trying for the spoiled, privileged persona that could get me the answers I wanted. "This room you gave us just won't do. Won't do at all."

"Sorry to hear that," he said smoothly. "You are in one of our finer junior suites."

"But it's not the room I reserved. I demand you switch us to another."

"I'm afraid that's impossible, ma'am. We're fully booked. Fully booked for the next three nights, in fact."

"Well, I reserved this well in advance. And I did not reserve a *junior* suite." I winked in Ellen's direction. If it hadn't been so serious, we would have laughed.

"Give me a minute. I'll pull up your reservation." After another thirty seconds of keystrokes . . . "Here it is. Yes. Yes, it appears you did reserve a junior suite. I can e-mail you a copy of the reservation if you want."

"Are you sure?" My words were full of accusation. "I made this reservation back in April and I'm sure I stipulated a full suite with a view of Union Square."

"No, ma'am. You made this reservation in May. May thirteenth. There's a note here saying it was our last available suite, so perhaps you did ask for a full suite but we were unable to accommodate you. I apologize if there was some misunderstanding."

I spent the next few minutes apologizing myself, the only

genuine part of my entire call, and got off the phone before he could insist on getting my e-mail address.

I turned to Ellen. "They reserved it three weeks ago. Three full weeks."

"So what? They planned a little getaway," she said. "Not all trysts are spontaneous."

"But how did they know they would be free? I don't mean 'free' as in being a widower. I'm talking about their schedule."

I went to my bag and pulled out the printed schedule. It was on page two. "Tonight Damien and Miranda were to hold a round-robin meditation workshop. It's the centerpiece of the retreat. Teresa had a nutrition lecture lined up after dessert, which sounds like an odd time to lecture about nutrition, but it's on the schedule."

I turned to page three. "Tomorrow morning, Damien has a nine a.m. lecture and Teresa starts her massage schedule at eight. I know because I'm her eight o'clock."

"Hmph. I don't get it. They were planning to skip out?"

"Not in the middle of a retreat. These things are twice a month, on the weekends. If they wanted to run off, they could do it any other time, without screwing up the schedule."

"I still don't get it."

If Monk had been here, I wouldn't have had to explain. Then again, if Monk had been here, he would have beaten me to it. "Ellen, they knew three weeks ago that the rest of the weekend would be canceled."

"How could they know?" She held out her hand flat, like a stop sign. "Wait. You're saying they knew this would happen?"

"And they knew they would want to get away afterward. Be together and avoid the press."

"You're serious? Three weeks ago they knew Miranda would commit suicide today? How?"

"Because they drove her to it. They made her."

"I hate to keep saying this, but how?"

I didn't know. But it made a lot more sense than the nonsense I'd been living with for the last six hours. Miranda Bigley didn't kill herself. She couldn't have. Someone forced her to do it.

CHAPTER FIVE

Mr. Monk and Number 99

I woke up the next morning surprised I had slept so well. I'm sure the wine had had something to do with it. And that fact that I had a theory now. True, it wasn't the most plausible theory. How exactly do you drive a person to kill herself, and on an exact, prearranged date? Nevertheless, I had a theory.

I started the day with a mug of Peet's French Roast, extra-strong, my usual remedy for the grape-induced cobwebs, but skipped the English muffin and granola. I figured I would save my appetite for Monk's kitchen, where I would perfectly toast his muffin, cover it evenly with one ounce of butter and get him on board with me, ready to tackle this new case.

Monk and I were full partners now. Almost. The exam was still more than a week away. But I had every right to bring in a case and have a theory about it. True, we didn't have an employer, per se. But there have been plenty of cases where we didn't start with an employer and still got paid. Besides, this was personal.

I used my key to get in, just like in the old days. And, just like in the old days, Monk was at the kitchen sink, using Clorox and rubber gloves and a bottle brush to clean out the garbage disposal. He didn't blink an eye to see me walk in, as if the last few months of upheaval had never happened.

"Why do you clean the garbage disposal?" I said instead of hello. "You never use it."

"Of course not. Garbage disposals are full of, you know, garbage. They're filthy."

"Not if you never use them."

"It's still a garbage disposal. It's like saying a pig isn't a pig because it's had a bath. Natalie, stand back. You're within ten feet of the switch. What in heaven's name are you thinking?"

"Sorry."

Luckily, the refrigerator and the toaster were twelve and sixteen feet away, respectively, and I could safely make our breakfast without endangering life and limb. "Mr. Monk, I've been thinking about yesterday. . . ."

As Monk cleaned already clean things and I assembled the muffins, I went on to explain. I told him all about last night with Ellen—about my hunch and the phone call and my deduction about the prearranged tryst.

"And Damien Bigley, according to the retreat brochure, is a licensed hypnotherapist." I said this dramatically. It was my big finish. "My theory is that he hypnotized her, maybe over a period of weeks, maybe giving her drugs, leading her closer and closer until finally he got her to jump.

"That's how he did it." I placed the toasted and buttered muffins, each half perfectly centered on a dessert plate, in front of him on the eat-in island.

Monk had remained silent throughout. Now, finally, he rearranged the muffin on the left and scrunched his face. "Ellen was at your place last night?"

"That's not the point. The point is, it wasn't suicide."

"Because I called Ellen every ten minutes and she never picked up."

"I know. Ellen and I needed to spend some time together. Alone."

"To talk about me?"

"No, not about you. Our mentor, our icon, our life coach just died. We were talking about her."

"Are you sure?"

"Yes, I'm sure." I wanted to shake him to make him focus, but I knew it would just make things worse. "Mr. Monk, it's possible, isn't it? I know a person can't be hypnotized to do something against her will. But if there are drugs involved? If the suicide is something as simple as jumping a foot or two forward?"

"Ellen's been getting more argumentative lately. The last time I tried to talk to her about her horrible shop . . ."

We could have kept going on like this forever. Luckily for my sanity, the phone rang. It was Captain Stottlemeyer with a fresh murder.

The crime scene was an apartment, occupying the lower half of a shabby two-story house on Willow Street on the edge of the Tenderloin. Even people who don't know San Francisco know about the Tenderloin. Despite the lure of gentrification, which had transformed other parts of town, it has proudly remained a sketchy neighborhood for the past hundred fifty years.

Lieutenant Devlin was waiting on the street. She didn't come over to meet us, but stayed by the front door. "The captain's in the back bedroom." Devlin is not the type to mince words.

As we walked past, I saw, out of the corner of my eye, a sign beside the door, perhaps a homemade business sign, with a colorful round design, like a balloon. It was mostly hidden behind Devlin's torso, so I didn't think much of it.

In the narrow hall, a row of three cops stood against the right wall, lined up, drinking cups of coffee and ignoring us. Again, as we passed, I noticed something half hidden behind them. A painting or a poster? Colorful again, with a striped tent and flags, although I couldn't really tell. Monk was preoccupied with keeping any part of his body from touching anything in this grimy hole.

Captain Stottlemeyer stood at the end of the hall, holding a set of plastic gloves in each hand. "In here, Monk. Natalie, good to see you. Put these on before you step inside. And don't touch anything, even with them on."

Lying in the middle of a multistained, rumpled bed was the body of Dudley Smith, late forties, curly dark hair, not unlike Monk, except he was dressed in a stained T-shirt and ratty jeans. Stottlemeyer neglected to tell us his occupation. Whatever it was, it must have paid well, because surrounding him on the bed were stacks of money, everything from singles to twenties. Hundreds of bills.

"He dialed nine one one, complaining of nausea, dizziness, seizures. When the EMTs arrived, maybe twelve minutes later, he was like this."

"Shouldn't the CDC be here?" I asked, taking a big step back. "If this is a disease . . ."

"You mean the CDC branch at the Department of Public

Health? Been and gone. They took their hazmats and left a few minutes ago. It's not viral or bacteria-based. It's a poison. Monk?"

This is one of the strange things about Monk. Well, there are plenty of strange things, but I mean strange as in "out of character." Here is a man who actually called the CDC when I had a cold and demanded I be quarantined. He's a man who's been quoted (by me) as saying, "Nature hates us. Nature wants nothing more than to kill us all." And yet corpses don't bother him.

He bent over Dudley's face, hands clasped behind his back so that he couldn't touch anything, even by accident. "Dilated pupils, massive sweating. Quick acting. Combined with the other symptoms, I'm guessing atropine. How was it ingested?"

The captain wriggled his mustache. When he had weird news to deliver, this was his tell. Not good news or bad news, just weird news, which in our world happened quite often. "The EMTs called our boys before trying to move the body. An hour later, both EMTs were admitted to their own ER. Same symptoms."

"Are you saying it's airborne?" Monk almost shrieked. "Augh. Why are we even here?" He slapped a hand over his mouth and began to hyperventilate, which of course made him breathe even harder.

"Not airborne." Stottlemeyer tilted his head toward a corner of the room. A trio of canaries fluttered in a large hanging cage, chirping and flapping their wings. "The proverbial canaries in a coal mine," he said. "If it was airborne, they'd be dead."

"What if they're immune?" Monk asked.

"The canaries are not immune."

"They could be super canaries. We could die any second—horrible, gasping deaths—and they'll still be chirping away."

"It's not airborne," Stottlemeyer insisted. "Get a grip."

And, surprisingly, Monk did. It took him a minute or two. But with a sheer force of will, he paced in a tight little circle, each time a little calmer. I was so proud. This was his job—more than a job; it pretty much defined him—and he was now willing himself to be a professional.

"Topical, then," he said, and returned to his normal breathing, at least normal for him. "The poison was on the body?"

"The EMTs said they didn't touch him, but obviously they did."

"Or maybe they didn't," Monk argued. "After all, they're pros. And no one lies to an ER doctor who's trying to save his life, especially something minor like an EMT touching a body. By the way, are they dead?"

"They both survived. Thanks for asking."

I'd like to say Monk ignored the sarcasm, but he probably didn't realize it was there. Instead, he held out his hands and framed the scene. "So the EMTs lied. They must have touched something. And it had to be something serious enough to risk their lives over."

Okay. Sure, when you phrase it that way and you're looking at a bed covered with money . . . "Money," I said before anyone could beat me to it.

"The poison's on the money," Stottlemeyer added. "Of course. Guess they couldn't resist a little fringe benefit." He turned to a CSI. "Bag a handful from the bed and take it in. Now. Devlin!"

The lieutenant appeared in the doorway, ready for action.

"Call the ER at St. Mary's. Have them isolate the EMTs, their clothing and equipment. Also the ambulance. We're looking for contaminated currency the guys may have filched from the crime scene. Also, anyone who may have come in contact with the bills."

"You think the poison's on the money?" Devlin asked, staring down at all the tempting cash.

"I do," said Stottlemeyer. "More important, Monk does."

"Good enough for me. Do you want me to make an arrest?" Devlin always seemed eager to slap on the cuffs.

"No, but keep them separated. I'll be there as soon as I can."

"I can question them." Devlin volunteered. She was stopped by one of Stottlemeyer's patented glares.

"Also, we need to clear this with the Secret Service and the Postal Inspection Service."

The lieutenant eyed the corpse and shook her head. "They're not going to want this one."

"Maybe not. But we need to inform them and keep them in the loop. I'll take care of it."

"I can do it," said Devlin, only to be met with another glare. "Okay," she said, and turned and walked away.

"What is that under the bed?" Monk was pointing to a pair of large bright yellow objects barely visible under the dust ruffle.

"Shoes," the captain said. "Our guy has big feet, huh? Look, Monk, our priority is finding out where this money came from."

"What did you say Smith did for a living?" I could hear his throat getting a little constricted.

"He's an entertainer. Small stuff."

Monk was suddenly alert. His hands went up again, framing bits of the room. "What's that?" He pointed to a shiny piece of tin sticking out of a bookcase shelf.

"Looks like a bike horn," Stottlemeyer said. "Our friend must have taken up biking. Now, Monk . . ."

"And that?" He pointed to what resembled a red rubber ball on the dresser behind the captain.

"That? Looks like a rubber ball."

"It's not a rubber ball." He was hyperventilating again. "It's a rubber nose."

Monk can move fast when he wants to. Within a second, he was out of the room. Within five, he was probably out of the house and across the street.

So much for being a professional.

"Dudley Smith was a clown?" I asked Stottlemeyer, dumbfounded. He shrugged yes. "You know Monk is afraid of clowns. It's a real condition. Coulrophobia."

"What?" Stottlemeyer chuckled. "You know the names of all his phobias?"

"Not all," I had to admit. "Some of them don't have official names."

"Because he invented them. What about his fear of milk?"

"That has a name. It's lactaphobia. And don't try to distract me. His fear of clowns is a real affliction. You knew that. You knew and you didn't warn him."

"Then he wouldn't have come in and we wouldn't have gotten to the money so fast."

"Well, now he's gone and is not coming back. Congratulations."

The captain seemed unfazed. "You can make it work, Natalie. Isn't that what you do? Monk is brilliant and you keep him controlled."

"Wrong. That's what I did when I was his assistant. Now I'm an ex-cop. I'm a week away from getting my PI license. I'm not his babysitter. If you want to fix the mess you made, do it yourself." I was almost ready to follow Monk into the street.

Stottlemeyer gave a thoughtful nod, then sent out the last CSI and closed the door.

"It's still your job to fix it," he said, looking me straight in the eyes. "Monk is making you his partner out of respect. Do you honestly think the force would hire you as a consultant? On your own?"

I wanted to say yes. I'd been involved in hundreds of cases by now. Many of them probably wouldn't have been solved without my participation. "Think carefully before you answer," said the captain, eyeing the clown in the T-shirt and jeans.

I knew what he meant. Was I ready to take over a crime scene, frame my hands in front of my face, and come up with some genius insight to kick things into high gear? "No," I had to admit. "No one can take Mr. Monk's place."

"Then I suggest you get him back in here."

"It won't be easy. He knows by now you betrayed him. I mean, having a row of officers blocking the painting? That was a circus scene, right?"

"Right. And Devlin was by the front door to body-block

the guy's business sign. 'J. P. Tatters. Clown to the Stars. Dudley Smith, proprietor.' I'm surprised Monk didn't see either one of those and put it together."

"That's because he trusted you."

"Okay," growled the captain. "Tell him I'm sorry." He sounded like he meant it. "I didn't think his clown thing was so bad. Isn't it like number one hundred on his list?"

"It used to be. Now it's ninety-nine. Aardvarks is the new one hundred."

"Aardvarks? Shouldn't that be at the top of the list?"

"That's what I keep saying."

CHAPTER SIX

Mr. Monk's Virtual Tour

"Monk, I owe you an apology," Stottlemeyer said.

"Sooo . . ." Monk paused.

"What are you doing?

"Waiting for the apology."

"I just said it."

"No, you didn't. You said you owed me an apology. That's like saying you owe me ten bucks. Just saying that you owe it to—"

"You're right. I apologize. I apologize."

"For what? For messing up your apology or for—"

"For everything!" The captain was sounding less and less sorry.

"Apology accepted," I ordered them both. "Let's move on."

The three of us sat in my Subaru, at the curb outside the clown's apartment. Captain Stottlemeyer was in the back. Monk was riding shotgun with his seat belt on, even though we weren't planning on moving.

The car was our temporary headquarters, since it had just started raining and Monk absolutely refused to go any closer to the scene of the crime—and by crime, he meant the residence of a clown.

In the half hour or so between Stottlemeyer's offense and his apology, the body had been removed, along with the poisoned money. Devlin was inside, finishing up some paperwork and preparing for Monk's upcoming inspection of the premises.

"No one likes clowns," said the captain. "They're like fruitcakes. Everyone hates them, yet they exist. But to be actually scared of them? And they're way down your list, number ninety-nine, so you can't be that scared."

"That's because they're relatively rare. If there were as many clowns as there are germs, they'd be right at the top. Higher than the top."

"Did a clown scare you as a kid, huh?" He snorted. "Look who I'm talking to. Everything scared you as a kid."

"If you must know"—Monk turned to face the captain—"my mother used to sit Ambrose and me in front of the TV and make us watch Fellini movies."

Ambrose was Monk's older brother. They'd been raised in a strange, sterile household, with a mother who withheld all affection and a father who went out for Chinese food one night and never came back. It was little wonder that Ambrose became an agoraphobe who never left his house and Monk became . . . well, Monk.

"You watched Fellini?" asked the captain. "I don't get it."

It took even me a few seconds to get it. "You mean the foreign films with those scary Italian clowns? What kind of mother . . . ?"

"She wanted us to learn a language. Ambrose actually liked them. When he was twelve, he decided to become a mime. He didn't speak for nearly a year. But I still get panic attacks when I hear Italian. It's the language of clowns."

A second later, my phone rang. It was Devlin, in the bedroom, paperwork done, ready to roll.

This was an emergency system that my daughter, Julie, had invented when she was acting as Monk's temporary assistant during my absence in New Jersey.

On one of their cases, Monk had refused to visit a crime scene on a high, uneven-numbered floor in an apartment building. This of course wasn't his problem. It was everyone else's. Julie's solution was to have Lieutenant Devlin tour the apartment holding her phone's camera out in front of her. On another smartphone, at ground level, Monk would take a virtual tour, with Devlin providing close-ups and a running commentary as she walked through.

I wiped my phone thoroughly and handed it to Monk. He squinted at the image on the screen. "Should I start in the bedroom?" asked Devlin from the other end.

"No need. I'll just review it in my mind."

"In your mind? You were only in the bedroom for a minute," she protested. "Then you got distracted by clown shoes."

"That doesn't mean I didn't see. Hold on." Monk put the phone in his lap, closed his eyes, and held up his hands. I guess he was framing whatever was running through his mind.

Stottlemeyer chuckled. "You just don't want Devlin showing you the clown shoes again."

Monk ignored him. "There's a wicker hamper under the window, which he never used. See it?"

"How do you know he never used it?" Devlin asked.

"Because 'A,' just look at the place. It's a mess. And 'B,' he kept something on top of it. You can see a crease line in the wicker, eight and a half inches long. That's a standard size for a picture frame. I assume it was a picture of a clown that you guys hid so I wouldn't freak out."

"Um," Devlin said. "That would be correct."

"Can you describe the picture?"

"Hold on. I put it in a drawer." A few seconds later, she was back on. Monk refused to look, so she described it in detail: a photo of the deceased, Dudley Smith, aka J. P. Tatters, dressed in full regalia at a children's hospital.

From her description, he was a cross between an Emmett Kelley hobo—dark, painted-on stubble, shabby suit, a hobo bindle over his shoulder—and a traditional Ronald McDonald—big red shoes, red fright wig. For Monk, it was the worst of both worlds. A hobo and a clown. I saw him turn white and thought he might even faint. But he didn't. He didn't even cover his ears.

"Those poor children," he moaned. "Was he responsible for putting them in the hospital?"

"No, Monk," Devlin said. "He was entertaining them. They're laughing."

"Laughing with terror. Okay, on to the next." He rolled his shoulders and refocused himself. "There's a blue push pin on the rug as you walk in the room. Turn left. Five feet down. About three inches from the wall."

"I don't see any . . . ," said Devlin. "Oh, yeah, there it is."

"Good. On the wall above the push pin is a rectangular mirror. There are a ton of smudges on both sides, slightly below eye level. Thumbprints, I'm guessing, since they're rounder than fingerprints. You can dust them but I'm sure they're the victim's."

Devlin's voice dripped with sarcasm. "The vic's prints. Gee, that's great."

"That's not my point. My point is he turned the mirror around a lot. Look on the other side."

We waited to hear her response. "It's a corkboard."

Of course, when I tell it this way, his deduction seems obvious: push pin, mirror, thumbprints from turning it around. But no one else had noticed. "Let me see what's on it," he said.

Monk picked up the phone and I glanced over his shoulder. In the corkboard's center, held up by another blue push pin, was a key on a string. A gloved hand entered the frame and turned the key around. "Do Not Duplicate" was etched in large letters.

"It's a Canada post key design," Monk said.

"A post office box?" Stottlemeyer asked. "Why would you hide your post office box key?"

Monk wriggled his nose and adjusted his seat belt, making sure it was still low and tight. "Well, that gives me a working theory."

"What's your working theory?" I asked.

"I'm working on it. Okay, let's move on to the stain on the ceiling above the bed, which I pray to God is unimportant. Then to the new Sharper Image catalog on the left nightstand."

The tour went on like this for nearly an hour. By the time we made our way through the living room, the kitchen, the hallway, and the apartment's only bathroom, my phone's battery light was blinking and ready to give out.

All of us focused on the details as Monk and Devlin went along. There was the manila envelope in the trash can, mailed to box 849 at the O'Farrell Street post office, a few blocks away. No name and no return address. There was the appointment book for the J. P. Tatters clown business. There were the ashes in the fireplace. There were the bookmarks on his Google homepage.

I turned the ignition key to auxiliary power. "Mr. Monk, give me the phone so I can plug it in."

"No need," he said, and handed it back. "I know what I need to know. The circus-loving police department can take it from here, what with their fiber reports and field work. It's patently obvious."

"What's obvious?" came Devlin's annoyed, disembodied voice.

"Monk, I hate to say this. Again." Stottlemeyer spoke slowly. He was trying to avoid doing his slow burn, partly because he knew it amused me. "But the reason we pay you is so you can tell us what's obvious."

"It's not your fault," Monk said graciously. "But you realize our clown is a blackmailer."

Stottlemeyer wriggled his mustache. I could see him mentally piecing it together: the secret post office box, the lack of names on the envelope, the cash in the mail. "Damn it, you're right."

Dudley Smith, we knew, did much of his business at children's parties. That was clear from his appointment records. And the "Clown to the Stars" had an impressive roster of clients. It struck me as rather ironic that San Francisco's wealthiest would hire a hobo clown for their impressionable children.

"Of course the key is significant," Monk added.

"The P.O. box key," I emphasized.

"No, I was thinking of the car key."

Stottlemeyer checked his notes. "What car key? Devlin, did you see a car key?"

"No, sir."

"Precisely," said Monk. "Dudley Smith didn't own a car. At least we found no indication. So he took public transportation or taxis, at least some of the time. And that means he had to change into his clown regalia at the client's home."

From this deduction, Monk's theory was fairly straightforward. While changing, Dudley had found something in one of his clients' homes, something worth blackmailing for. He said nothing at the time. Whatever the secret was, he thought he could get away with an anonymous blackmail system, hence the P.O. box key and the envelope without an addressee name.

"He probably used a disposable phone to contact his victim and changed his voice. Clowns are tricky—one might say diabolical. I'm sure he had some elaborate setup to retrieve the money at the post office. That's what I would do.

"When the blackmailee started being threatened, he or she had no idea it was the clown who had showed up for Jimmy's party last month. Their way of dealing with this unknown blackmailer? Send him poisoned money."

"Why didn't the victim send poisoned scraps of paper instead?" asked Stottlemeyer. "It would be a damn lot cheaper."

Good question. Tough question. I let Monk answer it. "Smith had to touch the bills in order for the poison to work. If it was me, I would have sent only half the requested amount. That would have ensured that Smith count the money over and over and get the atropine into his system fast."

"So, saving blackmail money wasn't the point of this murder," said Stottlemeyer.

"The point was to kill the blackmailer and make the problem go away."

"What about the ashes in the fireplace?" Stottlemeyer asked. "Did he burn some crucial evidence?"

"It was a Presto-Log," Monk said. "I recognized the texture."

"Right," said the captain with an embarrassed cough. "We've had some chilly nights."

"Should we keep this out of the public record?" I asked. "I mean, if the killer didn't know who his blackmailer was, why should we tell him?"

"Good thinking," Stottlemeyer agreed. "I'll call the DA's office and try to keep it out of the papers. See what develops."

A rear door opened and Devlin joined the captain in the backseat. She remained quiet, nursing a very serious scowl.

"If I were you, I'd find out when Smith rented his box," Monk advised. "That will narrow down your suspects to a manageable few. Then all you have to do is connect one of them to the envelope or the poison or the money. Or maybe you can uncover the scandal behind the blackmail. That's not really my problem." He frowned. "You lost me at 'clown.' I'm quitting this one."

"What? You can't refuse to work on a case. Natalie?"

Stottlemeyer was looking at me to intercede, but I couldn't. "If he doesn't want to, you can't force him. That's the beauty of being a consultant."

"No, that's not how it works. You guys are under retainer. We retain you to work on the cases we choose, not the ones you choose."

"All right," said Monk. "I'll work on the case but I won't solve it."

"Won't solve it?" the captain scoffed. "What is this, a strike?"

"You can't force me to work on a case that would harm my health. The very least you have to do is offer me hazard pay."

"Hazard pay?" Stottlemeyer snorted. "For one thing, you're a homicide consultant, so it's always hazardous. That's the job. And . . . it's a clown, for God's sake. A clown!"

"Don't say that!" Monk shuddered and sank away.

"Yelling 'clown' is not going to make things easier," I said, trying to restore some civility.

Devlin opened her mouth, about to say something—something scathing, no doubt. She closed it, then opened it again. "They found the body."

"There's a second body?" Monk was aghast. "How could you miss a second body? Was it under the bed with the clown shoes?" He shivered. "Was it under the bed *wearing* the clown shoes? This keeps getting worse."

"There was no second body."

"You just said there was."

Devlin looked me straight in the eye, though I could see she didn't want to. "Miranda Bigley. The call came in. Her body washed ashore. Here in town."

CHAPTER SEVEN

Mr. Monk Cleans a Cup Holder

Fort Funston Park is technically part of San Francisco, at the southern edge where the city blends into San Mateo County. A rugged, gorgeous seaside park. As far as I know, the only time it was ever really used as a fort was during World War Two, when they installed some huge cannons overlooking the Pacific Ocean, just in case the Japanese decided to invade the West Coast.

The sandy bluffs are similar to the ones at Half Moon Bay, which is only about fifteen miles south, as the crow flies or the fish swims. The cliffs and the steady breezes make the park a perfect setting for hang-gliding. And, in fact, it was a hang-gliding instructor who had called in the sighting.

He had been up there with a terrified, overweight novice who had come to cash in a gift certificate from her son and celebrate her sixty-fifth birthday with a once-in-a-lifetime thrill. They were strapped in side by side, instructor and novice, the instructor trying hard to compensate for the lopsided weight.

The woman was the first to see the yellow dot bobbing among the rocks and wondered aloud if this could be an oddly colored dolphin. She had only been convinced to go up in this kite because her son had promised her a dolphin sighting. The instructor saw it, too. He did several low passes over the yellow dot, then pulled out his cell phone and dialed 911. From this high up, he got remarkably good reception.

The trails from the cliff to the beach were treacherous. Narrow and rocky and steep, they wound back on one another until finally spilling out onto a narrow strip of sand. If you're wondering how in the world Monk could have made this trek, he didn't. He was back up in my car in the Skyline Boulevard parking lot, polishing one of my dusty cup holders.

The instructor was there when we stepped out onto the beach, along with the crew of the coast guard cutter that had responded to the call and pulled Miranda Bigley out of the water. These were probably the same men, I thought, who had been in their wet suits yesterday, searching for her fifteen miles down the shoreline.

Since the body had been found in San Francisco waters, it was brought ashore for a preliminary exam before being shipped to San Mateo County. Stottlemeyer took charge as soon as we arrived and Devlin took notes. I felt uneasy not having Monk there to raise his hands and do his thing. But in reality, the captain and the lieutenant had done this hundreds of times. It seemed fairly straightforward.

They noted the location, tidal information, broken bones, head trauma, and, in their professional opinion, probable cause of death. I tried to stay away during all this, preferring to remember the way Miranda looked in life. She had always been so alive that it seemed like a sacrilege to see her dead.

"Natalie, did you know her well enough to make an ID?" Devlin had come back to where I was standing. "I mean, I know what she looks like from the infomercials. But you knew her in person."

"Do I have to?"

I have never known Amy Devlin to be warm and fuzzy. Usually she goes out of her way to be hard-nosed, the total cop. But something made her soften. "You don't. But she's only been in a day, so it's not bad. Not much bloating. No fish nibbling to speak of."

"Please, stop." The image almost made me vomit.

"Is that my wife?" The voice startled us and we turned to see Damien Bigley, approaching us from the rocky trail end.

"Mr. Bigley, we didn't expect you so soon." She held out her hand and Damien shook it. "I'm Detective Lieutenant Devlin. SFPD."

"And I'm Officer Teeger," I said. "SPD."

SPD? I don't know why I said that. Technically I was still a member of the Summit Police Department, but only because the town fathers hadn't gotten around to finalizing my paperwork. It would never hold up in court.

"Officer Teeger." He looked at me a bit oddly, either because he recognized me from yesterday or because he noticed that I'd left out the "F."

As for Devlin, she took my half lie in stride. "Mr. Bigley, I'm very sorry for your loss. If you'll please come with me? Officer Teeger, please stay here."

From a distance, I watched as Miranda's husband walked up to the form in the sandy, soggy yellow top and looked down at the halo of short crimson hair. He nodded at the detective and she replaced a blue camouflage tarp over Miranda's face and upper body, as if tucking her into bed.

And then, for some reason, I found myself disobeying an order—well, disobeying a suggestion. "Mr. Bigley," I said, crossing his way, "do you mind if I ask a question?"

"Go right ahead," he replied.

"Where were you last night?"

He seemed thrown. "Me? I was in San Francisco. Things at the Sanctuary were a little stressful, to say the least. I managed to sneak past the cameras and reporters and get a last-minute room at the Belmont."

"Were you registered under your own name?"

It took him a moment to respond. "No. I had an employee make the reservation. I thought that would be smarter."

"A male employee?"

"Female, it so happens. The hotel understood my discretion. I'm sorry. What does this have to do with my wife's death?"

"Nothing, sir. I was wondering how you got here so quickly. But if you were staying at the Belmont, that explains it."

"Yes." He picked at one of his groomed eyebrows. "Do I know you?"

"I was at the retreat this weekend." There was no reason to lie, especially since he seemed on the brink of remembering me.

"I remember," he said, his brown eyes turning sympathetic. "I'm so sorry you had to be there and see that."

"If I hadn't seen it, I don't think I would ever have believed it."

"It's almost impossible. I know. I think that's maybe why she did it in such a public way, so that people wouldn't have any doubt."

This struck me, even at the time, as an odd thing for him to say. Why would Miranda want her suicide to be so undeniable? But at the time, with her body lying just a few feet, away, I let it go.

"This is a terrible time to mention it," he said. "But you should be receiving an e-mail from the Sanctuary. We're having a special weekend for the people who were there—to make up for the canceled retreat and to share some therapy and memories. It's going to be hard for everyone. I hope you can come."

"I'll be there," I said without even mentally checking my schedule. I would make the time.

"I noticed," he said haltingly. "She was talking to you right before . . . before the end. Do you mind me asking what you talked about?"

"We were talking about the preciousness of life," I lied. "I was with a friend who has trouble enjoying life. She stopped and talked to us, told him how special and precious every moment should be."

I guess I just wanted to mess with his head. He had no right to be so pulled together and calm. "Oh! Well, I'm sorry for your friend. I hope he's all right. Miranda really believed that."

"I'm sure she did," said Devlin warmly. "Sir, if you want to escort the body back to Half Moon Bay, the coast guard will be more than happy to accommodate you."

'Thank you, Detective. I think I will."

As soon as he was out of earshot, Devlin turned on me. "What was that about? Officer Teeger of the SPD?"

"He drove her to suicide. He's having an affair. And they knew the exact day that she was going to kill herself."

"Hey, hey, slow down."

So I slowed down and told her everything I knew. It wasn't much.

"You're saying that he hypnotized her and drugged her?"

"I don't know. All I know is, she would never have done it, not of her own free will. It goes against everything she stood for."

Devlin considered this, which was strange. Under normal circumstances, she would be mocking me. Then she did something even stranger. "Would a tox screen help you?"

"A tox screen? You can get a tox screen?"

"The San Mateo sheriff will be bending over backward on such a high-profile case. And it's the first thing the press will ask. Were there drugs involved? As for us getting the complete results . . . Well, she landed on our coastline. That gives us some pull."

"You would do that for me?"

"Not for you. For Miranda. She was a real force of nature. I actually sat through two hour-long infomercials in a row. Don't get me wrong, I didn't buy anything. But something about her made me feel better—just hearing her talk and try to sell it to me. It's hard to think that she killed herself."

"It's impossible."

From twenty yards away, we watched Damien Bigley talking to the coast guard captain. "What does Monk think of your theory?"

I shrugged. "He's not a fan."

"Really? He's usually all over this kind of weird, impossible crime."

"Not this time. Not yet. Amy . . ." I almost never called her Amy. "I changed my mind. I want to identify the body."

"Her husband just did."

"I know. But I want to see."

The idea just occurred to me, out of the blue, that this might not be Miranda Bigley under the tarp. It was a crazy, desperate theory, like something out of a Hitchcock movie. What if it wasn't Miranda who'd jumped, after all? What if they substituted someone else at the last second? I wasn't sure exactly how that would work.

Or what if Miranda had somehow faked her jump off the cliff and then they found a look-alike corpse somewhere and . . . Okay, this was getting crazy. But I had to know. Was she even dead?

"You really want to see?" Devlin asked.

I nodded and kept my gaze focused as she lifted the blue camouflage.

Devlin had been right. It wasn't so bad. There was a bit of bloating, plus the kind of wrinkly puffiness you get from being in the water too long. The strand of natural pearls was gone, probably broken and returned to the churning sea they'd originally come from. I tried to ignore her other landmark touches—the crimson hair, the colorful clothing, things that could be faked—and concentrate on her features.

"It's Miranda," I said. Unless perhaps Miranda had had a

twin, or they'd given some unsuspecting woman plastic surgery to make her look like Miranda, then killed her and dumped the body.

"No. It's Miranda." I had no option. I had to get used to this undeniable fact.

"Natalie, I'm sorry."

CHAPTER EIGHT

Mr. Monk Stays Out

In order to become a licensed private investigator in the state of California, you need to clear several hurdles.

First is the background check—getting a clean bill of health from the California Department of Justice and the FBI. This may seem easy for your average citizen. But thanks to my work with Adrian Monk, I have been arrested more than once, including on a murder charge. Never convicted, I'm proud to say. We've also gotten into a lot of hot water with the FBI. So the background check went through, but with more than one asterisk and request for further explanation.

The second requirement is an AA degree (whatever that means) in law or police science. This, of course, I don't have. But you can also qualify by logging in six thousand hours of compensated experience in investigative work. And, although I was not well compensated for my near decade of work handing out wipes and keeping Monk on track, I was compensated. Two down.

The third hurdle is the written exam. That's two hours of multiple-choice questions held at a Psychological Services testing center. You would think that with all my experience, this would be a snap. But the highest percentage of test failure, they say, comes from ex-cops. Maybe that's because they're overconfident or have a slightly different view of the law. I wasn't about to make that mistake.

Here's a sample question from the study guide, the twelve-pound study guide that cost hundreds of dollars and came with a no-fail guarantee:

"Henry wants to hire you to put a GPS system on his wife's car, to determine if she's been cheating on him. His wife is making the car payments, but the car is registered in Henry's name. Can you, as a private investigator, legally put a tracking device on her car?"

First of all, Henry seems like a scumbag whom I would never work for. But I wasn't given that multiple choice option. The possible answers were:

(a) No, because the wife has a reasonable expectation of privacy.

(b) Yes, because Henry is the registered owner of the vehicle.

(c) No, because they are married and both partners must consent, according to California law.

(d) Maybe, because the investigator is a third party and is presumed immune from liability.

Do you need to take a minute to think it over? Take your time. I'll just sit here and hum the theme song from *Jeopardy!* Dum, dum, dum, duh-duh . . . dum, dum, dum . . . Okay, time's up. The answer was b, and I got it wrong.

All this is a roundabout way of saying that I was at home the next morning, studying and taking advantage of the lull in business. Monk had stuck to his guns and refused to work on the clown case, despite the captain's threats. And the Miranda case was a case only in my imagination.

Around midday, my daughter, Julie, called, making a nice interruption. She was a senior now at UC Berkeley. It's just across the bay, an easy commute. But she had always insisted on living in Berkeley. Our interaction was now reduced to a visit home every few weeks and a phone call every few days. I felt lucky on days like this when she initiated the call.

It was boyfriend trouble. Her last one had shown his true colors by breaking up with her via a text message. This one, Maxwell, seemed to have the opposite problem. Julie said he was getting too serious too fast, but she was afraid of discouraging him. I hadn't yet met Maxwell. But long ago I had learned not to have an opinion, or at least to keep it to myself. This resulted in a lot of listening on my part, which I didn't mind and she appreciated.

After saying good-bye and tacking on one too many "I love you's," I returned to my study guide, only to be interrupted again, this time by a soft, rhythmic tapping on my door. Exactly ten knocks.

"How did you get here?" I asked as soon as I opened it.

"I have my ways," Monk said for the second time in three days. At some point, I had to figure out what his ways were because his mysterious mobility was starting to annoy me.

Brushing right past me, he strode into the living room and did a three-sixty. "Where's Ellen?"

"Not here."

"She always comes to my place on the day of chicken potpie night and helps me count the peas and pearl onions and cut the carrots into quarter-inch lengths. It's one of our fun traditions. Today she left a message saying she had other plans. I think she's avoiding me."

"She's not avoiding you," I improvised. Maybe she was; maybe she wasn't. It wasn't my place to say. "Ellen's busy. You should drop by her shop and say hello."

"Why? The peas aren't going to count themselves."

"Forget the peas. Go over there. You can help her polish the bars of soap or dust that hippopotamus-dung chandelier she's been trying to sell."

"Don't even say . . ." His hands flew up and covered his ears. "Augh! Now that image is in my mind. Get it out! Get it out before it cripples me for life!"

Monk had never even ventured inside Poop. He and Ellen had always agreed to meet nearby, often at Lush, a natural-soap store just a few doors away. Lush was much closer to his comfort zone.

"She would be thrilled if you showed an interest. Really." I wasn't exactly playing Cupid. But I knew Ellen had been feeling neglected. Having him actually walk through the door of her shop would be huge.

"Show an interest in fecal matter? This is the end of civilization. It's the fifth horseman of the Apocalypse."

"You mean the Apoop-alypse." He didn't appreciate my attempt at humor. "She's your girlfriend, Mr. Monk, or something similar. You need to make an effort."

"Oh, all right. Can you drive me over?"

"I thought you had your ways."

"I do, but . . . the idea doesn't seem quite as poopy if you're going to be there."

That was probably the nicest thing he'd said to me in a

while, which tells you all you need to know about our relationship.

Poop was in a storefront on Union Street, amid a stretch of trendy boutiques, galleries, and restaurants. The area is technically Cow Hollow, but it caters to the folks from nearby Pacific Heights, who can afford to live in a neighborhood with a nicer-sounding name.

I found a parking space a few doors down, in front of Lush. By the time I finished feeding the meter, Monk's nose was an inch from their display window, sniffing at the colorful piles of sweetly scented soap. "Wrong store, Mr. Monk," I said, and began to gently shove him toward Ellen's boutique. Then not so gently. For the last twenty feet, it was like pushing an anvil.

"Why am I doing this again?" the anvil demanded.

"To be supportive of the woman in your life."

We got within five feet when my strength gave out. "Close enough. I'll tell Ellen you're here. If she wants to come out, great. If not, that's your funeral."

"It's my funeral either way."

My stepping through the shop doorway set off a soft, civilized chime. "Ellen," I called out. The shop seemed empty. The hippopotamus chandelier was still there, unsold, throwing its soft glow over the perfectly organized shelves of soaps, doorstops, pot holders, and assorted knickknacks.

Brand-new since the last time I was in here was a rack of high-end vitamins. You wouldn't think sheep dung and monkey dung and six other kinds of dung would contain many vitamins and nutrients. Being a normal person, you wouldn't think about it at all. But, apparently, this V-8 blend of processed, concentrated, sanitized poo provided you with all the vitamins and minerals for a long, happy life, as long as you didn't think about where they came from. Then you'd be miserable.

On my previous visits, the shop had been crowded with a blend of the serious consumer and the simply curious. Even the curious usually bought something: a ten-dollar bar of Remains of the Gray whale soap; a twenty-dollar poodle-poo paperweight. So it was surprising to find the place totally empty. Then again, my previous visits had always been on the weekends and this was early afternoon on a Monday, hardly prime time.

"Natalie? Is that you?"

Ellen's voice had come from behind the counter. I circled around and found her on her hands and knees, scrubbing a section of marble floor left over from the days when the space had been home to a butcher shop. She was working with two wire brushes, one in each hand.

Ellen looked up, and her shoulder-length blond hair was half covering her face. "I've been meaning to do this for months," she said, smiling and sweating. "The dirt gets really ground in on these high-traffic spots."

"Are you okay?" I asked.

Like Monk, Ellen had a long history of OCD. She had worked hard to control her symptoms. Opening her unique business had been, in fact, an act of therapeutic defiance, proving to herself and everyone that all of life, even defecation, could be embraced and cleaned and consumed and sold at full retail.

"I'm fine," she said, getting up from her knees and sweeping back her hair. "I was just taking advantage of the lull."

"There does seem to be a lull," I agreed.

"Well, it's Monday. And the initial buzz has faded. My clientele is settling into regular customers and street traffic. That's perfectly natural. The store in Summit was like that, too." She removed her heavy-duty plastic gloves. "So, any news?"

"Nothing new." I had called Ellen yesterday after the recovery of Miranda's body. We were both still learning how to deal with the tragedy, and I wondered now, looking at her sweating forehead and raw knuckles, if this sudden need to polish the floor was a good thing for her or a bad thing.

"Nothing new?" She looked disappointed. "You just dropped by to say hello?"

"No, I brought a friend." When I cocked my head toward the door, she could see. There was Monk, framed in the open doorway. He was frozen, standing on one foot, with his other reaching forward, suspended in midair.

"Adrian." Ellen was shocked and delighted. She had never seen him so close to her shop. "I'm so glad you're here," she said, keeping her voice soft and raising it nearly an octave. "Come in. There's nothing to be afraid of." It was like coaxing a kitten.

Just to add to the fun, the door chime started going off. Every time Monk extended his leg into the shop, he would break the beam and trigger another round of chimes. It became like a self-generating accompaniment.

I've got to say this for Monk: He tried. He stayed on one foot, balancing forward and back, like a brown-suited flamingo. At one point, he lost his balance and had to reach out and touch the frame. Letting out a little shriek, he managed to push himself back into position.

"Don't worry," said Ellen. "I sanitized it this morning. The whole place is spotless."

But Monk remained in his tightrope-walking stance, one foot on the sidewalk, one foot hovering over the threshold, complete with tinny music . . . until Ellen took pity and met him at the door.

"I'm proud you came this far," she said. "Baby steps."

"I'm not taking baby steps. Or any kind." And with that, he lowered his leg and took a firm stance outside.

"This is the first time you've seen my San Francisco store. What do you think?" Ellen air-kissed him three inches from his cheek and I saw him fight the urge to wipe it off.

Peering inside, Monk examined the space, left to right. "It's empty."

"It won't be empty if you come in," I suggested. "Come on. We'll pick something and I'll buy it for your birthday."

"No one wants to come in here," Monk said. "You can tell because no one's in here."

"It's slow," Ellen admitted. "It picks up later in the afternoon."

"Why? Is that when the insane asylum lets out its patients?" No one laughed or cracked a smile. "So they can shop for animal poop?" Again, nothing. "Because no one would go into a poop store like this unless they were clinically insane."

"We get the joke, Mr. Monk."

"Because buying and selling animal feces is crazy."

"We get it," I said.

"I'm not sure you do."

"Adrian, we've discussed this." I could see Ellen's patience was wearing thin. "I'm trying to make the world cleaner. I'm reusing waste so it's no longer wasted. Making people reevaluate what they put down the sewers and into landfills. I thought you appreciated what I'm doing."

"I appreciate it," he said. "From a distance. Which is where I should have stayed. This is all Natalie's fault." He pointed at me with both index fingers.

"My fault?"

"If you hadn't physically dragged me here, Ellen and I could have met at the soap store or any other civilized place on earth."

"Natalie dragged you?" Without even looking, I could hear the disappointment.

"She said I had to make an effort. I told her that was nonsense."

"I suppose it is nonsense," Ellen said, "expecting an effort."

I should point out here that any normal person would have picked up on the warning signs. They were in Ellen's voice and on her face. Any normal person would have backed off or apologized.

"I told her no one should have to walk into a poop store. It isn't natural. There are sixteen people in the soap store down the street, seventeen people in the toy store, and twenty-one in the Starbucks. So it's not a slow afternoon. It's a slow Poop."

"A—slow—Poop?" Ellen pronounced each word like a

separate sentence. Any normal person would have been terrified.

"I meant the name of your store, not the other thing. Depressingly slow. It's a wonder you can stay in business."

"Adrian Monk." Ellen was seething. "Get out of my store."

Monk looked down at his feet. "I'm not in your store. I thought that was the whole point of this discussion—about why I'm not in your store."

"Get out," she said, then slammed the door in his face.

CHAPTER NINE

Mr. Monk Counts His Peas

Monk had been thrown by Ellen's anger. For a brilliant guy, he can be pretty dense. "I don't understand," he said over and over as I drove back to his apartment. "It was all part of our usual, witty repartee, our give-and-take."

"Where you give the insults and she takes them."

"It's an understood thing. If she was considering a change in format, she should have submitted it in writing."

"Maybe she just got tired of having her loved one putting her down and ridiculing her dreams."

"In writing!" Monk emphasized. "Then I would have known."

"The women in your life are too nice to you, Mr. Monk." I'd never said this before, but it was true. He brought out their mothering instincts and they were somehow willing to overlook an awful lot of insensitive behavior. Me included.

"I am as God made me," he replied, then sat back, crossed his arms, and pouted for the rest of the drive.

He seemed surprised when I dropped him at the curb and didn't get out. "Chicken potpie," he reminded me. "Don't you want to stay and count the peas?"

"I'll pass. I have to go see the captain and try to save our jobs."

"They're not going to fire me," he scoffed.

"It's not just you. It's me, too. And, yes, they have the right to fire us for not taking a case."

"The law makes an exception for clowns."

"I'll bring that to their attention," I said, tired of arguing. "See you later."

From Monk's place, it was a short drive to the station house, where I found Lieutenant Devlin in Stottlemeyer's office. One wall of it had been transformed into a small command center, with a dry-erase board and a bulletin board and several open files littering the chairs and floor. It's a decent-sized office and more than once has served double-duty like this.

Devlin looked up, an annoyed expression crossing her face. "Is Monk waiting outside? Tell him we're not straightening up just so he can come in."

"Not here," I said. "Where's the captain?"

"Not here, either. Angela Phister is recovering from her meat thermometer. The captain went over to San Francisco General to formally charge her and have her transferred to ward seven." The hospital's ward seven was a secure facility run by the county sheriff's department.

"So, the DA has enough evidence?"

"Thanks to good old police work. We picked up her DNA from a blood sample in Barry Ebersol's backyard and partial prints in his kitchen. We probably didn't need Monk on this one after all."

That was typical Devlin, trying to downgrade my partner's contribution. I couldn't let it pass. "First off, if it wasn't for Monk, you wouldn't have known his attacker had been stabbed, so I doubt you would have swabbed the yard for DNA. Second, a print is only as good as what you can match it with. And Ms. Angela Phister, your presumed second victim, wouldn't even have been on your radar."

"Yeah, yeah, I get it. You're protecting your paychecks. Fair enough. Oh, speaking of paychecks . . ." Devlin put down the file folder she'd been reading and picked up an envelope from the out-box on Stottlemeyer's desk. "Two days of consulting, for what was probably an hour's worth of work."

"You're paying him for his expertise," I said, snatching the check from her hand.

"I call it luck. He happened to get fixated on a couple of meat thermometers."

"Used twice in twenty minutes. Would you have been able to figure out the connection?"

"Maybe," she said with an unconvincing shrug.

"But it would have taken you days, wasting who knows how many man-hours. Meanwhile, your killer might already have been released and flown the coop. We saved the city a ton of money."

"Whatever. I'm busy." And she went back to her folder.

I slipped the much-needed check into my bag, then wandered over to the command center wall. On the city map, a red pin had been inserted into a familiar block of Willow Street on the edge of the Tenderloin. Other color-coded pins were scattered around the neighborhoods of Pacific Heights and Nob Hill and a few others.

"The clown case?" I asked.

"Uh-huh." Devlin's nose was buried in the folder. "We're

working on Monk's blackmail theory, our only theory at the moment. In the two months before Smith opened his post office box, he was hired for twelve private parties. We sent officers to interview all twelve households, on the pretext of following up on an accusation. We told them Smith was under investigation for stealing valuables from his clients' homes."

"Which is true," I pointed out.

"More or less. We didn't mention murder. Still keeping it out of the press." Devlin's nose emerged and she followed it to the pins on the map. "For five of those parties, he arrived fully clowned-up. Those households have been tentatively eliminated. For two more, he changed into his clown regalia in a powder room where he would not have had access to any private documents. That leaves five. Five houses where he was alone in bedrooms or home offices, where he may have had access to compromising information."

"That's a lot of suspects," I said.

"Especially since we can't get search warrants. We can't even interview them properly. These are wealthy, well-connected people." She adopted a deep bad-cop voice. "Excuse me, sir. Do you happen to have a blackmail secret you're desperate to keep? And were you being extorted by Mr. Smith? And did you send him poisoned money through the mail? Just asking."

I could understand her predicament. "What about investigating the other side of it?" I asked. "Smith must have had some record or information about his victim."

"We searched his apartment. Whatever he had, we can't find it, which means the killer was either smart or lucky. Or

Monk has led us down the garden path and we're in the weeds." She was mixing up her gardening metaphors, but I wasn't going to mention it.

"Mr. Monk can be wrong about a lot of things," I said. "But not murder."

"That's why we need him back."

I had been afraid that was where this conversation was heading. "As long as the corpse is still a clown, he won't do it."

"Then we're going to have to insist. Either he helps on the cases where we need him or we cancel his retainer. It's that simple."

"He won't do it. He can't."

"That's bull. I've seen him do plenty of things that frightened him. Well, not personally seen, but I've heard stories. Especially with you along. You can figure out how to make it happen."

"I'll try," I promised her.

"You know, every other city gets along without Adrian Monk. I don't know any other department, anywhere, that employs a consulting detective to wave his hands and make great leaps of logic."

She had a point, but then so did I. "And what is this city's national ranking for solved homicides?" I knew the answer. Just two months ago we'd been in this office celebrating the release of the annual report; Monk toasting with Fiji Water, the rest of us with champagne.

"San Francisco is a few percentage points above other major cities."

"San Francisco is number one by eight full points. Do you really want to give that up?"

"Monk can't pick and choose his cases. That's not how it works. At the end of the day, it's probably not a bad thing."

"What's not a bad thing?"

"To give up that crutch. It'll make us better cops. And we'll no longer have to deal with that invisible asterisk by our stats—'numbers may be skewed due to the use of a performance-enhancing consultant.' "

Devlin was serious. She had always resented Monk, and not just because he stole the limelight. Her notion was that he'd changed the game of law enforcement and somehow made the San Francisco homicide division lazier and more dependent.

I had never known Captain Stottlemeyer or anyone else on his squad to be lazy or dependent. But this was Devlin's view. She would have liked nothing better than to go without Monk and then take full credit at the end of a successful case. Even if there were fewer successful cases.

"I'll get him on board." What else could I say? I had no idea how I would do it, but . . . "I'll get him on board."

CHAPTER TEN

Mr. Monk Gets Threatened

Making an exit is not always easy. There have been times when I've found myself walking out shamefaced and in silence, or apologizing for something Monk said to a roomful of suspects or chasing him out the door that time when he happened to see a spider at a crime scene. The mutilated corpse didn't bother him. No, it was the spider crawling across the tip of a severed bloody tongue. That's what sent him running across three lanes of traffic with me in hot pursuit.

In this case, I tried to make my exit look dignified, perhaps even brave—a private eye with her job being threatened marching out to make things right. Then, as I stood by the elevator, waiting and waiting, still within view of the captain's office, refusing to make eye contact with anyone, I remembered.

There had been another reason why I'd come here. My temptation was to forget about it, leave it to another day. But then a familiar phrase popped into my head. "Why do you care what other people think? Care about what you think and you'll be fine."

It was one of Miranda Bigley's life lessons. I could almost hear her saying it in that voice that made everything seem simple and clear and right. I figured I had to follow her advice now, especially since what I had just remembered, what I needed to go back and talk to Devlin about, was her.

"I forgot to ask . . ."

Devlin was sitting, her feet up on Captain Stottlemeyer's desk, reading another file. She sprang up, embarrassed, like a kid caught trying on Mommy's shoes. "What? What did you forget?"

"The tox screen from the autopsy report. Did it come in?"

"Oh."

It was like a switch being flipped. All the coldness and protective animosity was suddenly gone. On this matter, we seemed to be on the same side.

"The San Mateo County Sheriff's Office posted everything on their secure Web site. I had to charm my way through three passwords." She reached for a paper-clipped document on top of the captain's in-box. "I printed a copy for you."

"Thanks," I said, and began looking it over. The first page was nothing but rows and columns of indecipherable chemical names and numbers. I pretended to study it.

"There's a summary on page three. The answer to your question is no. There were no chemicals in her system, outside of some Lipitor she took for her cholesterol. No stimulants or depressants. No alcohol. Not even residue from sleeping pills. Natalie, I'm sorry."

I had been preparing myself for this, but it still came as a letdown. "So her suicide was not chemically induced. It was of her own free will."

"I know how inexplicable this is. I admired her, too."

"Anything strange in the autopsy?"

"Starts on page four."

Page four was slightly more comprehensible than page one. At least it wasn't filled with numbers. "Nothing inconsistent with a fall or jump from a cliff," Devlin said, trying to be helpful. "Broken femur, a premortem concussion, probably from a rock. Then death by drowning."

I took a deep breath. "Was she conscious or unconscious when she drowned?"

"That can't be determined."

I decided to visualize Miranda Bigley unconscious when it happened. Yes, that was better. Drifting peacefully, sleeping in the deep, with no second thoughts or regrets over the senseless thing she'd just done.

Devlin brought me back to reality. "The suicide note's on page nineteen."

I flipped to page nineteen and found a photocopy of the handwritten note:

Dearest Damien,

I know my actions will cause such great harm and sorrow to my friends and followers. And you, too, dearest Damien. Most of all. I am so sorry.

If there were any other way to deal with this, I would. I've struggled for a long time with this decision. But there is no other way to avoid all the pain and heartache that is to come. As much as I long to be with you for even one more day, I must go.

In the grand scope of things, one can only live for one's self. And in my case, die for myself. Please forgive me.

Miranda

There it was, in her own handwriting, her intention to take her life. To avoid all the pain and heartache, as she said. I looked up from the note. "Was she sick?"

Devlin shook her head. "There's a medical report in there. Miranda had just had her annual physical, part of her company's insurance policy. A clean bill of health. And no markers for inherited diseases. She could have lived another forty years."

"Then why was she talking about pain? Avoiding pain and heartache?"

"The sheriff's office has a theory." From Devlin's tone I knew this wasn't going to be good. "They've asked the attorney general's office to look into the possibility of financial irregularities."

I was confused. "You mean like embezzling?"

"The Best Possible Me is incorporated in the state of California. There's a not-for-profit entity and then the business side. Miranda may have shuttled investor money around and used some of it for her personal investment portfolio." Devlin shrugged one shoulder. "Right now it's a theory."

"Miranda wouldn't embezzle," I said categorically.

"She wouldn't commit suicide, either."

"What about her husband? Do they think he was involved?"

"Damien Bigley says he's unaware of any shady dealings. Miranda was president of the BPM Corporation, so it's feasible that whatever happened she could have done it without anyone else's participation."

"Could he have done it without her?" I asked.

"Not without her signature on documents. Plus there are personal passwords she established. I suppose anything's possible."

"But they suspect her because of the suicide note. Avoiding pain and heartache."

"That's part of it," said Devlin. "Every suicide has a motive. The company was about to go through an audit. Starting this week, in fact. Any irregularities would have been exposed."

It was a lot to think about, and not very happy thinking. "Miranda Bigley stealing from her own company?"

"People are only human, even the best of them."

I headed out the door and for the elevator again. Then I turned back—again. "I didn't thank you."

"No need. Maybe it's a girl thing. I don't like the idea of powerful, competent women killing themselves. It's bad for all of us. Especially bad for her."

"Can I keep this?" I asked, holding up the paper-clipped pages.

"Sure. Just don't flash it around."

"Can you get in trouble for this?"

"Nothing I can't handle. They're going to release the highlights to the press, probably today, so we can expect another spike in publicity."

"Oh, dear." I hadn't thought of that part. The papers and TV entertainment shows were going to be all over this. Miranda would be instantly labeled a crook and a charlatan, no matter what the facts eventually turned out to be.

I sighed. And for the last time I headed out the door.

"Don't forget Monk," Devlin said as I retreated from view. "You guys are partners. We need you both on board."

• • • • • CHAPTER ELEVEN

Mr. Monk and Adrian

"Your goals are achieved moment by moment, one small act after another. What may look impossible is just one small everyday possibility on top of the last. Do you need to change your life in some big way? Start by changing a small thing. Before you know it . . ." Ring, ring, ring . . .

I didn't turn off Miranda's voice, but checked the clock on the mantel: seven twenty. Right on time. Monk had been calling since six ten that evening, every ten minutes on the dot. It didn't matter that I wasn't answering and he knew I wasn't answering. He would keep calling until his bedtime at exactly eleven p.m.

All the way home, through the afternoon traffic, I mulled over my talk with Amy Devlin. She had been right, of course, and Captain Stottlemeyer had been right the other day at the clown's house. Monk and I were partners. And it was my job, now more than ever, to figure out how to get things done.

As much as it hurt my ego to think Monk could do without me on the detection end, it was true. My half of the partnership was going to have to be organizational: to keep him in line, to keep his phobias from interfering, and to make our clients happy.

Of course our biggest client was the SFPD. No more excuses, I told myself. I had to find a way to make each case work, even if it involved a germ-infested spider zoo owned by an aardvark who liked to dress as a clown.

My first step in this personal transformation had been to put on a cup of Ginger Kiss organic tea and break out my favorite Miranda CD—number three, *Changing Your Life Moment to Moment.*

By nine forty-nine, I had savored a nuked portion of leftover Chinese, sipped two more cups of tea, and listened to two more CDs. I didn't care what anyone was going to say about Miranda Bigley. She helped me cope.

And then I was ready. At nine fifty, my cell phone rang. I waited a few seconds, then picked up. "Hello, Adrian."

I don't know what shocked him more: the fact that I finally picked up or the fact that I called him by his first name.

"Um," he said. I was enjoying his confusion. "I must have the wrong number."

"You don't have the wrong number, Adrian. This is Natalie."

"Natalie who?"

"Natalie Teeger, your partner."

"This must be some mistake. First, the Natalie Teeger I know isn't answering her phone. And second, she always calls me Mr. Monk. Always."

"Welcome to the new world, Mr. . . . Adrian." This was going to take some getting used to, but I was determined to make it work.

"Why are you changing? I hate change."

"Because I need change."

"You can call me Mr. Adrian if you want. That's a little better."

"No, that makes you sound like a nineteen fifties hairdresser. From now on, it's Adrian and Natalie. Unless you want to call me Ms. Teeger. We can be Mr. Monk and Ms. Teeger."

"I'm not calling you Ms. Teeger. You're Natalie. It's a tradition."

"Then you're going to be Adrian. We've got to be equal partners. The work we do is different but equal. Do you understand, Adrian?"

There was a long pause on the other end. "Can you put Natalie on, please?"

It went on like that for another eighteen minutes, which was good. I'd been expecting a lot longer.

"Good," I said at long last. "Now that we have that settled, let's talk about the clown case."

The next morning was a little hectic. It started with me showing up at Stottlemeyer's office and briefing the team—the captain and the lieutenant and two patrolmen who had been assigned—on the new ground rules. They were excited to have Monk back on the case and readily agreed to my conditions.

For the duration of the case, certain words couldn't be used in Monk's presence. The victim was Mr. Smith, not the clown. His profession was to be referred to simply as his job or profession. What he wore was to be called a uniform, not a costume. There were several other rules, but you get the picture.

I was even thinking of instituting a clown jar—like a swear jar, but where people would have to throw in a quarter every time they said the C word. But having something sitting around labeled a "clown jar" seemed to defeat the whole purpose.

We made similar adjustments on the bulletin board and dry-erase board. The most time-consuming change was with the files. Everything that Monk might read about the case had to be redacted with black markers to remove any reference to the circus world.

"Is this really necessary?" Devlin protested.

"It is if you want Monk," I said. "I know he's obligated to work with you, but you have to meet us halfway. I was up until midnight convincing him. That's an hour after his official bedtime. And this is as good as it got. Monk is going to try to go to his happy place and forget that the victim was clown oriented, or whatever you call it. And we have to help."

Captain Stottlemeyer understood. In fact, he was impressed. "You're really taking control. If this new attitude works . . . our lives are going to be a lot easier."

"That's our goal," I said. "Welcome to the firm of Monk and Teeger. Now, if you'll give me twenty minutcs, I have to go pick up Adrian."

"Who?" Stottlemeyer asked.

"Adrian," I said again.

"Adrian? Really? Is that allowed?"

"Of course it's allowed," said Devlin. She didn't quite beam with pride. It was more of a smirk. "About time, too. Good for you."

"Sharona calls him Adrian," I pointed out. "So do his mailman and his favorite grocery bagger."

"I know that," said the captain. "Is Monk okay with this?"

"He's going to have to be," said Devlin.

"No, he's not. Monk is not okay with a whole host of things. That's what makes him Monk."

I tried to explain. "When we first met, I called him Mr. Monk out of respect. Then he became my boss and it seemed right. But now we're friends and business partners. This will help everyone remember."

What I didn't say was that this would help me most of all. From now on, every time I said "Adrian," I would be reminding myself. And that would just make me work harder and take more responsibility.

It was like a final gift that Miranda Bigley had given me: the capacity to make one little change that would help lead to bigger changes and the woman I still needed to be. "Thank you," I said mentally, then walked out of the captain's office to go pick up my partner.

This time it was a perfect exit.

CHAPTER TWELVE

Mr. Monk Is On Board

So . . . am I going to continue writing about Monk, or start writing about someone named Adrian?

I've given this a little thought (not a lot; life is too hectic). I think I'll stick with Monk. I've been writing about Monk for years and it would feel kind of odd to change. But don't let this get back to him. It'll just start the argument all over.

When Monk walked into the captain's office that morning, he immediately got to work. The patrolmen who had conducted the interviews read their statements aloud, leaving Monk to close his eyes and just listen. I knew what he was doing, trying to convince his inner child that the victim had arrived at these homes, changed into a plumber's uniform, not a clown suit, and spent the next two hours talking to six-year-olds about kitchen drains and S curve shower pipes.

After hearing the five statements, Monk glanced through the files, then spent half an hour staring at the bulletin board and the dry-erase board and the map with the color-coded pins. He was focused and making a real effort. I was proud of him.

"Theories?" he asked, finally looking around and facing the rest of us.

"That's why you're here, Monk," said the captain.

"I have a favorite," Lieutenant Devlin said, almost meekly. She ran a hand through her spiky hair and approached the map. "Dr. and Mrs. Weintraub on Nob Hill. They fit all the parameters. We need to concentrate on them."

"You're wrong," said Monk flatly. "But go on."

She was taken aback. "Why should I go on if you think I'm wrong?"

"Because this is the new me, cooperative and professional and not even aware that the victim we're wasting so much time and resources on was a sickening, disgusting clo—"

"Adrian!" I interrupted. My calling him that was still so new that I found it could shock him back into focus. "Go ahead, Lieutenant."

Amy Devlin cleared her throat, swallowed her pride, and started again. "Steven Weintraub is an anesthesiologist with intimate knowledge of poisons and how they affect the system. His wife, Dina, is a serious gardener." She pointed to a photo pinned to the bulletin board. It was a narrow marble mansion, one of the last of its kind in Nob Hill. "An examination of the side garden, conducted without permission but from a public leeway, reveals the presence of foxglove."

She pointed to a photo of a patch of stalky purple plants. I remembered them fondly from my childhood in Monterey. My Scottish grandmother had called them fairy fingers and shown us how to put the little flowers over our fingertips, like the fingers of a glove, which I suppose is how the plant got its name. We never dreamed they were poisonous.

"The berries and roots contain atropine. If you boil

them down and concentrate it, you'll get a poison strong enough to kill topically, like the murder weapon that killed Mr. Smith. Dr. Weintraub would have the expertise to do this.

"The Weintraub house is also just a block from the Polk Street post office, where the tainted money was sent from. And"—she ticked off the final detail on her list—"the Weintraubs let Smith change into his 'uniform' in the doctor's home office. According to Dina Weintraub, he took a long time in there with the door closed. Apparently he had a problem with a very long shoelace, which took him a while to fix."

I glanced at Monk but he didn't react to the big clown shoe reference. Good.

"Anyway," Devlin went on, "I think this puts them at the top of our list."

Stottlemeyer nodded, acknowledging her competent police work, then turned to Monk. "Obviously you disagree."

Monk rolled his shoulders and nodded. "The killer would never use his local post office. That's just dumb.

"Point two: Someone's home office is not the most realistic place to run across compromising information, even though it may seem so. Smith would need their passwords or have some idea what he was looking for. It's hard to fathom them leaving blackmail-worthy information in plain sight, especially since Dr. Weintraub was at the event and he's not a sloppy person." Monk pointed to a close-up front view of the house. "See? That window looks into the doctor's office. Everything's in place. Even the two pencils on the blotter are perfectly positioned and exactly the same length."

Stottlemeyer pressed his nose up to the photo in question. "How can you even see . . . ? Oh, yeah, I see it now. You're right."

"What about the foxglove?" Devlin asked, refusing to give up. "That's pretty incriminating."

"The house only has that one small garden. If the doctor distilled poison from foxglove, why are there still so many of them?"

"He's not saying you're wrong," I told Devlin.

"You're wrong," Monk told her.

"Adrian just has a different idea. Don't you, Adrian? Adrian?"

Monk choked a little and whatever snide rejoinder he was aiming at the lieutenant died in his throat. This "Adrian" thing was magic. I should have thought of it years ago.

"Different idea," he moaned, and walked to the other side of the bulletin board, as far away from me as possible. "I would focus your resources on another family, the Harrimans."

According to the report we'd just heard, John and Alicia Harriman were both stockbrokers, although Alicia worked internationally and was away from home half the time. They had an eight-year-old son, a six-year-old daughter, and lived on a spacious lot on Sacramento Street in the toniest section of Pacific Heights.

"First, the date is perfect," Monk explained. "Smith opened his post office box four days after the Harrimans' event, giving him just enough time to figure out his blackmail plan.

"Second, the Harrimans also have a garden." He crossed

to a photo featuring a front garden sloping up to an expansive Victorian porch. He pointed at the photo on the bulletin board. "It's not quite symmetrical."

For Monk this was damning in and of itself, but almost never did it prove the gardener was a killer.

"You can see it's almost symmetrical—the azaleas on both sides, the roses. Even the Japanese maples are evenly spaced and the same height. Very civilized. But look at the foxgloves." He pointed to the familiar stalks, these a little more pink than purple. "There are twice as many on this side than on the other. Someone removed some foxglove."

Stottlemeyer examined the photo. "It would be interesting to see if you're right." He turned to the officers. "Check out Google Earth Street View. That's the easiest way."

"Got it," said Officer Garcia, and made a note.

"But I think our biggest tip is the garage," said Monk.

"The garage?" Devlin picked up the Harriman folder and took a look. "Smith changed into his 'uniform' in their garage. Is that what you mean?"

Monk lifted the corner of his mouth. "I love garages. I mean, personally I hate them. All the filth and disorder and oil stains on the cement. But people are weird about them. They store all sorts of stuff there—things they don't want in the house and then never get rid of. If killers were smart, they would never buy a house with a garage. It's like a ticking time bomb."

"You think something's in the garage?" Stottlemeyer asked.

"John Harriman was not at the children's event that day. It was his wife who gave Smith access to the garage because she wanted him to make a dramatic entrance through the front door. Yes, something was in the garage."

"Well, kiddies. We have a suspect." Captain Stottlemeyer clapped his hands and turned to face us. "Nobody talks to the Harrimans. Got it? Our goal now is information. Whatever can help us get a search warrant for that garage."

"I'll focus on Harriman's personal history," Devlin volunteered. "Any crimes he could be covering up. Suspicious deaths of relatives or associates. Influxes of cash. How far back should I go?"

"Eight years, two months," Monk said. "Eight years, three months this coming Tuesday."

When he realized we were staring openmouthed, he explained. "I know I should say ten years. Ten is a more civilized number. But Harriman bought this house eight years and two months ago. I doubt he would have taken the trouble to have the movers pack up and transport incriminating evidence to a new place, so I'm guessing this happened after they moved."

"Thanks," said Stottlemeyer, including us both. "Good work."

"I'm going to need to visit Mr. Smith's house again," Monk said. "Personally this time."

"Really?" Devlin sounded dubious. "You don't need me to go in there with my camera and describe it?"

"No." He sighed, long and hard, as if carrying the weight of a thousand clowns. "I'm afraid I have to see it myself. Last time we missed something."

"What? What did we miss?" the captain asked.

"I'll tell you when we get there." And he started to leave.

"We didn't miss a thing," Devlin protested, but no one listened.

I followed my partner out of Stottlemeyer's office and to the elevator, but not before catching the captain's eye. The man was shaking his head, exhibiting a familiar blend of admiration and curiosity.

Two perfect exits in a row. I was on a roll.

CHAPTER THIRTEEN

Mr. Monk Gets Mail

I drove Monk to his Pine Street apartment building, and this time when he made noises about sharing a fun evening of washing and drying all his lightbulbs, I actually said yes. It was my way of rewarding him.

He'd been feeling a little lonely and disconnected, I could tell. Ever since Ellen slammed her shop door in his face, he'd been quietly entertaining the possibility that he might, just might, be wrong about some things. I think that, plus my brilliant maneuver of calling him Adrian, had made last night's marathon phone session a lot easier.

The call had begun with him refusing to do anything that made him uncomfortable, as if no one else in the world did uncomfortable things. I know it's much harder for him than it is for the rest of us. But somewhere around eleven thirty, he began to realize that his friends needed him to step up right now—the captain, Devlin, me, and especially Ellen—at least just a little.

"Are you going to tell Ellen about this?" he asked as we celebrated our day of investigation with two tall glasses of water.

"I will," I assured him. "She'll be so proud of you."

"It's your fault," Monk said, and he meant it. "I don't know what's gotten into you."

"It's called a partnership."

Monk tilted his head from side to side. "I could have walked inside, you know, except for that sign on the door. 'Poop.' In big brown letters. She should change the name."

"Adrian, this is not about her changing. It's about you changing." He still winced when I used his name. I had to remind myself not to overuse the magic.

"Me changing? Well, the first thing I'd change is the name of her store."

I didn't pursue it. He had already done so much I didn't want to overload him. I held up my glass and we air-toasted. Much more sanitary than a real toast. "Clink," I said, and he clinked me back. "Now, how about those lightbulbs?"

As Monk went to fetch his cleaning supplies from the closet, I switched on the TV and began to flip through to the music channels. Monk was fond of Bach when he cleaned. There was a mathematical precision to Bach's music that he found soothing. We had tried Mozart once, but Mozart can get a little crazy.

On my way to the classical end of the dial, I happened to slowly flip by CNN. A handsome, big-featured face was on a split screen with Wolf Blitzer and I made the mistake of stopping.

"Our books are open," Damien Bigley told the CNN host. "We intend to cooperate fully with any investigation. It is inconceivable that Miranda would have done anything to hurt the good name of BPM. Ours is a philosophy based on ethical behavior and honesty."

Wolf seemed unimpressed. "We have reports from an unnamed source that your wife admitted to these financial misdeeds in her suicide note."

"That is totally untrue," Damien replied, handling it more calmly that I would. Where do reporters ever get these inside sources? "Miranda mentioned the pain and heartache her actions would cause her family and friends. Nothing more."

"So, are you denying these charges?"

Damien brushed a hand through his salt-and-pepper hair and looked sincerely at the camera. "As far as I know, no charges have been filed. We are going through an audit, scheduled months ago. And we're cooperating fully with the state district attorney."

Wolf looked straight ahead on the split screen, which was his version of looking Damien in the eyes. "Mr. Bigley, do you believe your wife capable of embezzling from her company?"

Damien looked away. "The economy has been hard on everyone," he said. "But Best Possible Me was Miranda's life. How could anyone steal part of their own life?"

"He's lying." The voice startled me.

Monk stood behind me, his arms loaded with a lightbulb-cleaning kit he had bought online from Japan. "You can tell by his eyes. He knew what was going on, whatever it was."

"Exactly." I snapped off the set. To hell with Bach. "That's the great thing about her suicide. For him. His wife takes the blame and he gets to be with his mistress."

"It was still a suicide," Monk pointed out.

I cringed. "You don't think he could have hypnotized her?"

"It doesn't work that way. Even under hypnosis, you maintain control."

I guess Monk should know. He had once gone to a hypnotherapist for treatment. This was years ago. Through some mistake that only seems to happen to him, he found himself regressing to the age of seven, the last time in his life when he'd been truly happy.

For days, he'd gone around as an emotional seven-year-old, carefree as a puppy, playing in the trees and even adopting a frog. We thought he was under the spell of his hypnotism and didn't know what to do. But along the way, he solved a murder and, when he needed to, pulled himself out of his trance.

"Okay. Not hypnotism," I said. "But it had to be something. He knew she was going to do it—on that particular day. How do you explain that?"

"I don't have to. I was there when she jumped. It was her choice."

Monk circled around my chair to the coffee table. "Do you want to start on one side of the apartment and work across, or should we start with the twenty-five-watt bulbs and work up to the three-ways? You're the guest." He pointed. "What's that?"

He was talking about the state of his coffee table. His binder of phobias had been pushed aside and replaced by a manila envelope.

"Oh." I'd completely forgotten. "When I came to pick you up, I brought in your mail. This was the only thing." I hadn't mentioned it to him at the time because we'd been on a mission and I didn't want him distracted. "Who's it from?" I asked.

"No return address." He retrieved two wipes and held the

padded envelope at an angle to the light. "Gum residue," he announced. "There was a return address label but it came off. Handwriting isn't familiar. The postmark is smudged and almost out of ink." He held it out and I inspected the blocky letters, addressed to a "Mr. A. Monk."

"You open it," he said, which is his usual reaction to getting something unexpected in the mail.

I grabbed a pair of scissors from the scissor sanitizer in the kitchen (another online purchase from Japan) and slit it open. "It's money," I said, peering inside. Without thinking, I dumped the contents onto the coffee table.

It was money, all right, but not American. The bills were old and of various shades of brown and gray and green, all basically the same size as U.S. bills. The denominations ranged from one to one hundred. "What country are they from?"

Monk peered down at them. "From right here," Monk said. "Confederate money."

"Confederate? From the Civil War?" I was instantly fascinated. "Who would send you Confederate money?" I checked the envelope again but there was nothing more inside except two pieces of stiff cardboard to keep it from bending. I had expected at least a note. "Are they valuable?"

"Depends on the rarity. Ambrose used to collect them as a kid, until mother made him wash them all with Ajax. Then the bills disintegrated and he lost interest."

I turned over a five-dollar bill and found a beautiful engraving of an "Indian Princess." On the back of a fifty was a portrait labeled "Jeff Davis." I began to gently sift through them. Stonewall Jackson. A woman I'd never heard of named Lucy Pickens. "They're like little pieces of history."

"Natalie, what are you doing?"

"I'm playing with money."

"Stop!"

It never even occurred to me, not until I heard the panic in his voice. Money in a manila envelope, sent through the mail with no return address. Sent to the detective genius heading up the poisoned-money investigation. And here I was playing with it, like a kid in a sandbox.

"Augh!" I dropped the bills and froze.

"Go wash your hands. Don't touch anything. Here, follow me."

I held up my hands and followed him into the kitchen, where he quickly turned on the hot tap, unwrapped a bar of soap, and dropped it in my palms. "Scrub like the wind. Like the wind. And keep the water hot."

While I scrubbed away, he ran back into the living room and dialed 911.

CHAPTER FOURTEEN

Mr. Monk and the Headache

Obviously, I didn't die.

This is kind of embarrassing, so I don't want to drag it out and build up a lot of suspense. But it was totally a false alarm. The EMTs showed up at Monk's apartment, this time with their own hazmat masks and gloves. Stottlemeyer and Devlin showed up a few minutes later to take the money and envelope into custody. Meanwhile, Monk and I were whisked away to the emergency room at San Francisco General.

By midnight, we'd been released with a clean bill of health. There was no poison on the bills or on the envelope. Never had been. And that was a point I had to continue making to Monk as the captain dropped him off in front of his place. I could see him eyeing the window of his second-floor sanctuary.

"You don't have to spend all night cleaning," I told him. For the tenth time.

"People in hazmat suits were in there. Hazmat!"

"Yes, but they didn't find anything."

"But they were wearing them. Imagine where those suits were before they came here. Those men don't wear them to tea parties."

"Fine." I sighed. "Do what you want. Just be bright-eyed and brilliant when the captain picks you up. We're revisiting Dudley Smith's house. You promised us you'd find a clue."

All three of us got out of the car, and the captain and I watched as Monk disappeared into his building. "He's going to clean all night, isn't he?" the captain said.

"I'm not my partner's keeper."

"I'm glad you guys are okay. That's the important thing." He brushed his mustache, which was his tell for being sincere.

"I feel so guilty wasting everybody's time."

"No, you were right. It was a weird situation. Any idea who might have done it?"

I'd spent the last few hours mulling that question. "If the money had been poisoned, I could understand—a murder attempt. But this was totally harmless. Maybe the killer had meant it as a warning. Get off the case or next time you're dead."

Stottlemeyer frowned. "An odd warning. And why Confederate money? It's harder to get and more expensive. I could understand if he wanted to poison you. Sending Confederate money would almost guarantee that it gets handled."

"Exactly the way I did," I said, still a little embarrassed.

"But it wasn't poisoned, so what's the point?"

I didn't have an answer. "Can't you do something with the envelope?" I asked. "At least figure out where it was postmarked?"

"We have our tech guys trying to lift residue ink. I'm not sure how much that will tell us."

I stretched and yawned. I couldn't help it. "Well, I should get home. If Mr. Monk . . . I mean, Adrian. If Adrian has a big day tomorrow, then I have a bigger one."

The captain chuckled. "I like the way you're doing this."

I smiled, took my keys from my bag and crossed to my Subaru. I was parked in Monk's private spot, which he never uses because he has a chauffeur instead of a car.

The next morning started early, at least for Devlin and me. The stress from yesterday's poison scare and the lack of a full night's sleep had combined to give me a headache that only seemed to get worse. I took two Tylenols, my last two from the bottle, and hoped for the best.

We met at the seedy apartment on Willow Street with our supplies and worked from the front door inward. Along the way we checked on the canaries in the bedroom. After Monk's visit, Devlin was going to take them to her niece and nephew in Alameda, where they'd be sure to get a good home.

The trick was to prepare the crime scene, hiding or minimizing the clown references without compromising anything that might be critical. The business sign by the front door was easy, as was the circus painting in the hall. We draped them in black plastic, cut from garbage bags, making sure that all the corners were cut straight and the tape evenly spaced. It wouldn't be smart to cover them up, only to have Monk fixate on the covering.

The clown shoes under the bed took more thinking. We decided to hang a sheet of construction paper in front of their offensive presence and write "shoes" on it in big letters.

If Monk wanted to lift up the paper and examine the yellow monstrosities, he could. Otherwise, they'd be out of sight.

Devlin and I wore plastic booties and rubber gloves, since the place was an active crime scene and might still have some atropine residue lying around. By ten o'clock we'd finished, just in time for the captain and Monk.

"I know this is a clown house," Monk whispered to me as soon as he saw the covered-up sign.

"I know. But you're powering through it. Out of sight, out of mind."

He rolled his shoulders, put on his booties and gloves, and walked into the building. "You'll tell Ellen I'm trying, right? I'm capable of change."

"You're doing great, Adrian. Great." My morning headache, which had never really left, was starting to work overtime.

The captain led our little parade into the front hallway. "Okay, Monk, what are we looking for?" It was what we all wanted to know.

"We're looking for a reason," he said. "The reason the killer felt safe."

"What do you mean?"

"Put yourself in his position. He's being blackmailed by someone who's been in his house. It could be a maid or a repairman or a friend. He doesn't know. All he has is a post office box where he's supposed to send the money—"

Devlin interrupted. "The boxes are protected under the Privacy Act. Our guy could have hung around the O'Farrell Street branch to see who opened box eight forty-nine. But that's far from a sure thing, and he'd only get one shot."

"Why didn't he hire someone to monitor the post office twenty-four-seven?" I asked. "Some sleazy PI," said the woman who hadn't even passed her PI exam.

"Involving someone else is a loose thread," said the captain. "So, instead, our guy poisoned the money, hoping it would do the job, which it did. What did you mean about the killer feeling safe? Monk?"

Monk had walked right past the plastic-covered painting and into the living room. "Mr. Smith took something from that garage, some piece of evidence he could send to the police or the guy's wife or whatever . . . in case Harriman refused to be blackmailed."

"Sure," said Devlin. "You always need leverage."

"So, the killer knows there's evidence floating around. But he still feels safe enough to go through with his anonymous plan."

"So, what is this invisible evidence we haven't been able to find?" I think I was speaking for everyone.

"I'll know it when I see it."

The rest of the morning was a fascinating type of torture. The four of us squeezed our way from room to room, avoiding contact with everything, staying out of Monk's framed sight lines and, most important, keeping his eyes and mind away from anything remotely clownish.

"Do you have any aspirin?" I asked Devlin as we made our way out of the living room. She didn't. So I asked Stottlemeyer. "Aspirin, Cemedrin, Tylenol . . . ?" He didn't either. What is it with cops? Don't they ever need pain relievers?

In the bathroom we had another close call when Monk opened a cabinet and found the top shelf lined with clown makeup. His face instantly froze. I called him Adrian and begged him to concentrate. But we only really got through the moment when Devlin suggested that he visualize it as Kabuki makeup.

"Smith was a Japanese actor in traditional white face," she said.

"Or a drag queen," Stottlemeyer said. "Maybe Smith did a drag show somewhere in the Castro. Don't even think clown."

"Clown?" Monk gasped.

"Not a clown," I corrected him. "Think of a drag queen . . . who does Kabuki."

The two detectives managed to rush him out of the clown's claustrophobic bathroom. I could hear him wheezing in the hall as they talked him down. Meanwhile, I had a head that was ready to explode.

"Aspirin, Cemedrin, Tylenol . . ." I said to myself, repeating the words like a mantra. If I could just get hold of some aspirin, Cemedrin or Tylenol. And then I saw it. It was on the top shelf, beside the row of makeup. A single lifesaving bottle of Cemedrin lying sideways in a ziplock baggie.

I was sorely tempted. That tells you just how much pain I was in. I was inches away from tampering with a crime scene and filching a couple of Cemedrin from the victim's bathroom. My hand was halfway up to the baggie when a thought struck in the very back of my brain. Why did he keep his Cemedrin in a baggie? It struck but it didn't stick.

Suddenly I found the baggie in my hand, my other hand fiddling with the zipper. "Natalie, don't." I nearly jumped out of my skin.

It was Monk, right behind me. He was focused now, not a

whiff of fear or distraction about him. He held out his hand for the zip-locked bottle.

"This is it," he said, turning to face the others in the bathroom doorway. His face was triumphant. "I was distracted by some Kabuki drag queen's makeup. That's why I didn't notice. Stupid, stupid."

"Notice what?" asked the captain.

"This. A 2009 bottle of Cemedrin," he announced. "Early 2009."

"If you're telling me it's past its expiration," I said, "I don't care."

"You should." He was serious. "They redesigned the bottle in 2009. Four months later, they were forced to redesign it again. Do you remember why?"

There was maybe a five-second pause. "Dear Lord," said Stottlemeyer.

"Oh, my God," I said a second later. And to think, I'd been this close to taking one. "You don't mean . . ." My head began to throb even more.

"What? People didn't like the first design?" Devlin laughed. We didn't laugh.

She hadn't been living in San Francisco back then, hadn't lived through it. It was an FBI case that Monk hadn't been involved with, given his testy relationship with the bureau at the time. If he had, the homicides might not have gone unsolved.

"You never heard of the Cemedrin murders?" the captain asked his lieutenant. "Three deaths in one week, all in the Bay Area. It was like the Tylenol murders in Chicago back in the eighties."

"Yes, of course I've heard of them."

Everyone had. In response to the seven Tylenol deaths in Chicago, the industry had invented tamper-proof containers. Two decades later, some sicko copycat in San Francisco figured out how to bypass the plastic cap seals on a few bottles of Cemedrin and place them in stores. Two children and an older man died.

I remembered it vividly. Julie was a senior, and at her high school, there were posters showing the bottle and telling everyone to turn them over to the FBI. Two more poisoned bottles were discovered, one in a grade-school nurse's office.

Cemedrin's parent company nearly went bankrupt as a result. And the sicko was never caught, just like in Chicago.

"It was a solid cyanide compound," Monk told us, holding up the plastic baggie and the bottle. "If I'm not mistaken—and I'm not—that's what's in here."

"You're saying this is what Dudley Smith found in the Harriman garage?" asked Devlin. "When he was changing into his . . . entertainer uniform."

Monk nodded. "John Harriman, maybe his wife, tampered with the bottles back in 2009 in the garage. Somehow he or she didn't dispose of all the evidence. That's how it is with garages. They're insidious."

"And when Dudley Smith saw this, he knew what it was?" Devlin asked.

"It was on every channel. In every paper," said Stottlemeyer. "I would have recognized it myself if I hadn't been so distracted by Monk getting so distracted."

"Now we know why the killer was willing to take a chance," said Monk. "Without someone's eyewitness testimony about finding the bottle, it doesn't mean much."

Stottlemeyer lifted the baggie gingerly from Monk's hand. "Smith was smart enough to preserve it. Maybe we can lift some prints or DNA. Good job, everyone."

"At least we have motive," I pointed out, more than a little proud of Monk and me. Yes, me. I'm the one who found it. Let's forget for a second that I was about to open it and pop a couple.

"This guy likes his poison," said Stottlemeyer. "I have to believe we're on the right track."

We were all kind of giddy at the prospect. A dead case, a famously dead case. And it was coming back to life in front of our eyes.

"This is wild," Devlin said, almost in a hush. "The FBI works for years hunting the Cemedrin killer, thousands of hours of work. And he's caught on a fluke by some clown in a garage."

"Don't say 'clown,'" said the rest of us, pretty much in unison.

• • • • • CHAPTER FIFTEEN

Mr. Monk Shakes on It

The captain gave us the rest of the day off, although for him and Devlin I'm sure the work day was just beginning.

I dropped Monk off for his regular session with Dr. Bell. He was down to once every Thursday, which was quite an improvement. For many long years, he'd seen his psychiatrist three times a week. And when things were unusually stressful, four.

Ever since he had solved his wife's murder, Monk and Dr. Bell have had less and less to talk about. So it was a bit of a surprise when I finished my hour of power-shopping at the nearby Real Food and picked him up in front of the two-story medical building.

"I need to go back Saturday," he announced as he got in, and fastened his seat belt. "Dr. Bell doesn't normally do Saturdays. I had to spend half of today's session talking him into it."

I was tempted to point out that he might not need a session on Saturday if he hadn't spent half of today's session talking the doctor into it.

"I can't bring you on Saturday," I said, shifting into gear and pulling away from the curb. "I'm going away."

"Another weekend with the girlfriends?"

"Same as before, yes. BPM is doing a special retreat at the Sanctuary. And, no, you can't come. Not even for lunch."

"I have a session anyway. And don't worry about driving me. I have my ways."

"You keep saying that. What ways? No, don't tell me. I prefer not to know."

Monk shrugged and changed his grip on his seat belt. "Dr. Bell says Ellen is being unreasonable."

Oh, so that was what triggered his sudden need for analysis. "I'm sure he didn't say that."

"He said someone was being unreasonable. I assumed he meant her."

"He meant you, Adrian."

"He also said you should start calling me Mr. Monk again."

"I don't think he said that."

The next morning at exactly nine, we met Stottlemeyer and Devlin at the station. The fact that the captain closed the door to his office and the fact that the patrolmen, Garcia and Chandler, weren't in attendance should have been a signal that something was up.

"All right, we've made progress," the captain said, settling behind his desk. "First off, we lucked out with Google Earth." He turned around a photo and shoved it over. "This street view was taken eight months ago. Ain't technology grand!"

He also shoved over a magnifying glass, the one he kept in his bottom drawer beside his emergency bottle of scotch.

It was a remarkably clear street view of the house on Sacramento. And the purplish pink stalks on both sides of the garden were lush and perfectly symmetrical. "It's foxglove," I confirmed.

"We put a rush on the pill analysis," the captain added, turning around and shoving across a one-pager. "A solid cyanide compound, just like in oh-nine. Just like Monk said." And another one-pager, turned and shoved. "The bottle. There were prints all right, but the oils had decayed and they were smudged. We'll be lucky to get one or two points of comparison, which means nothing. Not even a search warrant."

That was one factoid I'd learned over the years. Fingerprints don't last forever, no matter what they tell you on cop shows. They're basically made up of skin oil and sweat. In some cases, they last for years. In most cases, not.

Monk raised his hand, like a kid in school. "I hate to be the party pooper, but can you rule out an innocent origin of the bottle?"

I'd thought about this, too. A defense attorney could argue that John Harriman had bought the tampered bottle in a store, like the victims, and just never used it or turned it in to the authorities.

"We can," said the captain. "The plastic seal was on the bottle but loose. It hadn't yet been heat shrunk."

That seemed good enough for me. "How about Smith himself?" I asked. "Could he have been the Cemedrin killer?"

Devlin shook her head and checked her notes. "Not possible. In 2009, Dudley Smith was living in Vincennes, Indiana, going to school."

"At his age?" I asked, although I have nothing against adult education. I was doing it myself. But why Indiana?

"Clown school." Monk closed his eyes and did a full-body shiver. "Dear God, the man was a worse pervert than I thought."

"Monk's right," said Devlin. "About the school. Vincennes is home to the Red Skelton Clown Academy. It's part of the university."

"Really, Monk?" asked Stottlemeyer. "How did you know about the school?"

"It's the first rule of phobias," Monk said. "Know your enemy."

"Okeydokey." Stottlemeyer turned to his lieutenant. "So, we've eliminated Dudley and an innocent origin of the bottle. What else you got?"

Amy flipped to her next page. "I'm running a background on Harriman and his wife, focusing on a connection to any of the victims. Also any history of mental-health issues."

"Excuse me." Monk raised his hand again. "Isn't this technically an FBI case?"

"Half of it," said Stottlemeyer. "It's also an SFPD homicide. We're just following the leads."

"But aren't we required to turn over evidence? It's an open federal case."

"Technically, yes," said Stottlemeyer.

"What did the lab say when you gave them the bottle?" asked Monk. "They must have known."

"Are you familiar with Ms. Jasmine Patil?"

I didn't know about Monk, but I wasn't.

"I asked for her personally." The captain brushed his mustache. “A twenty-three-year-old CS technician who was raised and schooled in New Delhi. Moved here two years ago and doesn’t ask questions.”

Monk got it. “You’re not turning this over to the FBI.”

Of the four of us, not one had had a good experience with the bureau. For instance, during our last encounter, less than a year ago, they’d accused Monk and me of laundering money for the Italian mob. That was also the case in which Monk accused an FBI special agent of murder and the theft of half a million from the evidence room. Monk of course had been right.

The bane of our existence over there was Special Agent Joshua Grooms, a beefy, intimidating man with an off-centered widow’s peak that drove Monk crazy. Hold on! Can you have more than one bane? Because our second bane would have to be Special Agent George Cardea. We had embarrassed both agents professionally on more than one occasion.

“Do you really want to deal with them?” Devlin asked. She and Stottlemeyer had obviously discussed this before we arrived.

“Of course not,” I agreed. Grooms and his macho crew had always been a thorn in our side. Plus—and I couldn’t help thinking it—a high-profile case like this would be a perfect way to inaugurate the new team, Monk and Teeger, PIs extraordinaire. On the other hand . . . “Won’t we get in trouble?”

“Not if we play it right,” said Stottlemeyer. “We arrest Harriman for the Smith murder, then quite by chance make the connection to the big oh-nine case. No one but Monk would have made the connection to begin with.”

"Grooms is going to be pissed," I said, although I couldn't help smiling.

"If he ever finds out we had the Cemedrin bottle and knew what it was and didn't turn it over . . ." Monk shuddered.

"That's why officers Garcia and Chandler are no longer on the team," Devlin pointed out. "The only ones who know are in this room."

"Monk, I need you to promise me something." Captain Stottlemeyer got up from his desk and faced my partner. They were still two feet apart, but to Monk it was the same as being toe-to-toe and eye-to-eye. "I need you to promise you'll stay on this case."

"He'll stay on the case," I said.

"I need to hear it from Monk."

"I'll stay on, Captain," Monk said with a hard swallow.

"Are you sure? It's a clown case, Monk. Before it's over, you may have to deal with squirting flowers and clown cars and God knows what else."

"Stop saying the C word," Monk croaked.

"I'm serious," said Stottlemeyer. "If you can't promise me, then we'll call it off. We'll turn everything over to Grooms and just hope his people can pull it off."

"Even though they haven't pulled it off for the past four years," Devlin said.

"Don't pressure him. It needs to be his choice. No matter what, Monk. Can you promise?"

"Yes, sir," said Monk, as determined as I've ever seen him.

"Good. Let's shake on it." The captain stepped back and

extended his hand. "And no wiping afterward. I want a real shake."

"No wiping?" Monk shivered. "What is this, some barbaric ritual, like becoming blood brothers?"

"Worse. We're germ brothers. Joined by our hand germs. What do you say, buddy?"

Monk stepped up to the captain again, toe-to-toe, two feet apart. And they shook.

CHAPTER SIXTEEN

Mr. Monk Stays at Home

For a while, I thought I wouldn't be able to get away. Monk and Stottlemeyer had become germ brothers, as Monk kept calling it, and the case looked like it was ready to swing into gear. But Lieutenant Devlin still had more research to do.

Our immediate goal was not to raise any flags, either in the department or with the FBI. And then there were the Harrimans. Within the San Francisco financial community, these fat cats were very well connected, which also meant politically connected.

Killers, and this is just from my experience, get sensitive when you start snooping around. We couldn't afford to get on the Harrimans' radar, not until we had enough evidence to go in front of a friendly judge and get a search warrant for their garage.

Anyway, this is a long way of saying that I still had my weekend.

When I first drove into the BPM Sanctuary, the iron gates had been open and welcoming. On this visit, they were closed, with a temporary guard checking photo IDs against names on a list. It was understandable.

Although I'd tried not to turn on a TV for the last few days, it was hard not to know what was happening. As Damien had predicted, the irony proved irresistible, at least to the late-night hosts. Bill Maher did a comedy monologue about the hypocrisy of the self-help movement. Jimmy Fallon, dressed in Miranda drag, did his version of her infomercial.

And there was one I overheard in the shower. I was just waking up to my golden oldies when they rebroadcast David Letterman's Top Ten list: Top Ten Life-Improving Suggestions from Miranda Bigley. "Number Ten: Live each day as if it's the last day you walk up to a cliff." I raced out of the bathroom and nearly took a tumble on the tile, just to keep myself from hearing the other nine.

The faces arriving at the Sanctuary were mostly familiar, the same ones I'd seen on the cliff a week ago, looking so shocked and lost. The few additional attendees were probably her most loyal fans who couldn't stay away. Combined, we made a full contingent, with every cottage on the property occupied.

Teresa Garcia was working the front desk when I checked in. It was hard not to think of her differently now, as something more insidious than the beautiful, bubbly woman who could work out your kinks.

It didn't help when Damien Bigley walked up to us. "Teresa, you remember Natalie Teeger."

"Of course," Teresa said. Her sad smile looked practiced. "We never got around to that massage you had scheduled."

"I was hoping you'd have an availability tomorrow." I don't know why I said it, except that it would have been awkward not to. Did I really want this woman touching me? God help me, I felt as skittish as Monk.

"I'm sure I can work you in. I'll check the book and leave a note on your door."

"Did you know that Natalie here is a police officer?" Damien said.

"I believe you mentioned it."

"Natalie was on the scene in San Francisco when Miranda's body washed up."

"I happened to be with Captain Stottlemeyer," I said. "He and I were working a homicide when the call came in about Miranda." You'll notice that everything I said was true, if perhaps misleading.

"Well . . ." Teresa seemed taken aback. "I'm glad you could take time away from your homicide . . . I mean, to deal with her remains."

"I wouldn't have missed it." If that sounded a bit edgy, I meant it that way.

Dinner that evening was a subdued affair. No speeches or greetings. For me and the other meat eaters, there was a simple grilled salmon. For the vegetarians, it was something with sautéed eggplant and broccolini.

Half an hour later, we gathered in the meditation center. The building was packed by the time I got there. Apparently, other guests had been invited just for the memorial and had begun filling the seats while I was still fiddling with my lemon curd mousse.

The stage was a festival of flowering plants, overflowing from a hundred or more oversized pots. Miranda had spoken more than once about the sadness of cut flowers. "How is it possible to celebrate life by killing so much beauty?" It must have taken them all day to set them up. In the center was a simple black podium backed by a framed photograph of Miranda, about the size of an emperor's portrait in a museum.

I meandered through the rows, searching for a single seat in the somber throng. I gave up and found a spot to myself by a side wall, not far from the stage. I was there, leaning against the wall, when Damien got up.

"Thank you for coming. There have been several memorials around the world to Miranda's memory, from London to Mumbai, where she had been such a beloved figure. But this one, at the peaceful retreat she called home, would have meant the most.

"I can't help wondering how Miranda visualized this moment. It may not be the most pleasant thought, but to me, it's comforting. She knew we would be here, in this room, celebrating her life. I wonder what she would say to us."

For an awful second, I thought he was about to play a recording, with Miranda explaining everything, like the CDs that had made her famous, only this time dealing with the senseless thing she was about to do. I wasn't sure I could have dealt with that, and luckily I didn't have to.

Damien's eulogy was brief and heartfelt. He ended by inviting anyone who wanted to say a few words or to share a memory to come forward. He then took a seat on the dais, half hidden by the living flowers, alongside Teresa Garcia and a few other members of the BPM staff.

I'm not fond of this part of a memorial. Mourners at a microphone can be long-winded and self-serving and—I know it's a terrible thing to say—boring. But this was actually wonderful. So many people loved Miranda and had been helped by her.

My sight line for all this wasn't the best. I was basically staring at the sides of the speakers' heads, but the sound was good. And the view? I could look through the dozens of flowering pots to see . . . Well, this was interesting. Very interesting. I could see Damien and Teresa playing footsie.

At first I thought I was wrong. I had to be wrong. From the torso up, Damien and Teresa were mournfully solemn, sitting side by side but focused totally on the speakers. The widower and the friend. But below the waist, shielded from view by pots and foliage, they were playing footsie like a couple of teenagers in chemistry class.

I don't need to tell you how outraged I was. Anyone would be. From Monk's first deduction about the blood drop to their reservation at the Belmont, I'd known about the affair. But to be carrying on like this at a memorial service . . .

I desperately wanted someone to be standing close to me, someone I could reach out and tap on the shoulder who would bear witness to this, so it wouldn't just look like I was making it up. But the nearest standee on the sidelines was over two arm lengths away.

I don't know exactly what I was doing during this moment of outrage. Staring? Angling for a better view? Making angry little noises in the back of my throat? Whatever I did was enough to draw Damien's attention. For the first two seconds, he affixed me with a sympathetic little smile—at the exact same time he was playing teenage footsie. Outrageous. Then he saw where my eyes were really focused.

He reacted, and it was like reversing a pair of magnets. Two feet that couldn't seem to get enough of each other suddenly flew off in opposite directions. Teresa's foot continued to reach out but Damien's was now swinging wildly trying to avoid hers, all the while his brown eyes boring into mine.

I don't know what I would have done if a speaker hadn't just left the stage. But one had, a doughy man in his sixties who had just talked himself into big, gasping tears. There was a lull now as he cried his way off.

And that's when I took my turn. Before I knew it, I was up on the stage at the podium, adjusting the microphone, without a clue as to what I was doing.

"Hello. My name is Natalie Teeger, and I'd like to say a few words."

CHAPTER SEVENTEEN

Mr. Monk and the Massage

All right. Once more I left you in a state of suspense—only to come back and confess that nothing much happened.

After taking the stage with such purpose, I didn't accuse anyone of anything. Nor did I expose the footsie in the potted plants—not out of concern for them, but out of respect for Miranda.

What I did do was stand in front of her closest friends and admirers and go on about a woman I barely knew and how she couldn't possibly have killed herself. "Something's horribly wrong," I sputtered into the microphone. "Miranda would never do that. Something else was going on, something we don't know about. And we owe it to her memory to find out."

I may also have said something about calling their congressmen and demanding an investigation. And maybe starting a petition. Even at the moment I could sense how irrational I was. And I kept on going. I'm estimating between three minutes and an hour. I have no idea.

I turned out to be the last person speaking. After my emotional rant, I think everyone was pretty much shell-shocked and ready to leave. As for me, I just wanted to get back to my little cottage and hide.

People were being helpful in that regard. As I stumbled out of the meditation center, everyone stepped aside and gave me a wide berth. Except for the last person I wanted to see. Damien Bigley was right outside, waiting. He took me gently by the elbow.

"Natalie, I know how hard this is to deal with." The other mourners were going out of their way to walk around us now, giving us a berth wide enough to dock the *Queen Mary*.

"I've worked plenty of suicides and homicides," I whispered, playing the cop card again. "I know when something isn't right."

"You've heard the rumors about financial irregularities?" he asked, matching my whisper. "I know you have."

"Miranda would never do that."

"You didn't know her." He seemed reluctant to say this. "The Miranda you knew was a manufactured image."

"That's not true."

"It's going to come out. My wife took funds from the corporation and from the nonprofit. It's a sad, familiar story. I don't doubt for a minute she intended to make everything right. But the economy and the real estate crash made that impossible."

"And you knew nothing of this?"

"You'll see. Everyone thinks I was the money guy and she was the guru. It was the opposite. BPM was my idea. But I never had the personality to sell it. Miranda had a way of connecting. But they were my words, my philosophy that people fell in love with."

"So you're the real Miranda Bigley?"

He checked to make sure we were alone, and we were. "I don't want her memory tarnished more than it already is, but . . . Miranda was the face and the finances. The rest was me."

"That's a lie. I've seen her deal with people. She helped thousands."

"I'm not arguing. She was a wonderful woman. She believed everything she said. But look at her background. A Stanford MBA. I was a double major in psychology and philosophy. Who do you think ran the business?"

The look in his George Clooney eyes was deep and sincere. I didn't want to believe him. It was easy for him to blame his dead wife. And—I had to remind myself—bad guys lie. It comes with being a bad guy. Their lies are often more convincing than any truth could be.

"Her plans just got too big." Damien leaned back against the building and let out a deep sigh. "It's partly my fault. If I'd been there for her, if I hadn't gotten involved with Teresa there toward the end . . ."

"So you admit the affair."

His deep eyes hardened. "Miranda wasn't the saint you think. But maybe we could have worked it out. Maybe she would have turned to me and told me about her problems. Maybe we could have found a way out. Instead, she was alone."

"And the documents are going to back this up?"

"Miranda was the CEO. I personally haven't written a check or signed a paper in years."

"We'll see about that." Bad guys lie, I told myself again as I turned and walked away. That's what makes them so bad.

"Natalie!"

I didn't turn around.

That night in my cottage, with the windows open and the sea breeze rustling the gauzy curtains and the soothing rumble of the waves beyond the green lawn, beyond the cliff's edge . . . I didn't sleep a wink.

The best lies are partly true.

I don't know who said that. Maybe me. It popped into my head the next morning, so maybe I dreamed it when I thought I wasn't sleeping. Maybe some wise cop spirit was telling me I didn't have to believe Damien Bigley just because he made sense and could possibly prove a little of what he was saying.

Had he been the real Miranda? Had she been simply the face that drew in the gullible customers, who wanted to believe in a strong, caring, mildly eccentric leader?

Put in this light, it was easier to imagine her walking up to a cliff, in full view, and jumping. And yet . . . the best lies are partly true, I told myself. An ounce of what he said might be true. But only an ounce.

As promised, Teresa left a note. She was keeping a slot free from eleven to noon, she said, and recommended the hot stones. Yuki, Ambrose Monk's wife, was studying different types of Asian massages. She had told me about the hot-stone massage and it sounded interesting. Plus, after my little meltdown last night, I felt guilty enough to make an effort. So I called the front desk and confirmed.

I got to the massage cottage a few minutes early. An assistant, Maxine, had me fill out the paperwork (No, I don't have arthritis or a sports injury. I just want a massage, okay?) and advised a quick steam in order to open up the pores. That's what they tell you.

The cottage was built of stacked stone, a small version of the main building but with fewer windows. The slate floors were cool but comfortable, with colorful hand-woven rugs, probably from Mexico, lying in all the right places.

I emerged from the steam directly into a massage room, where Teresa was waiting. She was all in white, clinical but fashionable, and a great complement to her perfect light brown skin. A few feet away was a shallow steel sink full of water with broad, curved black stones sitting on the bottom.

Teresa followed my gaze. "They're basalt," she gently explained. "Volcanic. The iron and magnesium let them absorb and disperse the heat evenly. We heat them to one hundred twenty degrees, which is quite comfortable. Don't worry."

"I'm not worried," I said. Well, not about the stones.

"Good. How are you, Natalie? Feeling better this morning?"

Teresa had heard about last night, of course, from the footsie incident to every word of my confrontation with her boyfriend. "Much better."

"Memorials can be emotional."

Especially when the widower is playing games under the smiling photo of his suicidal wife, I wanted to say.

As she washed her hands and prepared the stones, I removed my robe and lay facedown on the table, clad only in my white Give-n-Go bikini briefs. A stone massage is performed totally on the back. It makes sense, although I'd never really thought of it. The back is flatter and more conducive to the placement of stones, at least on most women.

The process began with two large stones, one placed horizontally right above my Give-n-Go and one just below my neck. Smaller stones were added in rows on either side of the spine. Almost immediately I could feel the muscles start to warm and relax.

The usual spa music helped lull me into a blissful state. But I was still aware enough to figure out the process. Teresa took two smaller stones, coated them with scented oil and used them to start massaging my arms. By the time she got to my legs, I was asleep.

I know, I know. What a waste, dozing in the middle of a massage. My only excuse was the release of tension from last night and the total lack of sleep.

When I woke, the wall speakers were still echoing with harps and breezes and bird sounds, but most of the stones were gone. There was still one, the largest, across my lower spine. I don't know if the first one had been replaced or not, but it was as warm as before. I lay there for a minute, trying to sense how much time had passed or if Teresa was even in the room.

The room had one small window with Venetian blinds, which were closed. As I tuned my ear, listening past the harps and the breezes and the birds, I thought I could hear the faint sound of voices. Not in the room but from the window.

Could that be Damien mumbling somewhere outside the

cottage? It was a man's voice, certainly. I'd been thinking about Damien so constantly that I would probably identify Winston Churchill's voice as Damien's. But, yes—now that I listened again—it was Damien's. And the other voice was Teresa's.

Before I could think, I was on my feet, not even considering the stone balanced on my back. I froze in place as it took a soft bounce off the massage table and landed with a light thump on a Mexican rug. I breathed again and left it there.

I didn't dare touch the Venetian blinds, although I was tempted. I had no idea how close they were or where they were facing, but I assumed any movement of the blinds could draw their attention. Instead, I crossed to the sound system and clicked off the harps and breezes and birds.

Back at the window, I leaned my head as close as possible and listened. I listened like the wind, to borrow a phrase from Monk.

"I have to get back," Teresa said.

Just my luck, catching them at the end. They were maybe fifteen feet away, on the side facing away from the cliffs and the surf.

"Did she mention anything?" asked Damien.

"Not a word. Why the hell did you even invite her?"

Damien snorted. "How would that have looked? The only person not invited back and she happens to be a cop. One more day and she'll be gone."

"What if she wants to come back again? Another retreat?"

"We'll tell her we're booked."

"I don't like the idea of her snooping around. The woman works homicide."

"Homicide? Listen to you. No one's suggesting homicide, not even her."

I was still trying to process this last sentence when the voices began to come closer. "I have to get back," Teresa repeated.

Uh-oh. Think fast, Natalie. At this point I had two options: stand far from the window and start getting dressed; or hop back on the table and pretend I was still asleep. I chose the wrong one, of course.

I was halfway up on the massage table when I realized my mistake. The stone. Again I had two choices. Leave it on the Mexican rug, like it had just fallen off; or try to get it back onto my lower spine. Again, wrong choice.

I grabbed the flat, oblong stone in my right hand—still warm (how does it do that?). Then I lay facedown and reached behind me and placed it in position, trying to keep it low and straight. I didn't get a second chance. The doorknob turned.

My face was plunged inside the doughnut-shaped headrest, so I could only tell what was happening from the sound and my view of her feet.

For a few seconds, Teresa stood by the door. Next, her feet traveled to the sound system. Damn, I'd forgotten. The music machine clicked and the harps started back up, informing her that it hadn't run out. Someone—guess who—had gotten off the table and turned it off.

A few seconds later and I could feel her hand on the stone, straightening it and placing it slightly lower on my back.

Well, I had to wake up sometime, right? So I began to

move and stretch a little and yawn. "Ah, that was wonderful," I said in a relaxed, breathy voice. "Thank you so much, Teresa. I was totally zonked out."

"Yes, I can see that."

What else could I do? I smiled innocently and left her a big tip.

CHAPTER EIGHTEEN

Mr. Monk Goes Flush

It took all my self-control to stay the full weekend. For one thing, I needed to talk to Monk. And, to tell the truth, without Miranda, the self-help wisdom being handed out like peanuts in a bar began to feel a little hollow. I kept imagining Damien's voice instead of hers, and I didn't like it.

As for Teresa and Damien, avoiding them was easy. I just didn't take any of Damien's classes and never scheduled another massage. During the other hours of the day, I think they were as eager to avoid me as I was to avoid them.

After the last kumbaya on Sunday evening, I drove directly from Half Moon Bay to Monk's apartment and knocked once before barging in. I found him sitting centered on his living room couch reading a manual. "Guess what I did this weekend," I gushed.

"Guess what I did this weekend," he gushed back.

"I overheard Damien Bigley admit to murdering his wife."

"I got a new toilet."

Needless to say, in this crazy world, Monk's news trumped mine.

Monk dragged me down the hall to his bathroom. For a man who hated touching, this consisted of pulling an invisible rope, like a mime playing tug-of-war. "There it is," he said as he stopped pulling and opened the bathroom door. I don't know what I expected, but a toilet had to be pretty special for him to even acknowledge its existence.

It looked just like a toilet, perhaps a little more substantial, with a square control box mounted next to it on the wall. "Walk up to it. Go ahead. But don't use it, for Pete's sake. Don't use it."

"I'm not going to use it," I said, stepping up to the porcelain bowl. I have never used Monk's bathroom, even when I've been there for twelve hours straight. But those are stories for another day.

"See?"

And I did. The lid was magically easing up, like a clamshell. "If you don't turn around in five seconds, the seat will lift up, too. You know, for number one. For boys doing a number one."

"Where did you get this?" I asked. "Wait. Don't tell me. Japan."

If there was one culture that Monk admired above all others, it was the Japanese. At least he had the most in common with them. He had discovered their customs through Yuki, his brother Ambrose's young bride.

To my mind the Japanese took cleanliness to an obsessive level, but to Monk they were people who barely got the picture. So far they had supplied him with a dust magnet, which was literally a magnet that attracted dust, plus the lightbulb-cleaning kit, the scissor sanitizer, and other gadgets I couldn't even begin to guess at.

"It warms the seat. Then it washes your rear and dries it. It even has a stream of warm water aimed at your front parts. I don't know what it's for, so I didn't push that button."

"You don't know?"

"About washing the front? I think it's a prank. You know, for when you have guests and they press the wrong button. Those crazy Japanese."

"You honestly don't know?" How does one try to explain douching to a man like Monk? I decided not to try. "Neither do I."

"Plus it cleans itself after each use and it plays music. Nice music, not rock and roll."

"Why would you need music?"

"For encouragement. Oh, and look." He took a little gadget out of his pocket. "It has a remote control."

"And why does a toilet need a remote control?"

"So you can operate it from a distance."

I was confused. "But you're not doing it from a distance. You're already on the toilet."

He thought for a second. "This gives you a chance to operate the toilet when someone else is on it."

"Why would you want to do that?"

"As a prank? You can combine it with the prank that sprays you in front. A person sits down and . . . surprise!"

"I don't think so."

"Natalie, you're killing the buzz."

"You're right, Adrian," I apologized. "This is the nicest toilet I've ever seen. It's nicer than my house."

"We're not at work, Natalie. You can call me Mr. Monk."

I smiled. "Nice try. Now, do you want to hear about my homicide or not?"

"If I have to." Reluctantly he left his new gadget and we settled on the sofa.

I've had a lot of experience telling him things. I've learned exactly what to include and how much detail to go into and how not to set him off on a magpie tangent. For instance, I went light on the details about the massage, but I repeated word for word everything that Damien and Teresa said.

"'I don't like the idea of her snooping around,'" Monk said, repeating what I'd overheard Teresa saying outside the window. "'The woman works homicide.'"

"Yes, and then Damien said, 'No one's suggesting homicide. Not even her.'"

Monk shrugged. "That's true. You weren't suggesting homicide."

"I know. But she was freaked out because I'm a homicide detective. Why would that freak her out unless she's hiding a homicide?"

"Homicide detective?"

"Okay, I'm not technically. But I do investigate homicides and I am a private detective—at least I will be once I pass the exam. That's not the point. I need you to focus."

And he did. "Okay," he said. "Best-case scenario: Damien and Teresa killed someone else and that's why they're freaked out."

"Who?"

"That's not my problem. Most probable case scenario: They have something to hide, nonhomicidal, and are freaked out that you, Natalie, the crème de la cops, hate them and are snooping around."

"No, no," I insisted. "The guilt was in their tone. 'The woman works homicide.' 'No one's suggesting homicide. Not even her.' " I repeated it several times, lowering my voice, trying to make it as evil as possible. I wound up sounding like a bad Bond villain. "Look, I know it's not possible. But you solve impossible cases all the time."

"But there's no case," he said. "The San Mateo sheriff is happy. The captain's happy. There's no client asking us to investigate. No one thinks anything is wrong but you."

"That should be enough. Adrian, I'm your partner."

"Do you want to see my toilet again?"

"No! I want you to be a partner and help me. Just look at the files from the sheriff's office. See if you notice anything odd. I'll bring them over early tomorrow."

"How did you get the files?"

"Devlin gave them to me."

"How did Devlin get them?"

"She worked her charm."

"Is this the same Devlin?"

"She went out of her way, okay? She's on my side, Adrian, like you should be."

"All right, I'll look at the files."

"Thank you." I would have been even more grateful if I'd thought he was paying the slightest attention. "What are you doing?"

"Nothing."

"You're playing with something in your pocket."

"No, I'm not."

"Yes, you are. What is that? Is that the remote for the toilet?"

"No. What makes you think . . . ?"

A second later, when the toilet flushed and the music started to play, I punched him on the arm. Then I punched him on the other arm, just to make it symmetrical.

CHAPTER NINETEEN

Mr. Monk Gets Mail 2.0

Monk had promised to examine the file, and I meant to hold him to it.

Years ago, I memorized his morning routine. Shower. Exfoliate. Shower again. Floss. Brush teeth. Exfoliate the gums, whatever that means. That's just the first twenty minutes of a two-hour process, starting at six a.m. on the dot—except for daylight saving time. That's when the whole schedule gets pushed up to seven a.m., although Monk would argue that he's still starting off at six while the rest of the world plays fast and loose with the natural order.

Except for emergencies, like crime scenes or death threats or the menace of a spider or aardvark, the routine is sacred. I remember one night when the city underwent a blackout. By the time Monk woke up, he was eight minutes behind. For the entire rest of the day, he was exactly eight minutes behind and we had to reschedule a meeting with the mayor from four to four-oh-eight in the afternoon.

I had calculated exactly when to knock on his door the next morning. I had to squeeze in after he finished his routine, but before Captain Stottlemeyer showed up to discuss the clown-Cemedrin case. Our secret team was having as many meetings as possible outside the station, just to be safe. I tacked on an extra ten minutes for Monk to play with his toilet and arrived at the perfect moment.

"Well?" I was sitting across from him, the file on the coffee table between us.

Monk thumbed through the paper-clipped pages. "The good news is motive," he said. "All of Miranda's money will be taken by the courts to pay off her embezzlement. The same with the assets of the cult of the Best Possible Her."

"Best Possible Me."

"Sorry. Best Possible You."

"Whatever." I'm not always sure how much of Monk's behavior is naturally irritating and how much is an act. This, I'm pretty sure, was an act. "Go on."

"It looks like the Bigleys, alive or dead, will be wiped out."

"So where's the motive?"

"Insurance," Monk said. "Miranda had three policies, one personal, one as CEO of the company, and one as president of the nonprofit."

"Her insurance pays out for a suicide?"

There was a case we had worked on a few years ago. I don't think I've ever written about it. But a famous ventriloquist was deeply depressed and in debt and committed suicide. He tried to make it look like murder—specifically, a mugging gone bad—so that his wife would get the insurance payout.

The wife, it turned out, had no clue about the suicide and wound up being at the wrong place at the wrong time. She came to Monk when the San Francisco police arrested her for her husband's murder. It was one of those impossible crimes where no on else could have done it. Except the victim, who just happened to be a ventriloquist.

The ending was bittersweet. The woman was exonerated by Monk's brilliant work. But she lost the insurance settlement and wound up broke. She never could pay her bill.

"Some policies will," he informed me. "In Miranda's case, there were suicide provisions. After you have the policies three years, your heirs can claim full suicide benefits."

"All of her policies were like this?"

"Not so unusual," said Monk. "I have four policies like that myself."

This could have been the start of a two-hour conversation about Monk and insurance and his beneficiaries, et cetera. You'll be glad to hear that I refrained from going there.

"So, all three of Miranda's policies pay out."

"Yes. And since Damien inherits as an individual and not as a part of Best Possible You, he won't be forced to pay off the debts. It'll be his, free and clear. A little more than five million."

"You see?" I felt vindicated. "That's a great motive. Kill the wife and start a new life with your mistress and a ton of money."

"Now all we need is a murder. That's the bad news that comes with the good news."

I'd been prepared for this, but it still stung. "Are you sure?"

"I'm ninety-seven percent sure, yes."

"Ninety-seven percent?" All right, there was hope. "What's the three percent?"

"Allowing for the existence of magic."

"No. There has to be something or you wouldn't have said three percent. What is it?"

Monk rolled his eyes. "The cult leader's cell phone. When the body washed up, they found a cell phone twisted in one of her pockets."

"I remember from the report. Is this important?"

"Not important. Three percent." He twisted his neck and rolled his shoulders. "It seems slightly odd to make a premeditated jump with a cell phone on you. Most jumpers divest themselves of things—glasses, wallets, phones. It's not like you're going to twitter your fans when you're freefalling off a cliff."

"So, what does that mean?"

"It means nothing. It means ninety-seven percent instead of a hundred. Still . . ."

"Still what?"

"It might be a good idea to check with the phone company. See if any calls were made to the woman's cell phone after she died. Between her jump and when the body washed up"

"And if I find something? If someone called her phone? You'll be willing to work on the case?"

Monk responded by growling under his breath. He actually growled. It might have even developed into a bark, but we were interrupted by a knock on the door. It was Captain Stottlemeyer.

"Monk, Natalie." He walked in, right past us. "Bad news about the Harrimans."

Okay. Time to change gears. From the suicide to the Cemedrin murders. Just like that. Dealing with multiple cases seemed to be a regular part of our lives.

"Devlin couldn't find a motive," Monk guessed.

"None. Neither John nor Alicia had any connection to the oh-nine victims."

The captain settled into Monk's favorite white leather chair. "The first, you might recall, was Craig Tuppering, a nine-year-old boy in Damien's Point. He woke up one morning complaining of a headache. His mother thought the boy was faking it and didn't want to go to school. But she gave him a Cemedrin just in case. Two hours later, little Craig was dead.

"The second case was two days later. A girl in Excelsior got hit on the head by a softball. Ginny Costello." The captain knew all the names, probably by heart from 2009. I half remembered them myself; the cases had been that traumatizing for the city. "Her Little League coach gave her two Cemedrins and sat her out for the rest of the game. An hour after her team won, Ginny died.

"This time the medical examiner could trace it. The poison was quick-acting and Ginny hadn't eaten anything that morning except the pills. Within twelve hours, the city was on alert. Within twenty-four, the parent company had cleared the shelves of their product.

"The third victim was Harold Luckenby. He was an older man, a Vietnam veteran who lived alone and was a bit of a hoarder. Hated spending money or throwing things out. His daughter came by every day to check on him. Harold regularly took pain relievers for his arthritis. She discussed the scare with him. She made him promise to throw away any bottle of Cemedrin. The next day, she came and found him dead in front of the TV. All because he wouldn't throw things away."

The three tainted bottles had been bought from two drugstores in the Mission District, both of them Walgreens. So had the two other tainted bottles that were caught in time. The police deduced, from the estimated dates of purchase, that the bottles had been tampered with and placed on the shelves two weeks before the first death.

"The Harrimans had been in San Francisco during that period," Stottlemeyer continued, still not referring to any notes. "Along with eight hundred thousand other citizens."

"And they had no connection to any of the victims," I said, just to be sure.

"None. And according to their insurance records, neither Harriman has been treated for any mental or emotional disorders, which doesn't rule out anything. Jeffrey Dahmer had a clean bill of health, as far as I know. Look what happened to him."

"How about their investments?" Monk asked.

The captain scowled. "You mean the Harrimans'?"

"They were both stockbrokers at that point. Did they have any investments that might have profitted from the Cemedrin scare? Did they own stock in a rival company like Tylenol? Or in a rival drug store like CVS?"

"Are you saying they killed three people, including two kids, just to manipulate the stock price?"

"It's money," Monk said. "People kill for it. And they had no idea that kids would die, only that someone would."

The captain shook his head. "I'll get Devlin on it. If it was a business investment, there'd be a record at their brokerage house. If they did it on their own, there are all sorts of ways to hide it."

"How about their tax returns?" I said. "If there was any profit or loss declared from a transaction . . ."

"And how do you suggest getting their returns?" the captain asked. "You can't even make presidential candidates show their returns. The whole point, Natalie, is for us to get a warrant without arousing their suspicions."

"Oh. Right." I'm sure I would have known this if I'd spent the weekend studying for my PI exam instead of eavesdropping and getting a massage. My embarrassment was tempered by the ringing of Monk's bell.

"Adrian?" came a voice from the other end of Monk's intercom. It was Andrew, the mailman. "Got a package for you to sign for."

"Is it from Japan?" Monk asked.

"I don't think so."

Monk was disappointed. But he started down the stairs, leaving the front door open behind him. Stottlemeyer watched him go, then lowered his voice. "Monk tells me you spent the weekend in Half Moon Bay." His tone sounded a little accusing.

"Not that it's anybody's business. But yes."

"And that you're trying to make her suicide into something more."

"Adrian thinks it might be more," I said. "He's going to help me look into it."

"Don't do this, Natalie."

"What do you mean?"

"I know you admired this woman. But this clown case is big. We have families still looking for answers. Not to mention me and Devlin putting our jobs on the line. If it blows up and the FBI discovers we were withholding evidence in one of their biggest cases—"

"We can handle more than once case," I assured him. "We do it all the time."

"Maybe. But we need his full attention. I can't order you to stop—"

"That's right. You can't."

"But I can appeal to you as a friend. There's a lot on the line. Life is not just about you and your personal fulfillment, no matter what this guru told you."

I was thrown by his attitude, to say the least. And it really hurt. Miranda's philosophy wasn't about selfishness. It was about taking control over your choices. And that's what I thought I was doing here, taking some control.

"Natalie?" Monk was coming back up the stairs, holding the open box Andrew had just delivered, about twice the size of a shoebox but shallower. There was confusion in his voice.

"What is it?" But I already knew. "Mystery package?"

He held it out and I reached in past the bubble wrap. "Stones."

"The handwriting is the same," he said. "Addressed to Mr. A. Monk. And there's no note or return address, like the other."

"You mean like the Confederate money?" Stottlemeyer said, pushing his way to see. "Put it down. It could be dangerous."

"No, I had Andrew open it. There's no bomb. Just stones."

"Stones?" Stottlemeyer took the package anyway, brought it in, and placed it on the kitchen counter. "Who would send you anonymous stones?"

Before unwrapping the stones, Monk insisted that we put on rubber gloves. He kept them in a drawer in all our sizes—small, medium, and large.

Neither the captain nor Monk knew what they were dealing with, but I did. Flat, black volcanic stones with rounded edges. Eight of them of various sizes. "They're massage stones," I said.

"Massage stones?" Stottlemeyer asked.

"It's a technique where they heat up stones and massage you with them," I explained. "From Japan, I think."

"Then it must be good," Monk said. "Except the massage part." He shivered with disgust, then turned to me. "How do you know this? What kind of massage did this Teresa give you?"

"A hot-stone massage," I said. "You don't think . . . Why would she send me stones?"

Monk was already checking the postmark. This time it was inked and clear. "Hot Springs, Arkansas. It wasn't Teresa."

"Who is Teresa?" Stottlemeyer asked.

"She's Damien Bigley's mistress," I told him. "And she was involved in Miranda's suicide."

"Says you," Monk scoffed.

"Says me," I confirmed. "Where was the Confederate money sent from? Could your guys lift the postmark?"

"They could," Stottlemeyer said. "I got their report this morning. Tupelo, Mississippi."

"Not Hot Springs, Arkansas."

"But the same person sent both," Monk said. "The handwriting is the same."

"What are we going to do about this?" I asked the captain.

"Do about it?" He tilted his head. "Okay, let's review.

You're receiving anonymous stuff in the mail. There's no note. There's no threat. There's no charge. I'm not sure what we can do to stop this heinous crime spree."

"But isn't it a little weird?" I asked.

"Last time I checked, weird wasn't a crime."

It was a puzzlement, all right. We get into a case with poisoned money, and a few days later, someone sends Monk a package of Confederate money. We get into a case where I eavesdrop during a hot-stone massage, and days later, someone sends him massage stones. From across the country no less.

My first thought was that our cases might be connected. This has happened more often than you might think. Dozens of time. It's almost a pattern. We work on two impossible cases, and by the end, they wind up being parts of the same case. But I really didn't see how that could be happening this time.

On the upside, since Monk will never, ever have anything to do with a massage, I now had my own set of massage stones.

• • • • • CHAPTER TWENTY

Mr. Monk Skips Lunch

That afternoon I had a late lunch scheduled with Ellen, just us girls. We'd both been meaning to try the new Peruvian bistro on Steiner, one block over from her Union Street store. This would be the perfect time. Between her rocky relationship with Monk and my weekend at BPM, the two of us had a lot to catch up on.

This left me just enough time to visit Lieutenant Devlin.

I found her in Captain Stottlemeyer's office with the door closed. Ever since we started our special team, this had been our command center. And Devlin was getting more and more used to sitting at the captain's desk when he was away. She didn't even get up when I knocked, but just motioned me inside.

"Where's the captain?" I asked.

"At the courthouse," she mumbled, then went back to staring at her laptop screen. "He's throwing a Hail Mary Markowitz."

That was our nickname for it: a Hail Mary pass made in front of Judge Mary Markowitz, the most cop-friendly jurist on the San Francisco bench. We've gotten a lot of questionable warrants through her. I personally think she has a thing for the captain, even though they're both happily married.

"Trying to get a warrant for the garage," I guessed.

"Uh-huh. But he can't tell her about the Cemedrin bottle. All he can show her is our evidence that this clown Smith was blackmailing someone and that he had used the Harrimans' garage shortly before the alleged blackmail began."

"Is he going to mention Monk's theory that garages are insidious time bombs?"

"I don't think it matters what he says. But he's giving it a shot." Devlin lowered her laptop lid and emitted a groan. "If we can show the Harrimans profited from the Cemedrin murders, then we can tell her about the bottle and maybe get a warrant. Maybe. Even then we'd have to make the argument that this is our jurisdiction and not the FBI's."

"So, how's it going?" I asked, pointing at her computer. "Anything?"

"Nothing," she said. "I suppose we could get a tech in here to hack their financial records, but we'd need a search warrant for that. A search warrant in order to find something that might get us the search warrant we want."

I nodded in sympathy—make that empathy, since I was part of the team. "Do you have a minute?" I asked.

"Sure."

"Totally different case." I cleared my throat. "Do you need a warrant to get the phone records of a deceased person?" I knew the answer from my PI study guide but figured this was a good way to bring up the subject.

"Not if it's an active investigation. Why?"

I sat down in the guest chair and explained about the phone in the pocket and Monk's three percent hunch.

"So he thinks someone called Miranda? How is that important? A lot of deceaseds get calls. We had a case last month. The victim got three dozen texts from her BFF in Cincinnati before we called back the number and gave her the bad news."

I shrugged. "You know Adrian. He has this whole grading system on crime scene anomalies. Anywhere from 'Huh, that's odd' to 'He's the guy.' This one is three percent, so it's barely worth checking out. Still . . ."

"Sure I can get it," Devlin said. "I was the officer in charge at the recovery."

"But it's not an active investigation."

"Yeah? Who's going to protest?"

My mouth fell open. "Well, you, for one. I gave myself an hour to beg and argue and talk myself blue. And you just said 'sure'?"

"Natalie, I told you. I'm doing this for Miranda, not you. So don't get used to it."

"Don't worry. I'll never get used to it."

"Good. Do you know her cell number?"

"I can find out."

I remembered Ellen telling me about a bad emotional patch she'd gone through last year. I didn't ask what. But out of desperation, she'd called the BPM Sanctuary and they had put her directly through to Miranda. She had never expected that. Miranda spent an hour with her, talking her through whatever it was, then gave Ellen her private cell number. Just in case. Ellen had kept it on her phone ever since, as a reminder that a caring friend was always available.

"I'll text you the number this afternoon," I said, trying to keep the gratitude out of my voice.

By the time I got out of the station and drove to Cow Hollow and found a parking spot two blocks away and did the pay-and-display and started race-walking uphill, I was a few minutes late. I had just turned the corner onto Union Street and was all set to jaywalk across to Poop, when I saw him out of the corner of my eye.

You know how it is when you recognize someone. It's not just the physical features that you notice, but the attitude and posture and clothing. In this case, the clothing made it easy. "Adrian?"

He was in front of Dahlia's, an upscale flower shop directly across from Ellen's store, half hidden behind a central pole that helped support the building's iron awning. "What are you doing here?"

He saw me but stayed behind the pole. "I have my ways."

"I didn't mean how. I meant why. I couldn't care less about your ways." This wasn't strictly true. How was this man getting around? I was stumped. Was he using a sanitized taxi? Did he have a friend with a car I didn't know about? Had he gone crazy and bought a motorcycle? But right now I was more curious about why. "Are you spying on Ellen?"

"Please," he scoffed. "I'm not a loony. I just don't know how to get into her store."

"You could use the door."

"Let's eliminate that right off. I can't. I just want to be in there with her," he said wistfully. "In a different store. With her."

Ahh. I found this touching, I had to admit. He missed Ellen. He wanted to apologize in his own way and be with her. "Adrian, I know. Why don't you come to lunch with us?"

This was really the last thing I wanted. Ellen and I needed to talk about a whole host of things, including him. But what could I do? The man was in pain.

"Come to lunch?" he repeated. "Okay. Your place or mine?"

"In a restaurant. We're having lunch in a restaurant where you are welcome to join us."

"Is it Rassigio's?"

Rassigio's was the one restaurant where Monk would eat. It's a long story, but it involves several kitchen inspections, a very kind man named Tony Rassigio, a menu that never changes, and a fake, nonexistent AAA rating from the board of health, posted in the window whenever Monk shows up.

"It's not Rassigio's," I said. "But it's a nice place. Very clean. With an A rating."

"Not a triple-A rating? What's wrong with it?"

"Look, if you want to come, it's totally your decision. I'm sure Ellen would love to see you."

He cricked his neck and rolled his shoulders. "I'll think about it."

"Well, don't think too long. We're already late."

"You mean today? Not possible. It'll take me at least a day to think about it."

I tried for another minute to convince him, for his own

good if not mine. At the end of the minute, I left him behind his pillar and crossed over to Poop.

Ellen was waiting for me in a nearly empty store. There was one middle-aged couple, browsers not buyers, in my expert opinion, and a fascinating-looking girl with a half-shaved head, several piercings, and a tattoo running up and around her neck. She was at a counter sniffing a bottle of guano perfume and turned out to be the part-time help.

"Suzie," Ellen said. "I'm going to lunch."

"No problem," Suzie said, then went back to sniffing the bird-poop.

"So, what's Adrian up to?" Ellen asked as we emerged onto the street. I could see the top of Monk's head as he peered around his post.

"Nothing. Just hanging around."

The Peruvian bistro was a midpriced white-tablecloth establishment that used to be a French café and still looked a little French. We settled in with a couple of Diet Cokes and took our first look at the menu.

"I wish I could have come to the memorial," Ellen said. "I tried to get a reservation. Was it everything you expected?"

"Everything and more," I said without exaggeration. "What are you having?"

Most of the dishes seemed familiar enough. Pork and fish, yuca and beans. A lot of things with garlic. Ceviche was a popular item, as was some type of meat called *cuy. Picante de cuy* and *Cuyes en salsa de mani.*

"What's *cuy*?" I asked. I'm never shy when it comes to menu items. How else do you learn?

Ellen leaned across the table and whispered, "I wouldn't recommend it."

"Why?" I whispered back. "Isn't it fresh?"

"It's guinea pig."

I yelped and almost dropped the menu. "Guinea pig? We used to have one when Julie was growing up. Ralphie. I can't imagine eating Ralphie."

"It's their national dish. They probably think it's weird we keep them as pets."

"I hope these didn't come from a pet store."

"Why? Do you prefer your guinea pigs free-range?"

"I prefer none of them. I'm glad Adrian's not here. He'd be halfway home."

Ellen chuckled and shook her head. Then she blinked. "Wait. You're calling him Adrian? Since when?"

And so, for the next fifteen minutes, through the ordering process—no guinea pigs, although the waiter said they were the daily special and very fresh—and our second round of Diet Cokes, we discussed Monk.

"If he would just give me a little support . . . ," Ellen said.

"He never gave you any support," I pointed out. "Since the day you met."

"I know," she admitted. "But I used to be strong enough to deal with it. Now, ever since Miranda's suicide and . . ." She took a break and sipped from her fizzy brown drink. "I may have to close the San Francisco Poop."

"Oh, my God. Really?"

I don't know if this was a complete shock or not. I knew business was bad. Anyone who'd been in her store lately could have figured that out. But closing it? That had all sorts of implications, especially for Ellen and Monk.

"Does this mean you're leaving?"

"If I close the shop, there's no reason to keep my house. And I should be spending more time in Summit. The store there is doing well enough, but it needs more attention than I'm giving it."

"So the answer is yes. You're leaving."

"Maybe. I opened a San Francisco branch because it seemed a good idea and because Adrian was here. I'm not sure either plan is working out."

I could only imagine what she was going through. You devote your life and all your savings to a daring new concept. And then, when you take a chance and move cross-country to be with the man you love . . . Well, you'd expect a little support. Instead, Monk seemed to be almost gloating at her failure.

"I'm surprised you only slammed the door. I would have done more."

"I still believe in Poop," Ellen said. "It adds such a fun, earthy element to the whole idea of recycling and conservation. But if I concentrate on the one store and focus more on our online presence . . ."

What she was saying seemed smart and logical and absolutely right, but . . . "Don't go," I pleaded. "Adrian will miss you terribly. I'll miss you."

"I haven't made any decisions."

"And you'll be thousands of miles away from BPM," I added, without really thinking, "which might not be a bad thing."

"I know." Her face clouded over. "I can never look at those cliffs the same way again. Can you? My guess is Damien will shut the place down and sell it to a hotel."

"Speaking of Damien Bigley . . ."

"What?" She could hear the hesitancy in my voice. "Tell me everything. What have you found out?"

So I told her everything, from the footsie incident to Damien's claim to be the real Miranda to Teresa's talk of homicide out of the clear blue. I ended with Monk's question about Miranda's cell phone and the three percent chance.

"I don't know what he's looking for, but he wants to know if anyone called her cell. And for that, we need the number."

"No problem. I have Miranda's number right here. She made me promise not to give it out, but it doesn't matter now."

Ellen reached into her purse for her own phone, and within a minute, I had texted the number to Amy Devlin.

"I can't believe Damien would say that." Ellen was angry.

"About being the real Miranda?"

"It's inconceivable." The more she thought about it, the angrier she got. Not about murder, which was still a far-off concept, or about infidelity, which was none of her business, really. But the idea of Miranda being a fake. "There was nothing phony about her."

"He's not saying she didn't believe it."

"No." Ellen's jaw was clenched. "He's saying she was a conniving schemer who saw BPM as a business she could exploit. Well, that wasn't the woman I knew. That wasn't the woman who kept me on the phone at midnight, helping me try to make sense of my life."

"People are complicated," I said, which was lame but true.

"I hope Damien is responsible somehow. Then Adrian can go after him and make his life a living hell."

"It's only three percent," I reminded her.

"I don't care. If Adrian doesn't go after him, we will. You and I. There's something fishy about this whole thing."

"Exactly." I lifted the dregs of my second Diet Coke in a toast. "To vindicating the good name of Miranda Bigley."

CHAPTER TWENTY-ONE

Mr. Monk and the Test

"Jane, a private investigator, is hired by a lawyer to gather information for a liability case. While interviewing witnesses, Jane enters the garage of one witness and is attacked by the man, a registered sex offender. Jane sprays him with pepper spray that she carries openly on her belt and escapes unharmed. She has not taken any training courses for the use of pepper spray. What are the consequences of Jane's actions?"

My first reaction on reading this was "Monk was right. Garages are dangerous." My second reaction was "It's happening in two hours. I should have prepared better." As my study guide says in big print: seven out of ten people who take the California Private Investigator Exam fail. It's far from a sure thing, even for someone like me.

My third reaction was "Concentrate, Natalie. You can do this."

My multiple choice options were:

(a) Pepper spray is not illegal. It was smart of her to be prepared.

(b) Jane has violated the B&P code and the Penal Code and may have her license suspended.

(c) Jane has not violated the law, which allows for private investigators to use such sprays as long as they are carried openly.
(d) Jane was required to take a course in the use of any tear gas spray. The standard penalty is a citation and a fine.

Ah, this brought back fond memories. How many times have I been in situations with a bad guy where I would have given my eyeteeth for pepper spray? Not having a can of spray, however, I usually made do with a wine bottle or a kick in the groin or, on one memorable occasion, the wand of a heavy-duty vacuum cleaner. So, striking a blow for Janes everywhere, I answered c.

I was wrong. The answer was b and I would have my license suspended, if I was ever lucky enough to get it in the first place, which remained to be seen.

The phone rang and I was not at all in the mood to pick up, until I saw it was Julie.

"Hey, Mom. Just called to wish you luck."

"Thanks, sweetie." Just hearing her voice was enough to lower my heart rate by ten beats. "I needed that."

"Just remember, it's multiple choice, so answer everything, even if you don't know. Personally, I like to alternate between b and d, unless I knew the answer right before it and that was b or d. Then I go for a."

"Are you telling me you guess? I thought you spent every night studying."

"Yeah, just like you." She laughed. "When was the last time you took a test?"

We went back and forth like this for a while. It was a welcome break. And I got to hear more about Maxwell the boyfriend and how, after she told him he was getting too serious, now he didn't seem serious enough.

"Is Mr. Monk going with you to Hayward?" she asked. That's where the test was being administered.

"No. His way of being supportive is to stay home and clean something in my name."

"Did he at least call and wish you good luck?"

"Of course." Of course, he hadn't. But I never expected him to.

Julie had just hung up and I was gearing myself up for one more crack at my study guide, when the phone rang again. For some reason, I assumed it was Julie, so I didn't even check the display.

"Natalie?" It was Amy Devlin, calling from the captain's office. "I just got the file from Verizon."

My heartbeat went back up ten beats. "Did someone call Miranda? Who?"

"We're talking about a twenty-six-hour period, between the jump and the body's recovery."

"That's the period Adrian's interested in. Yes."

"Okay." I could tell she was reading it as she spoke. "This is her personal iPhone, which seems to be the only phone she owned . . ." Devlin paused. "Nothing."

"What? That's impossible."

"Not so impossible. From the rest of her records, it seems Miranda wasn't much of a texter or a talker. There were a few calls early on Saturday. But nothing in your time frame."

I was confused. "Are you sure?"

"I'll send you the file." She paused a second. "There. You can see for yourself."

"Thanks. And I know. I can't spread this around or let anyone know where I got it."

"Sorry about the bad news. It was just a three percent chance."

"Right." I guess, having dealt with Monk all these years, I'd gotten spoiled. Somehow the three percent chances and the far-out theories have almost always paid off. Except in this case.

Over on the dining room table, my computer dinged. "Got it," I said. "Thanks, Amy. Oh, and don't forget to pick up Adrian for the meeting this afternoon."

"That's right. You have your exam today. Good luck. And don't forget. If you don't know an answer, pick c. It works for me."

After Lieutenant Devlin hung up, I should have returned to my cram session. Instead, I checked out the Verizon attachment she'd just sent. Like she said, no texts or e-mails or voice mails. That would have been extremely unusual on my own phone, but everyone's different. And Miranda's phone records seemed to confirm that she wasn't a smartphone junkie like the rest of us.

As long as I was on my computer, I went to YouTube and clicked on my least favorite video, which I couldn't keep myself from watching.

It was the Saturday before last, a bright, warm day by the sea, when the world still made sense and Miranda was alive. Someone having lunch on the Sanctuary lawn—a Joshua Council from Seattle—had been filming her with his phone.

I don't know how much he'd caught, but the part he'd uploaded—the part that had garnered more than three million hits and had been showed on every news program in the world—was of Miranda in the distance, standing by the cliff, doing a slow, relaxed yoga stretch, then walking to the edge and jumping.

The aftermath wasn't nearly as clear. The phone jiggled and bucked, turning away and back again. The audio was a confusion of disbelief and screams. And it ended with Damien running, leading the way. The phone ran behind him. In the last moments, it was pointing down to the empty sea and the crashing waves. The minute and thirty-seven seconds that were starting to dominate my life.

You would think with all the private eyes roaming these foggy streets that San Francisco would have its own PI testing facility. Or maybe I'm thinking of Sam Spade and those fictional guys in trench coats. The closest facility is actually in Hayward, across the Bay Bridge and south about half an hour. It's a nice little city, the skyline dominated by a water tower left over from when the Hunt's cannery was the biggest local employer.

The job of testing had been farmed out to a private firm in an unimposing one-story building in an industrial park right beside another industrial park. Seven of us were taking the test that day. We nervously compared notes in the parking lot. I was surprised to see that four out of the seven were women, two of them very young and attractive. My guess was these girls could make a nice living just from wives hiring them to see if their husbands were the cheating type.

All of us were seated at individual desks, with plastic dividers in front and on the sides to prevent a wandering eye. There were five possible tests, chosen at random, and all five were changed every year.

The first few questions were easy. "How many counties are there in California? Fifty-eight." "In what U.S. city are the majority of military personnel records stored? St. Louis, Missouri." "What type of camera lens 'sees' the same as a human eye and should be used when shooting accident scenes? Fifty millimeter."

Toward the bottom of page two, there was a question about police reports. I think I got it right. But it also got me thinking about Miranda's police report. Why was I suddenly thinking about her police report? There was something odd. . . .

Before I knew it, five minutes had passed, and I hadn't even looked at the next question. What was it about the report that was distracting me? I'd had a copy of it for days now. I'd looked it over a dozen times. Why was it sticking in my head?

The subconscious is funny. It's aware of stuff that you're not, not on the surface. But I find that if I look back and try to find the trigger . . . What prompted this? Was it the YouTube video I'd just seen? Was it my drive down here? Was it something in the test? Was it my conversation with Devlin about the phone?

Eureka! The phone. I'd have to check the report, but I was sure I was right.

I didn't know what it meant. No idea. But I'd just discovered something odd about Miranda's phone and couldn't wait to let Monk figure it out.

For the next hour and a half, I tried to force myself to concentrate. But it wasn't happening. Whatever focus I'd had at the beginning was gone.

"HIPAA is a federal law about the privacy of medical records. What does the letter P stand for?"

It probably stands for "Privacy," I thought. No. Too easy. Was it Policy? Or Plan? It certainly couldn't be Portability. Where did that choice come from? I knew I had seen the answer somewhere in the twelve pounds of study guide. But I wound up going with Julie's suggestion: b.

It went downhill from there. Between my general unpreparedness and Miranda's phone and my desperate need to get back to town and talk to Monk, I turned in my test and didn't even wait for the results.

I knew I'd failed miserably.

The answer, by the way, was Portability. Is that crazy? What the hell does portability have to do with medical privacy?

CHAPTER TWENTY-TWO

Mr. Monk and the Breakup

While I'd been away in Hayward, choosing random Bs and Ds, the other members of the task force had been at the station house. A quick text to Devlin assured me they were still there. That was good.

The blinds in the captain's office were artfully drawn. Fully closed, they might arouse suspicion, but they were just open enough to prevent a passing officer from seeing too much. I knocked on the door and eased it open. Monk, Devlin, and Stottlemeyer all shot me quick, startled glances, then went back to work. They seemed energized and excited, even Monk. It was good to see him so involved in a case.

Devlin tried to catch me up. "I combed through the local financial news from 2009. That was a year or two after the crash, so there was a lot."

"The lieutenant's been busy." Stottlemeyer smiled. It was as close to beaming as he got.

Devlin continued. "Harriman Brokerage, of which both John and Alicia were partners, was on the bubble, like many companies. Really overextended. A lot of firms were being investigated for misuse of funds. But Harriman made good. All his clients were paid in full."

"How?" I asked.

"That's the big question. Whatever Harriman did to get out of the hole couldn't have required a lot of capital and had to happen quickly. On a hunch, I checked the public record of short sales of Cemedrin stock or, more specifically, the parent company, Medical Mills."

I basically know what short selling is. That's one of the advantages of growing up rich, where half the talk at the dinner table is about how Uncle Walt made a killing in the market. I'll try to keep it simple.

Let's say I think Cemedrin stock will go down. So I "borrow" ten thousand shares from Investor Bob and promise to return them to him in a month. I pay Investor Bob a small fee, which is the only cash I need to play this game. Bob's happy because he didn't want to sell the stock anyway and he's making money.

Right away I sell the Cemedrin; let's say for a hundred bucks a share. Then I hold on to my million bucks and wait.

Cut to a month later and the Cemedrin stock has tanked. It's now ten bucks a share. I buy Cemedrin at this new price and give it back to Investor Bob, as agreed. He has his ten thousand shares, same as before. And I have close to $900,000 in profit.

I looked at Devlin. "You're saying they shorted Medical Mills right before the poisonings."

She grinned. "John was the borrower of record. He placed it through six different brokerage houses, just to keep it under the radar. But once I knew what I was looking for . . ."

"John wound up with an eighteen-million-dollar payday, and his firm stayed in business." Stottlemeyer looked to his lieutenant. "Great work, Amy." He only called her Amy when it was something very good or very bad.

Devlin tried not to blush. "This confirms that Harriman's our guy. It's not just based on some Monk mumbo-jumbo anymore. No offense. Unfortunately, if we take this in front of a judge, the FBI will find out."

Monk held up his hand. "The FBI doesn't have to be involved, not if we put this in our back pocket and go after Harriman for killing Smith."

"I would love to, Monk," Stottlemeyer said with a sigh. "And how do you suppose we do that? Harriman probably doesn't even know that Smith was his blackmailer or that he's dead. There's nothing to tie him to it."

Monk winced and lowered his hand. "I'll come up with something."

"Make it fast. The longer we wait, the more trouble we'll be in when we have to go to Special Agent Grooms."

I think we all shuddered in unison at the thought of being chewed out by the FBI bully with his off-centered widow's peak.

It was an awkward moment. And it was only broken when Stottlemeyer suddenly recalled why I was late. "Natalie. I forgot. How was the test? Hold on. Save the details. I'll break out my emergency bottle and we'll have a toast."

"I flunked," I said quickly, ripping off the proverbial Band-Aid.

"What? Is this a joke?" Devlin seemed truly puzzled.

"Sorry, Natalie," said the captain. "I hear the tests are hard." I didn't know which was worse, having everyone sorry for me or disappointed.

"How could you flunk?" Monk asked.

"Oh, don't start with me. You'd still be back there sharpening pencils. The reason I flunked was . . . Okay, maybe I was a little underprepared. But I found the cell phone clue," I told Monk. "The clue you were looking for."

"Mr. Smith had a phone?" Stottlemeyer asked.

"Not that case. The suicide at Half Moon Bay. The so-called suicide."

"Natalie, please," said the captain. "We don't have time for this."

"But Adrian said there was a three percent chance."

"That was if someone called Miranda's phone while her body was in the water," Devlin corrected me. "No one did."

"I know. But that wasn't her phone." The excitement I'd felt during the test had faded since walking through the door. But now, as I paced the floor and explained, it came back.

The thing that had subconsciously bugged me about the police report was the phone found twisted in Miranda's pocket. It was a small T-Mobile, not even a smartphone. But Miranda's phone, her only one, was an iPhone.

Devlin could back me up on this, and she did. "You're right. I should have noticed the discrepancy."

"So, where is Miranda's real phone?" I continued. "And what was the other one doing in her pocket?"

"Monk?" Stottlemeyer was looking impatient. "Is this a case or not?"

Monk cricked his neck and rolled his shoulders. "I was humoring her. Natalie needed humoring."

"Humoring? Since when do I need humoring?"

"Since you joined that cult and went overboard."

"But you said the phone was important."

Monk frowned. "It was a tiny oddity, so I said three percent. Have you seen three percent lately? It's small. Doesn't mean a thing."

"Yes, it does," I insisted. I went to the dry-erase board and, without thinking, grabbed an eraser. "First, we need to get hold of the T-Mobile phone. Find out who bought it, who has it now. Probably Damien, since it was in Miranda's possession and he's the next of kin. The phone itself is probably useless from the water—"

"Natalie!" Stottlemeyer's voice boomed. "What are you doing?"

It turns out I was erasing the board, the one covered with bullet points from the Cemedrin case. "Sorry. We'll get another dry-erase board in here. We can work on both cases at the same time."

"Natalie, step away from the eraser. Devlin, fix the board before we forget."

"Sorry." I gave Amy Devlin the eraser and stepped away. But that didn't stop me. "Our step after that is to find Miranda's iPhone. Damien probably has that, too."

"Stop now!" the captain barked. This time I stopped. "Natalie, take a look at yourself. Do you even see what you're doing?"

To be honest, I couldn't see what they saw. I saw a case like any other Monk case—puzzling, impossible, but one that was going to get solved. The fact that I was so emotionally committed didn't seem material. Obviously it was.

"You're obsessing over a suicide in another jurisdiction,"

the captain said, lowering his voice to a patient growl. "The sheriff's office closed the case."

"I understand," I said, thinking I did. "You don't have to help. Adrian and I can do it ourselves."

"No, you can't," said Stottlemeyer. "We're working a series of high-profile murders that had the city in a panic. Now we have a new victim and a viable suspect. And we have this sword called the FBI hanging over our heads. Every moment counts. I can't let Monk get distracted with trips to Half Moon Bay and little inconsistencies in a case twenty miles away that doesn't even exist."

Captain Stottlemeyer can be very eloquent when he wants to be.

"You don't even know what you're looking for," said Devlin, pitching in. She had just repaired the board and was trying to look sympathetic.

But I was having none of it. "I know what this is about. You think the Cemedrin case is going to make your career."

"Maybe," Devlin half agreed. "But it could as easily ruin all our careers if we don't do it right."

"So I just have to forget about Miranda Bigley? I can't."

"You don't have to," said Stottlemeyer. "But Monk does. We have a contract with him. We would love to have you on this case, Natalie, but if you can't let go of this suicide . . ."

It sounded like he was getting suspiciously close to firing me. There's been more than one time when Monk has been fired from a case and, by extension, me. But never me alone. "Are you firing me?"

"No. I'm just laying down the law."

"You can't do that. Adrian and I are a team. If we want to work on this case on our own time, you can't stop us."

"Actually, I don't." Monk had said it so softly I almost didn't hear.

"You don't?"

"Like the captain said, it's a distraction. And a cult. And I have a chance to solve four murders and show up Special Agent Grooms, which is something I like doing. It's, like, my favorite thing."

"But we're a team. We're partners."

"Actually, we're not. Not until you pass the test."

"I'll pass the next one."

"When?" Monk asked. "I don't even know when the next one is." Neither did I, since I'd never expected to fail this one. "Until then, you're my assistant and you don't get a say."

I couldn't believe it. "Yes, I get a say. We've been together almost ten years."

"Monk made a promise," Stottlemeyer reminded me. "We're germ brothers. He's staying on the Cemedrin case."

"We're germ brothers," Monk said, as if that meant something. "You can't abandon a germ brother."

"Adrian, please."

How did we get to this point? In just a couple of minutes, I had backed myself into this corner and now I couldn't see a way out. "Mr. Monk, please."

I don't know why I said that. It felt like cheating. But it didn't make any difference. "Sorry, Natalie."

So there it was. I'd thought we were partners. I thought by now they all trusted my cop instincts. Apparently not. The lure of a big case and the impossibility of a small case were just too much.

"Fine," I spat out. "If you want to get along without me, that's your call. Have fun with your clowns—clown noses and clown shoes and clown cars and little clowns in diapers."

"Natalie," Devlin warned softly.

"Clown, clown, clown, clown, clown, clown!" I shouted. Then I turned on my heel and walked out.

I could hear a little whimper escape from Monk's lips right before I slammed the door.

• • • • • CHAPTER TWENTY-THREE

Mr. Monk Loses It

Now that I look back on it, on that day six months ago when Monk and I were in the car and I was about to fly off to New Jersey, I realize it had all been my idea.

I was the one who impulsively turned and said I was leaving the Summit Police Department and coming back. I was the one who insisted on becoming partners and getting my PI license. Monk had no concept of a partnership or of treating me as an equal. He just wanted things back to normal.

There have been many times when I'd threatened to quit and once when I actually did. But this felt different. First, I hadn't technically quit. It was more of a work stoppage. I wanted to take on a case I thought had merit. They said no. And second, I had no idea how this was going to get fixed. If I was going to be Monk's partner, then I felt I had to be taken seriously. It was my line in the sand.

On arriving at the cocoon, I scrounged around the freezer and found a Lean Cuisine left over from when Julie, an even more serious noncook than her mother, was staying at the house. I nuked it, toasted an English muffin as a side dish, and sat down in front of CNN. A pretty sad picture, I must say, made slightly happier by the fact that tonight's newscast did not once mention Miranda Bigley.

I had just rinsed the plastic container and put it in the recycling bin when there was a knock on the door. Three knocks, not ten.

The porch light revealed Ellen Morse, with a box of tissues in one hand and quart of Swensen's hand-packed Rocky Road in the other. Her face was wreathed in a big, sympathetic grin. "I have a DVD of *Working Girl* in the car. If things get bad, we can put it on and yell back at the male-chauvinist workplace."

This was pure Ellen, always there at the right moment with just the right touch.

"It's been quite the day," I had to admit.

"How did your test go?"

"Not bad. I was somewhere around the seventy percentile."

"That's pretty good."

"The seventy percent of people who don't pass." I shrugged. "It's all right. I was distracted. I can always take it again."

In all my excitement about the phones and disappointment about the case, I'd already blocked out the earlier trauma of the day.

"I'm so sorry. Here." She handed me the box of tissues and we laughed. Then she held out the Swensen's. "Let's get this into us before it melts."

I got bowls and spoons from the kitchen, divvied up two scoops for each of us, and put the rest in the freezer. We didn't want to peak too early.

"I would have brought dinner," Ellen told me, "but I got sidetracked for a few hours by Adrian."

"You're seeing each other again?"

"He popped up at my house after work. I don't know how he got there."

"Apparently he has his ways."

"That's what he said."

We settled in at my small dining room table. "What else did he say?"

Ellen blushed and gushed. "He was being very cute. He showed up at my door with a bouquet of ten perfect long-stemmed roses."

Okay. You and I know that roses come by the dozen. But not with Monk. We also know that real roses aren't perfect. "Were they artificial?" I asked.

"Of course they were," said Ellen. "He went through four local florists and bought and discarded their entire rose supply before he settled on this. I assume there's going to be more than one angry woman in town who's getting gladiolas for her birthday."

"Well, at least he made an effort. And artificial roses don't have that annoying smell."

"He pointed that out," Ellen said. "Although he still doesn't understand what he did wrong. All women, according to him, are flighty, and he doesn't know what's gotten into any of us."

"You're feeling sorry for him," I warned her. "That's not the basis for a good relationship. I'm learning that the hard way."

Ellen nodded and started on her second scoop. "He also

said you refused to work on one of the biggest cases in a decade because you're obsessed with Miranda Bigley's suicide."

"He said that?" It was annoying to hear Monk describe me as obsessed. Okay, maybe I was being unreasonable. But he had been unreasonable about so many things over the years, and I had always supported him. "Do you think I'm obsessed?"

Ellen shook her head. "They didn't know Miranda. They're looking at the facts, not the person. Damien is guilty of something. That much is undeniable."

We had just returned to the kitchen to dish up our second helping of Rocky Road when my cell phone rang. I checked the display. "It's Monk." I let it ring. If he apologized in his message, then maybe I'd call back.

But it didn't go to voice mail. It rang three and a half times and stopped.

Then Ellen's phone began to ring and it was the same thing—three and a half rings. Then mine did the same again, almost immediately. Then Ellen's. On the fourth cycle, we knew something must be wrong. Not that Monk wouldn't play this game for hours just to annoy us. But there was a kind of urgency to the quick succession of calls.

On the fifth cycle, I picked up. "Adrian?"

"Come over, right now." There was sheer panic in his voice.

"What's up? What's wrong?"

"I'm trapped in the kitchen and can't get out."

"Is it a spider? Or an ant? We've been through this a hundred times. Just kill it."

"No," he wailed, but his wail was a little hushed, as if

someone might overhear. "Clown," he said, choking out the word. "In my living room. Cloowwnn!"

A clown in his apartment? "We'll be right there."

It's funny how you react in an emergency. My anger at Monk vanished. He was a friend in trouble—threatened, it seemed, by some maniacal clown. Ellen reacted the same way.

I ran into my bedroom and dove into the closet for my lockbox. Inside was a Glock 22, fully loaded. Lieutenant Devlin had recommended it—a simple, inexpensive gun with decent firing power and enough bullet capacity to make up for my imperfect aim, not that I hadn't been practicing at a firing range. I had.

I'd been saving this .40 caliber beauty for when I was officially a PI and could take another course and pass another test, this one for a permit to carry a firearm on the job. That's a different can of worms from just owning a gun.

Anyway, in less time than it took you to read that, I grabbed the Glock, threw it in my purse, and was out the door.

In five minutes, we were at Monk's building. Not knowing quite what was up, we didn't ring the bell. I used my keys on the building's front door and at the top of the stairs on Monk's door.

Inside, the lights were on and a Bach harpsichord played softly. Everything felt normal, but of course it wasn't. I dipped into a slight crouch and lifted my Glock with both hands, just as I'd seen Captain Stottlemeyer do on hundreds of occasions. Then I walked slowly and silently down the short hall and turned quickly into the living room.

It was empty.

The great thing about Monk's apartment is that you immediately know when anything's out of place. In this case, it was a large, shallow, opened package centered on the coffee table. I relaxed a bit and lowered the gun. Ellen was right behind me.

The bubble wrap in the box had been pushed aside, and we stared down at a coffee table book about half the size of the coffee table. A larger-than-life face stared back up. A clown with a white face and red nose and a painted grin that was enough to unsettle anyone. The title above and below the face was *The Big Book of Clowns and Mimes.*

"Natalie?" It was a whimpering voice coming from the far side of the kitchen.

"Are you okay?" I called softly. "Is it just the book?"

"It's not just the book, Natalie. It's the clown book."

I put the safety back on and tucked the Glock in my purse. Ellen and I both took deep breaths.

We found him in a corner, trying to squeeze himself into the gap between the refrigerator and the wall. "Get rid of it," he said. "Flush it down the toilet. No, don't do that. I love that toilet."

Monk and I waited in the kitchen while Ellen took the book and the package and put them in the trunk of her car, as Monk insisted. Monk insisted that she lock the car, too, just in case the book had some plan to escape.

By the time she got back, Monk had sanitized the coffee table and we were sitting around it, drinking from bottles of Fiji Water. I could have used something stronger.

Monk explained the history of mysterious packages to

Ellen—the arrival of Confederate money from Mississippi, massage stones from Arkansas, and now the diabolical clown book from . . .

"I checked the postmark before opening it," Monk said, still shivering as he sipped his Fiji. "That should have been a warning. Sarasota, Florida."

"Why would that be a warning?" asked Ellen.

"Sarasota used to be the winter home of Ringling Brothers and Barnum & Bailey—names that will live in infamy alongside Cirque du Soleil and John Wayne Gacy. You know, that serial killer who did the clown paintings."

I'm not sure which Monk considered worse: the fact that Gacy had been a serial killer or that he'd painted clowns in his spare time. Probably clowns.

"The town has a circus museum," he continued, "with a gift shop, which is where I'm sure he bought the book."

"Who?" I asked.

"My tormentor," Monk moaned. "He must be a clown, probably a friend of Dudley Smith's. I'm being stalked long-distance by a Confederate clown who likes massages."

"Adrian, you're not thinking straight." Ellen turned to me. "Can't the police do something?"

"There's no law against sending anonymous presents," I said.

"You call that a present?" said Monk. "It's a threat, Natalie. There are too many clowns. You have to come back."

I'd been expecting this ever since I saw the book. "No, Adrian. I have my own case to work on."

He scoffed. "That's just silly. If there was a case with the suicide, which there's not, you couldn't solve it without me."

"I'm going to have to try."

"And I can't do mine without you," he said magnanimously. "So let's compromise and do mine."

"That's your idea of compromise?" I put down my Fiji Water and headed for the hall. "Well, this has been fun. Good luck with your clowns. And remember, you can't quit when things get tough this time. You promised Captain Stottlemeyer. Your solemn word. You're germ brothers."

"Come on, guys," said Ellen. She tried to block my way. "I hate to see you like this. Maybe there is a compromise. You can do the captain's case first. And then you can do Miranda's. How does that sound?" She held out a hand to each of us.

Hmm. It wasn't a great idea but it wasn't horrible. Most crimes are solved in the first few days. But Monk has solved plenty that had some age on them. Once he'd even determined that a skeleton in a museum had been murdered. He even knew the killer's name. Miranda's case might be able to wait a few extra days.

"Adrian?" There was new hope in my voice. "What do you think?"

"Um." Monk hemmed and stammered. We could see him struggling. "It's a waste of time."

I groaned. "No, it's not. Are you saying you don't trust my judgment?"

"No, no. I trust your judgment. Implicitly. You're just wrong."

That was it, I guess. There was nothing more to say. Ellen stepped out of my way and followed me into the hallway, almost as disgusted as me.

"By the way," I shouted over my shoulder, "I know who's sending you the packages."

That was a great tease, right? Hitting him with a line like this right before walking out? And the best part was, I did know. It had come to me a few seconds ago while Monk was busy hemming and stammering and being a jerk.

"You do not."

"Fine. Have it your way."

I could hear him scampering up from his chair. His head popped around the corner. "That's impossible. How could you?"

"Because I'm a detective. And a smart one. I'm going to solve my case while you're still huddled in a corner crying over dead clowns."

"Impossible. There's no way you know, not unless you have secret information."

That was, in fact, true. I did have secret information about the packages. I just hadn't pieced it together until now.

I laughed. "Secret information? You wish!"

And with that, I was out the door. I didn't slam it because Ellen was right behind me.

She slammed it.

CHAPTER TWENTY-FOUR

Mr. Monk Phones It In

Ellen and I went directly back to my kitchen, picking up where we'd left off and dividing the last of the Rocky Road. "How long, do you think?" Ellen asked, leaning back against the counter and enjoying the first bite.

Monk had a thing against letting anyone use a phone in a moving car, one of his few quirks that made perfect sense. I'm sure he'd been timing us, figuring out exactly how long it would take us to get home. Unbeknownst to him, we had gone slightly faster than the limit and hit all the lights.

Ring, ring, ring . . . "Right about now," I said, and picked up my phone.

"All right, I give up. Who? Who's been threatening me?"

"You're a bright boy, Adrian. You figure it out."

"But you've got secret information. Did you find out from your pals at the cult? No, wrong. Your cult wasn't involved with poisoned money or the clowns. Was there something at the clown house? No, that wouldn't account for the massage stones." He was thinking out loud, and it was kind of fascinating. "Does Ellen know? Or is it just you?"

"This isn't twenty questions."

"If the next package is a bomb and I get killed, I'll never forgive you."

"It won't be a bomb."

"Does that mean you know what it's going to be?"

"Not a clue."

"But the fact that you know it's not a bomb means it's nonthreatening, not in a life-and-death way, so . . ."

"Good night, Adrian," I said sweetly, and hung up the phone.

Ten seconds later, Ellen's rang. Without exchanging a word, we turned off our phones and returned to our melting ice cream.

"Don't tell me. I don't want to know," said Ellen as she led the way to the living room sofa. "I'm curious, of course. And amused."

"Adrian could figure it out," I told her. "But it's connected to one of those subjects he blocks out."

"Good. Serves him right. Brilliant is as brilliant does."

"I think the line is, 'Stupid is as stupid does.' From *Forrest Gump*."

"Same thing," Ellen said. "Adrian may be brilliant, but he doesn't always act that way. You may not be as brilliant. But my money's on you."

"Thanks." It was a very supportive thing to say. But I had no idea what I was going to do next.

"So what are you going to do next?"

"Augh!" My hands flew to my head. "I don't know."

"If you were with Adrian, what would you do?"

Good point, I thought. If I act brilliant, maybe I'll be brilliant.

"Wouldn't Adrian go back to the Sanctuary?" asked Ellen. "Look for clues?"

"The only trouble is Damien and Teresa know that I'm suspicious. They wouldn't let me through the gates."

"Well, then Adrian would send his trusted assistant, to be his eyes and ears and report everything she sees."

It took me a second to get her drift. "You would be willing to do that?"

"Sure. There's a retreat this weekend. From all the e-mail blasts I'm getting from BPM, I know it's not completely booked. Not like in the old days."

Wow. This might actually work, I thought. Ellen knew how the Sanctuary operated. She was friendly with both Damien and Teresa. And, as far as I knew, they were unaware of her connection to Officer Natalie Teeger.

"I can get Suzie to cover at the shop," she added. "Not that there's a lot to cover."

"You really want to do this?"

"I've always wondered what it was like. To be honest, sometimes I get jealous when you and Adrian are out there chasing the perps. I could use a little adrenaline rush."

"Ellen, this isn't fun and games." I tried to sound serious, not excited by the prospect. "We don't know what Damien's really up to."

"Natalie." She put down her bowl, looked me in the eyes, and matched my seriousness. "Miranda was my mentor. You're not the only one. Do you know what it's like, listening to you talk about going in there and peeling away the layers and not being a part of it? Let me help."

What could I say? She was right.

"Okay. But only if I can split the cost." Like I said, a weekend at the Sanctuary wasn't cheap. "I wish I could pay for the whole thing. But I'm not even sure if I'm still on the payroll."

"Don't be silly," she countered. "I'm the one staying there, taking their seminars, and eating wild salmon. Business isn't so bad that I can't treat myself to a little adventure."

"Fine," I said. "But if we ever get paid for this case, you get half." I couldn't imagine that kind of thing happening, but it was my way of saving face.

"Agreed," she said. And we shook on it.

To seal the deal, I opened a bottle of Coastal Fog, a chardonnay bottled in the hills just above Half Moon Bay. I'd found it a month ago in a local wine shop and considered it a good omen at the time, a promise of a wonderful weekend to come. Now I considered it a promise to solve this case. "To Miranda," I toasted.

"To Miranda," she toasted back.

We sipped in silence and then both apparently had the same thought. "Do you want to see how he's doing?" Ellen asked. I laughed and nodded.

At the count of three, we powered up our phones. Ellen's was a little faster than mine. "Fifteen calls," she said, checking the display.

"Fourteen," I said, checking mine. "You win." And then, of course, mine rang.

"No, you win," Ellen giggled.

We were still giggling on the third ring when I answered. "Hello, Adrian."

"Who's sending me stuff?" he demanded without a word of greeting.

"Nice talking to you, too."

Making a reservation was as easy as Ellen had thought. In fact, they were giving a twenty percent discount this week, which made me feel better about her paying.

For the rest of the week, I didn't go into work and work didn't come to me. And by work, of course, I mean Monk. I guess we'd come to some unspoken agreement. He would solve his case and I would solve mine. And the results would determine our future partnership, whatever it was.

I'm not sure that's what Monk had in mind, because, like I said, it was unspoken. But he was mad enough not to call again or show up on my doorstep.

For the next two days, Ellen came over and we prepped for the weekend. My number went onto her speed-dial list, as well as those of the San Mateo County Sheriff's Office, Captain Stottlemeyer, and Lieutenant Devlin.

We downloaded a Google map of the compound and quizzed each other on every nook and cranny of the place as well as possible exits and escape plans. Ellen practiced taking secret photos, regular and close-up for documents, then sending them off by touch, with an innocent smile on her face and a phone hidden in a pocket.

She scheduled a massage with Teresa for Saturday and another on Sunday, which she could always cancel if they weren't needed for general spying or conversation.

She Facebook-friended both Damien and Teresa and the

Sanctuary itself, and we pored over their comments and timelines, just to get to know them better. It turns out they were both fans of Bon Jovi, Holistic Homes, and Oliver Stone movies.

On the last evening, we sat down over another bottle of Coastal Fog—decent but a little sweet—and mulled over various scenarios. What if we lost cell service or they took her phone? What if she couldn't get off the premises and I couldn't get on? I toyed with the idea of lending her my Glock 22. But she nixed the idea as being dangerous and illegal, and I had to agree.

In short, we did more prep work than I'd ever done in my life for any case. But then I was going to be working with an amateur this time, not with the seasoned pros who'd always had my back.

And not with Adrian Monk.

CHAPTER TWENTY-FIVE

Mr. Monk Is Defriended

I was born and raised in Monterey, another picture-perfect seaside town, less than two hours south of Half Moon Bay. My hometown is a bit larger, but both places were settled as Spanish missions. Quaint, touristy storefronts, built during the California gold rush, decorate the main street, although only theirs is named Main. Ours is Alvarado.

A few steps away from the art galleries and restaurants and boutiques is the great outdoors, miles of craggy, foggy coastline and every possible activity: horseback riding, surfing, hiking. But you would think from all the ads posted around town that most of the native population is made up of whales who like to be watched by people who like to stay in B-and-Bs. You'd probably be right.

Ellen and I arrived late Friday afternoon in separate cars. We parked at a scenic lookout about a mile north of the BPM Sanctuary and compared notes one last time.

"Oh, look what I picked up at Target." Ellen reached into her bag and pulled out a small cherry red clamshell of a flip phone. "It's prepaid and pretty cheap for just a couple of days."

"You're not taking your iPhone?"

"Sure. But this is my backup. You know, like cops carry an extra gun strapped to their ankle, just in case."

It made total sense, although I hated to think of a situation where she might need a phone strapped to her ankle. She gave me the number. I tried it and it worked. Then I added the number to my speed dial and rearranged my list, making them one and two and dropping Monk to number three.

After exchanging hugs and saying our good-byes, I watched her drive south on the Cabrillo Highway. Two minutes later I followed her, stopping half a mile south of the BPM Sanctuary at the closest place to spend the next two nights. This would be my one-woman command center—the Myrtle & Thyme, a charming B-and-B that had been highly recommended on TripAdvisor.

I met my hostesses, Cathy and Darlene, a sweet middle-aged couple who asked a few questions about my visit but not too many. They did happen to see my binoculars in the backseat and handed me one brochure for a bird-watching tour and three for whale watching.

I settled into the upstairs back bedroom, a bright and cozy hideaway decorated in floral prints and possessing an unobstructed view of the ocean. I proceeded to unpack, make myself a cup of chamomile tea with the electric kettle on the sideboard, and go about my main job for the evening: worrying myself to death.

I've always been the type to second-guess my decisions. The Best Possible Me CDs had been helpful in this regard, teaching me how to trust myself and move forward. But now, alone and with someone out there trusting me as her backup, the doubts were starting to return.

I eyed my Glock, sitting prominently on the bedside table. What if Ellen got hurt? Or killed? That would be a tragedy. For her, obviously, and her family and friends. But also for Monk. He had already lost one woman in his life to a violent death. The loss of a second would be devastating. And I would be indirectly responsible.

The other option, on the opposite end, was that nothing would happen.

What if there was no danger at all? I wondered. No Damien-Teresa conspiracy to reveal? What if, like Monk said, we were just a couple of cultists, trying to deny the sad truth about our cult leader? That would have its own implications.

Among other things, it would mean I probably shouldn't be a partner, that I don't have the instincts or skill, and that I should just fade into the background, content with handing out wipes at a crime scene. My expired police badge and all my work in Summit, New Jersey, would suddenly mean nothing. And I'd be back where I'd been nine years ago.

But at least Ellen would be safe. I had to think of it that way.

I put the gun away in a drawer. Much better. Then I gravitated to the only reading matter in the room: a three-punch binder filled with fliers from the local restaurants, including a separate section for restaurants that delivered.

When my phone dinged, I threw down the binder and flew across the room. It was a text from Ellen. "Anyone up for a game of footsie?"

A second later, it dinged again, this time with a photo. It had been taken under a tablecloth, probably at one of the larger tables facing the sea. It was a shot of a leg in a stylishly distressed pair of jeans curled seductively around a shapely bare brown leg in a white Dansko sandal with a two-inch heel.

I immediately texted back. "What are you doing?"

Twenty seconds later. Ding. "Meet and greet. With feet."

Yes, of course. The meet and greet. "Hope you had your flash off," I texted.

Ding. "Not to worry. This ain't my first rodeo." Ten seconds later, she dinged again. "Actually, it is."

"BE CAREFUL!" I shot back. Do people take you more seriously when it's all in caps? I hoped so.

I knew firsthand the euphoria of being undercover and getting away with a few little jokes. Before you know it, you've drawn some unwanted attention to yourself. I could have kicked myself for not warning her.

I waited a few minutes. But she didn't text back, which I took as a good sign.

As long as I was on the phone, I did a quick Facebook check and was just in time to catch a new post from Lieutenant Amy Devlin. "I need a martini. Hold the ice, vermouth, and olive. Make it a double."

This made me laugh—not because I wanted her to drink, but because I knew the cause. I checked back on her Timeline and saw her earlier posts for the day. One other mentioned alcohol, one mentioned prescription medication, and one was a copy of the Serenity Prayer, printed over a pair of clasped hands. "God grant me the serenity to accept the things I cannot change. . . ."

I called her up to commiserate.

"So, how's Adrian? You guys having fun?"

She almost reached through the phone and grabbed me by the neck. "You wouldn't believe it. It was a clown meltdown. How do you deal with him?"

"I don't, for now."

"Natalie, you have to come back."

"I'm not a partner, remember?"

I felt bad for Devlin and Stottlemeyer. They were people I liked and admired. In a perfect world, I wouldn't have had to abandon them just as Monk was facing down one of his top one hundred. But I was not going back.

On the other hand, I felt I could use some entertainment. "Okay. Tell me all about your day."

And she did.

CHAPTER TWENTY-SIX

Mr. Monk Faces the Lair

I had seen this coming. With the Cemedrin angle blocked, Monk had been forced to focus on the clown's murder. Hey, what could go wrong?

Devlin told me the fun had started that morning at the crime lab when Monk let something slip. He was standing in a corner, averting his eyes, and running out of patience. "You're not going to find anything on those shoes." He'd emphasized the word "those" and Stottlemeyer picked up on it.

The captain's favorite new technician, Jasmine Patil from New Delhi, was at the steel table, dissecting the size twenty-two soles of a yellow clown shoe, trying to find any connection to the Harriman garage where, according to our theory, Dudley Smith had changed clothes and stumbled upon the bottle of solid cyanide compound. It was a long shot.

"What do you mean, 'those' shoes," demanded the captain. "You're saying Smith had other shoes?"

Monk didn't answer. But Devlin walked over to a steel desk where she checked an inventory list, then checked again. "There were no other clown shoes in the house."

"Yes, I'm sure you're right," Monk said meekly. "My mistake."

"No," said Stottlemeyer. "I'm pretty sure it's our mistake. What other shoes?"

Monk tried to dismiss it. "Well, look at them," he said, pointing to the scuffed yellow banana shoes. "They're old and the soles are cracked. They're like his everyday clown shoes. For a gig as important as the Harriman party, he would have worn his new red shoes."

Stottlemeyer sighed. "What new red shoes, Monk?"

"The ones in the picture on top of the wicker hamper."

It turns out that in the framed photo Monk had never seen, the one Devlin had described to him over the phone, Dudley Smith was wearing shiny red twenty-twos, not the yellow ones. "It was a recent photo," Monk added. "I called the hospital and found that his alter ego, J. P. Tatters, visited there just two months ago. His first visit."

"And this means something?" Devlin asked. But she knew it did.

"It means," Stottlemeyer said, "that Dudley Smith probably has a storage unit somewhere or an office or someplace we haven't searched yet. Isn't that right, Monk?"

"Yes, sir. The man had a clown lair."

The captain scowled. "You weren't going to mention this?"

"I don't want to go to a clown lair. Don't make me go."

"Let me get this straight. You held back a vital piece of information because you don't want to go to a clown lair?"

"If you put it that way, yes. A thousand times yes."

"No, it can't be," Devlin protested. "I checked. There are no properties owned by a Dudley Smith. Or properties rented to him."

"Did you check J. P. Tatters?" Stottlemeyer asked.

"Damn." Devlin felt like smacking herself on the forehead. Now that she thought about it, there had been a suspicious lack of business material at the clown's home. No business cards. No promotional material. Only the appointment book.

Devlin borrowed the CS lab's computer and, after a few minutes on a real estate database, had located an office on Willow Street, three blocks away on the edge of Little Saigon. It had been leased to a Jackson Pollock Tatters.

As you might imagine, Jackson Pollock was Monk's least favorite artist of all time. We were once almost arrested at the San Francisco MOMA when he tried to clean a corner of *Lucifer*, one of Pollock's most spectacular drip paintings. Another minute and it would have been ruined. We both had had nightmares after that experience. But for different reasons.

"Jackson Pollock Tatters?" Monk said when they found the name on the lease. "Is this some sick kind of clown joke?"

"Apparently so," Stottlemeyer said as he led the way to the door. Then he turned back to the woman standing over the size twenty-twos. "Thank you, Ms. Patil. We look forward to reading your report."

It took them less than an hour to get a search warrant. And a key from the landlord wasn't necessary. Dudley Smith had kept an unlabeled, unaccounted-for key on his key ring, which fit the lock perfectly.

The clown's lair was a narrow one-story office wedged between a Vietnamese restaurant and a fitness center. It had probably been an alley once. The building had no storefront presence and no sign, and it was too small for any real business.

The captain once more reverted to the "Julie method," leaving Monk out on the street with a smartphone and sending Lieutenant Devlin inside, warrant in hand, to give the virtual tour. This time, wisely or not, Stottlemeyer joined her, perhaps to make sure that nothing was missed.

If I had been with them, what happened next might have turned out differently. Maybe not.

The first few minutes went smoothly. The lair, as suspected, was a combination office and storage space. One section of wall, as Devlin described it, held a pegboard covered in various noses, from big to small, from red to flesh-colored to a red, white and blue model for patriotic occasions. There was a clothes rack devoted to tattered, threadbare trousers, a few of them in dry-cleaning bags. The wigs had a low shelf to themselves, all on Styrofoam heads. And this time there were two with American flag motifs.

Stottlemeyer kept Monk in constant contact, talking him through the space, working to keep his anxiety at a relatively low level of panic. All was going well. They had just inspected a helium tank and five boxes of red balloons. And then . . .

"Mr. Smith? Dudley Smith?"

Monk raised his eyes from the phone and immediately recognized the man. "Um," Monk replied in an uncommitted voice that could have been interpreted as a yes.

"You're a hard man to contact, Mr. Smith. You're not answering your phone. And I must have dropped by here three times. My name's John Harriman."

"How did you find this place?" Monk was still holding the phone in front of him like a walkie-talkie.

"The address was on your receipt."

"Oh, that makes sense."

On the other end of the line, Devlin and Stottlemeyer heard everything and were scrambling.

"My wife says you were fantastic at Thaddeus' birthday party. I was sorry I couldn't be there."

John Harriman, according to Devlin, was in his midforties, of average height with thinning brown hair, and the thuggish features of a boxer. Even in a richly tailored suit, he wasn't a man you would peg as a stockbroker.

Monk recognized him from a photo. And while Harriman must have seen dozens of photos of Dudley Smith smiling alongside Thaddeus and his friends, it was easy to see how he could mistake Monk for the man behind J. P. Tatters.

"It's not easy having kids who are so close together in age," Harriman said. "Celine's birthday is coming up. You remember Celine."

"Celine is your six-year-old."

Harriman smiled fondly. "Turning seven next week. And everything Thaddeus does, she wants to do, right? Including a party. Including J. P. Tatters, Clown to the Stars."

Monk was aghast. "Are you asking me . . ."

"Please? My wife's been in Hong Kong for a month, so it's been hard. I kind of let the ball drop. Celine is adamant about having you there."

"I hate clowns," Monk said.

Harriman stepped back and laughed. "You picked the wrong job, pal. But you gotta admit, kids love you. Now, I know it's short notice. I've been trying to contact you for a week."

"Jackson Pollock Tatters is dead," Monk announced.

"Jackson Pollock? The artist? Yes, I think he died in the fifties."

"No, I mean . . ."

"Dudley? Dudley, how are you?"

Leland Stottlemeyer was just rounding the corner, followed a few seconds later by Amy Devlin, just putting away her phone. They'd found the rear exit and had raced around the block through a back alley.

"Hello," Monk said, which was about as much as he could improvise.

"Sorry I'm late. But I had another client to deal with. You know this business. A bunch of Bozos, present company excepted." The captain turned to Harriman and held out his hand. "My name is Randy Disher." I guess it was the first name he could think of. "I'm J. P. Tatters' booking agent. And you are—"

"No," I said, interrupting Devlin's story right at the crucial moment. "They didn't do what I think they just did."

"Yes," said Devlin. "That's why I need a pitcher of martinis."

"You're kidding me."

"Oh, how I wish I were."

I tried not to laugh. Poor Amy. I could see where this was heading. And I was amazed and tickled and horrified all at the same time.

Adrian Monk was about to go undercover.

As a clown.

• • • • • CHAPTER TWENTY-SEVEN

Mr. Monk and the Cliff-hanger

That night I slept under a fluffy down comforter with the windows open.

The next morning, in the fog of waking up, I felt like a kid again in Monterey, alone in my room facing the ocean view, a thin layer of dewy mist covering everything in the world. I snuggled under the covers and enjoyed the feeling, then started thinking about Monk and his predicament.

Right now the investigation was at a standstill. The clown's lair had produced nothing. The only chance for progress lay in the Harrimans' garage. And Monk now had a chance to get in there and snoop around, with the owner's permission, which was the only way that it could legally work. He could happen across something as big as another bottle of Cemedrin or as small as a milligram of cyanide residue on a shelf.

The circumstances were almost eerily perfect. Alicia Harriman was away in Hong Kong for the month, while John, desperate to keep the kids happy, had never met the deceased clown. The kids had met him, of course. But that wasn't such a big deal. If things went according to plan, Monk would be able to get in and out without ever having to blow up a balloon or honk a bike horn.

All he had to do was arrive at the Sacramento Street home and ask John if he could use the garage to change. Monk would never even have to open his costume bag. At least that was the plan, as Devlin kept insisting. What could go wrong?

The smell of apple-cured bacon finally roused me from my downy heaven. The breakfast room was directly below mine. It was late by the time I made it downstairs, and I was the only guest left unfed. A table for one by the window had been reset and was waiting.

I placed my phone on the table and just stared at it. My arrangement with Ellen was that I wouldn't initiate a call. She would call or text at certain prearranged times—after morning yoga, after lunch on the lawn. The report from yoga had been upbeat if unexciting.

"So what are your plans for the day?" Darlene poured my orange juice and delivered a small carafe of coffee. She was probably the younger of my two hostesses, although it was hard to tell. Like many couples who'd been together forever, they'd wound up looking and dressing alike.

"Just relaxing. Hiking. Maybe some bird-watching," I added, remembering the binoculars in the car.

"Well, you picked a good time. You should have seen this place two weeks ago. What a zoo."

"That's right," I said vaguely. "It was just down the road, wasn't it?"

Darlene nodded. "Every cubbyhole in town was booked after that. Soledad O'Brien, from CNN, she was in your room for two nights."

"Really? In my room?" I felt honored.

"Lovely girl, although she doesn't look Irish. Smaller than you'd think. And skinny. I guess they're all skinny."

Darlene obviously like chatting with the guests. I suppose that comes with the dream of opening a B-and-B. "Did you know her?" I asked. "Miranda Bigley?"

"Not well," she had to admit. "The two of them used to show up at town meetings, but only when it was about zoning or beach access."

"What was she like? Was she as inspiring as they say?"

"She was nice." Darlene paused, perhaps torn between her need to be pleasant and her need to gossip. "When she was speaking or really interested, you could see her energy. It was just like watching her on TV. But at a town meeting, with all the local characters—you can imagine—there's a lot of downtime. If you looked at her then, it was like a lightbulb turned off. Seemed a little phony, if you know what I mean."

"You could say that about anyone," I suggested.

"You're right," Darlene said. "Who am I to judge? The poor woman had her demons."

I was all set to argue the point, a silly, pointless argument. But I was saved by a ding to my phone on the table. "Excuse me."

Okay, I hate it as much as you when someone interrupts a conversation to look at their phone. But this was different. This was a text. And it was Ellen. "I just have to see . . ."

"By all means," said Darlene.

They were close-up photos, four of them. A row of vitamin bottles in a mirrored medicine cabinet. A hand towel, monogrammed MGB, on a bathroom rod. A close-up of a round pink pill on the white tile of the bathroom floor. At the end of the third was a caption. "From the Hers bathroom. Woo-hoo!!!!"

"What the hell is she doing?"

I didn't mean to say it out loud. But now Darlene was eyeing me quizzically. "Sorry," I said. "A friend of mine is actually at the Sanctuary this weekend. She just texted me some photos."

"Inappropriate photos?"

"No," I lied. They weren't inappropriate in a sexual sense, only in a legal one.

Darlene's brow furrowed as she processed my situation. "So your friend is at the Sanctuary and you're here, half a mile away? Without her? On a beautiful weekend like this? You don't like the Sanctuary?"

"No, I like it a lot. I've been there twice."

"Were they all booked up this weekend?" She frowned, and whispered. "Or is she with somebody else?"

"No, she's alone. We felt it would be better if she went alone."

"I understand," Darlene said, and laid a comforting hand on my arm. "Relationships are complicated."

It was maddening, being so near and yet so far away.

My consolation was that I knew Ellen or thought I did. She wasn't the type to go crazy and endanger herself. On the other hand, she did send three photos from Miranda's bathroom with four exclamation points.

Her first evening at the Sanctuary had been fairly ordinary. Or so I later heard. She tried her best to blend in, perhaps asking a few more questions than normal and showing a tad more curiosity. By the end of the day, she was growing impatient and promised herself to be a little more proactive the next day.

During the deep meditation part of Saturday's sunrise yoga, Ellen formulated a plan, one borrowed from a hundred old episodes of *Charlie's Angels.* She would break into the Bigleys' private residence on the main building's second level and see what she could find.

She'd chosen the morning's Actualization-Visualization session as her cover. Everyone would be there, including Teresa, who was leading the group, and Damien, who would be circling the floor monitoring their progress. Ellen would find a place at the rear, partly hidden behind a pillar, and sneak out during the last half hour, when even Damien and Teresa would be in a lotus position on a mat with their eyes closed, visualizing. Probably visualizing each other naked.

For Ellen, the session went on forever. But finally, all eyes were closed, all voices humming contentedly. Her exit from the back of the room went perfectly, as far as she could tell. Seconds later she was quietly bounding up the stairs, past the red velvet "Staff Only" rope, to a door marked "Residence." It was the floor's only residence and was armed, she discovered, with a state-of-the-art keypad system. So much for trusting your trusty followers.

Without even trying her luck, Ellen looked for an alternative and spotted a balcony at the end of the hallway. The French doors were unlocked and revealed a stunning view. In an act of architectural hubris, the entire building had been cantilevered out over the seaside cliff. On the main floor, this was impressive. On the second level, with the support beams extending the floor plan out over the cliff, it was breathtaking.

Ellen emerged onto the small balcony and, looking to her left, saw a matching balcony, less than twenty feet away, that opened off of the Bigleys' private apartment. She also saw that this balcony's French doors had been left tantalizingly open. Less than twenty feet away.

What had made Ellen think this was even possible? Maybe she was an experienced rock wall climber. Maybe she'd spent every weekend at Planet Granite in the Presidio, going up from one tiny foothold to another. I doubt it, but maybe. Whatever her rationale, Ellen was over the railing in an instant, climbing sideways across the stacked stone wall, the surf pounding a hundred feet below her.

I don't mean to diminish the suspense of the next minute or so, but there's more suspense coming, so let's cut to the chase. Her foot slipped once or twice on the narrow footholds but she made it across.

Ellen grabbed the iron railing with both hands, pulled her torso over and found herself staring into Miranda and Damien's spacious bedroom.

After all the derring-do of getting in, the suite itself was a letdown. A king-sized bed provided plenty of room for spreading out. The furniture was Mission style, probably Stickley, probably originals. The suite had two bathrooms, his and hers. Ellen focused on hers, snapped photos of pill bottles and monogrammed towels, and took the time to send them to me.

On a bedside table, she thumbed through a well-thumbed copy of *Spiritual Solutions* by Deepak Chopra and didn't quite know what to make of it—one self-help guru using another one for her bedtime inspiration. She took another photo, decided not to send it, and proceeded to open drawers.

The very last thing she found made the danger of the climb worthwhile. It was in the top dresser drawer, underneath a pile of Damien's folded socks. It was an odd place, Ellen mused, to stash a pearl necklace worth a couple hundred thousand dollars. Especially odd since it had last been seen on Miranda Bigley's neck, vanishing off the edge of a cliff.

The police assumed the necklace had been torn free, the pearls spread out over the ocean floor. But here it was, safe and sound and lying underneath her husband's socks.

Ellen laid it out on the bed and was about to take a photo when she heard a soft whir coming from the living room. She assumed it must be the heating system kicking in. A moment too late she realized what it was: the electronic key system.

Rushing to the bedroom door, she was just in time to see Damien Bigley walking in. He must have left early, she thought. But why? Why would he leave an Actualization-Visualization session early?

Bathroom break. It was an educated guess and Ellen faded back into the bedroom and hid behind the open door.

Did I disturb anything? she wondered, frozen in her shoes. Yes, right here. Damien's sock drawer, gaping wide. It was on the opposite side of the room from his bathroom, so maybe he wouldn't notice. Through the crack by the hinges, Ellen watched as a large man in a forest green polo strolled past her and toward his bathroom.

Yes! Bathroom break. Just as she thought. Being a detective wasn't that hard, she reasoned. It was certainly something she could handle. Climbing around a building perched over a cliff. Finding a big clue. Making an escape while the bad guy's busy in his own bath . . . Oh, no! Damn it, no.

Damien must have seen it out of the corner of his eye. He turned, focused on the drawer, and crossed quickly to the bureau, just a few feet from the open door. Ellen didn't stop to think through this next part. She just ran.

Startled by the swing of the door, Damien was slow to react.

He was just coming out the door when Ellen reached the top of the stairs and started taking them two by two, steadying herself on the banister. Neither one called out or said a word. By the time Ellen reached the outside, Damien was halfway down the stairs. No one else was in sight.

The grounds, too, were deserted. Ellen didn't pause to think what her options might be: locking herself in her cabin and calling the police; running for the guard at the gate; trying to bluff her way out. She just ran toward the light and the open space, past the cabins and the great lawn, to where the promontory of land swung around again.

Toward the cliff.

"Miss Morse." They were out of sight and out of earshot from anyone. Just the surf and the sky and the edge of the world. "Ellen."

She had stopped running, while he had reduced his pace to a wary walk. "What were you doing?" he demanded.

"Nothing," she shouted back. "I was using the bathroom, like you."

"How did you get in?"

"It was open."

"It wasn't open." He was getting closer. "Give it back and I won't press charges. We'll pretend this never happened."

It wasn't until he said this that Ellen realized she was holding the necklace in her right hand. Not her phone, like she'd half thought in all her excitement, but the strand of perfectly matched pearls that could probably prove something, although she didn't know what.

"No," Ellen shouted back, then turned to face the unforgiving cliff.

"Miss Morse. There's no way out."

And that's when she jumped.

CHAPTER TWENTY-EIGHT

Mr. Monk and the Bullies

I wasn't surprised when Ellen didn't text again. I was relieved. Maybe she was finally listening to me and keeping out of trouble.

After a second helping of apple-cured bacon and a sourdough biscuit, I returned to my room to brush my teeth and figure out how to spend the day.

During a regular day, even on a weekend, my schedule was dominated by Monk, either work related or trauma related or both. Naturally, my thoughts turned to him now and by extension to Devlin and Stottlemeyer. Of the three, only Devlin had a Facebook page.

Her last entry, according to my phone, had been this morning. "I've got Cemedrin headache number twenty-two," it started, playing off the old TV commercials. "Better yet, give Monk a couple of Cemedrins. That would cure things."

It was a morbid inside joke only the four of us would get. And I couldn't help thinking it had been aimed my way. You can imagine how curious this made me. But I couldn't just call up and ask. That would go against my whole idea of a work stoppage.

As I later found out, Monk had arrived at headquarters

on his own that morning, shortly after nine. He knew something was up as soon as he entered Stottlemeyer's office and faced the off-center widow's peak of Joshua Grooms and the less annoying crew cut of George Cardea, FBI special agents.

Monk's list of phobias does not include individual humans. If it did, these two would be near the top. My experience with Grooms goes back to a time when he was holding Monk in protective custody in a cabin in the woods. Grooms wouldn't listen to us about a murder at a nearby cabin, and we wound up escaping by locking him in a bathroom. Our relationship went downhill from there.

The captain and lieutenant were already on the scene, shooting Monk the kind of looks that say, "Keep your mouth shut," which usually results in Monk saying, "Why are you looking at me like that?"

"Why are you looking at me like that?" he said.

"Monk." Stottlemeyer jumped in before they could. "You remember special agents Grooms and Cardea."

"Monk," said Cardea in his booming voice. "How's it going?"

"Living the dream," Monk said with a shudder. "It's not my dream, but it must be someone's."

"Monk, my man." Grooms locked eyes with Monk and held out his hand, like a snake hypnotizing its prey. He loved to make Monk shake his hand, just to witness his anguished reaction. "Where's your perky little assistant with the wipes?"

"Wipe," Monk shouted. Devlin came to the rescue, giving him a handful from a pack on the captain's desk. "Natalie is taking a personal day or week or whatever she's doing. I don't know." He finally stopped wiping.

"Our friends at the FBI dropped by to see if they could help us with a case." The captain was trying to gain some control of the moment. "The Dudley Smith case. Not the other case we're working on. Just the Smith case."

"What's the other case?" asked Cardea.

"It's none of your business, sir," said Lieutenant Devlin. "With all due respect."

"We got a ping from our database about a poison case involving U.S. currency and the U.S. mail. Imagine our delight when your names came up."

That couldn't have been a good feeling, knowing that the FBI's computer system was keeping tabs on your cases.

Stottlemeyer managed a smirk. "Far as I know, the FBI has no jurisdiction. We cleared everything with the Secret Service and the Postal Inspection Service, and they were happy for us to take the lead in what is a local homicide. So, thanks for the visit."

Grooms pursed his lips. "As long as you're sharing with the appropriate agencies. Isn't that the point of this post-nine-eleven world? We share our information and cover our butts."

"The second we have any evidence that involves the FBI's interests, we'll share," Devlin promised.

"Absolutely," Stottlemeyer seconded.

Monk's mouth was too dry for him to add anything but a grunt.

"I hear there're clowns involved," said Special Agent Cardea maliciously. "That's what your prelim says."

"Hey, Monk," said Grooms, "I thought you hated clowns.

Oh, maybe 'hate's' not the right word. 'Scared.' 'Frightened to death.' Are those the right words?"

"Monk's got it under control," said Devlin.

"Under control?" said Grooms, fixing Monk with another snake stare. "Really? Without little Natalie around to act as your human tranquilizer?"

"How do you solve a clown case?" Cardea asked Monk.

"Are you going to interrogate a roomful of them?" said Grooms. "Maybe you should do a lineup." They were on either side of him now, ping-ponging it back and forth.

"Or get a sketch artist. 'Yes, Officer, I think his nose was a little bigger.'"

"Just don't get into a car chase." Grooms went into a high-pitched clown voice. "Oh, the humanity!"

They could see the effect this was having. That's why they were doing it. It was the one way these bullies could get even after all the times he'd shown them up. They certainly couldn't outpolice him or outthink him.

"I can see the wreck now. A few unicycles. A tiny car. The world's smallest bike."

"Enough!" Stottlemeyer shouted, and pointed to the door. "Out of my office. If you have any more clever things to say, put them in writing and go through the proper channels. This meeting is over."

"No, Captain, they're right."

Monk was shivering head to foot. Devlin told me later that she'd never seen him shake so badly. "I thought I could do this, Leland, I really did."

"You can, Monk. Don't let these animals—"

"I can't. I know I'm letting a germ brother down, but— " And he turned and fled the room.

I don't know what I'd been planning to do for a full weekend, besides sitting around being Ellen's backup.

My first time killer consisted of taking a hike around the B-and-B. The gravel drive opened onto a dirt road that wandered behind the house, down to a small secluded inlet. It always surprised me how towns that seemed so overbuilt and that prized their priceless beachfronts would have so many secluded spots, little beaches like this with nary a house in sight.

I looked north along the cliffs to where I knew the Sanctuary must be, nestled between its tall stucco walls and the sea.

For the next hour I wandered the town's Main Street, going into shops crowded with antiques and knickknacks and making a mental list of all the adorable things I couldn't afford. Not that I'm complaining, but it gets a little old, always pinching pennies. I wondered how our partnership, Monk and Teeger, might positively affect my income—if there ever was to be a Monk and Teeger. At this point it looked iffy.

After sufficiently depressing myself, I strolled back to my Subaru and noticed my binoculars in the backseat. Ellen hadn't called or texted since breakfast. She wasn't scheduled until after lunch, so I was just a little bit anxious. I'm not sure "anxious" is the word. Concerned? Aware? I should ask Monk. He's like an Eskimo. You know, the guys who have thirty words for snow? Monk must have at least fifty words for his various levels of anxiety.

Before I realized where I was going, I found myself driving to a turnout not far from the white stucco wall that marked the northern boundary of the BPM Sanctuary. Two weeks ago, this had been the prime gathering point for the TV trucks and photographers. I bowed to the wisdom of professional snoops and pulled in.

Taking my pair of vintage Bausch and Lombs, I crossed the Cabrillo Highway and began to scout out a place in the sandy scrub, a little shielded from the road, but still with a view over the north wall.

Sure, this was a pointless exercise. So is Pilates, at least for me.

But it made me feel better. It gave me a sense of control, knowing that, if Ellen was in trouble and had the wherewithal to stand on the lawn and wave a colorful distress flag, I would be there to see it and come to her rescue.

I'd been sitting there for perhaps forty minutes, just long enough to have my left leg fall asleep, when I thought I saw something out of the corner of my eye. It was a flash of color—red, maybe—moving between my cubbyhole and the road above.

I trained my binoculars on the spot. A second later, I saw it again. Could those be roses? Growing in this sandy terrain? No.

But, yes, I decided after taking another look. These were roses, profoundly red ones. And they were bobbing up and down and coming closer. Not only roses, but long-stemmed. Exactly ten of them, being held above someone's head like a white flag.

"Natalie," he moaned from a distance. "Please come back."

I moaned as well. "Adrian." Then I got up to shake my sleepy leg. "How did you find me?"

Monk wobbled closer and closer, trying desperately not to let the sand get into his pant cuffs. "I knew you were still obsessed. So I called the Sanctuary and you weren't registered. So I had Luther drive me here and we saw your car parked off the road."

"Who is Luther?'

"He's this guy. Here!" Monk stood in front of me, pushing the plastic roses into my face.

I had to hang the binoculars around my neck to accept them. "What am I supposed to do with these?"

"I don't know. It's part of the ritual. It seemed to work with Ellen."

"Well, it's not going to fix this. Who is Luther?"

"He's this guy. What do you expect to see with those binoculars?"

"None of your business. Who's Luther?"

"This guy. Can we please discuss this someplace not so sandy?"

"Sure." Why not? This spying wasn't getting me anywhere, and I had to find out who Luther was. I stretched my dozing leg again and handed him back the roses.

"No, those are for you."

"I don't want ten artificial roses."

"Fine," he said sulkily. "I'll save them for someone else."

"You do that."

"Can you carry them back up to the car for me?"

"Carry them back yourself."

"I'd prefer not to. They set me off balance. We can leave

them here in the sand. Why don't we do that? They'll just return to nature."

"They won't return to nature. They're plastic."

I wound up carrying the roses in one hand and my binoculars in the other.

Up at the turnout, I was finally introduced to Luther and his car. "Good to meet you, Natalie." The man was in a black suit, a white shirt, and a black tie and wore a cap that he tipped my way. "I've heard a lot."

Monk nodded. "Mostly about how dirty your car is and how unreliable you are."

I took Monk a few yards away, although I'm sure Luther could still hear. "A chauffeur? You hired a limousine and chauffeur?"

"Not a chauffeur," Monk said.

You could have fooled me. The car was a black Lincoln sedan, spotlessly clean. Luther himself was a youngish black man, large, lean, and well-spoken, with just a little salt-and-pepper at the temples. Monk had created his own dysfunctional version of *Driving Miss Daisy*.

"It's a car service," Monk said, as if this explained everything.

"Since when can we afford a car service?"

"It's not so bad when the owner gives you a rate."

"Who's the owner?"

"I am."

"You are?" I was starting to sound like a straight man in a bad comedy sketch.

"It's a foolproof investment," Monk said. "You remember the reward I got from solving that billionaire's kidnapping?"

"No, I remember the reward *we* got. You said it was going right into our emergency fund."

"Transportation is an emergency. I believe it was one of FDR's Four Freedoms. Freedom of Transportation."

"What about my bonus?" I asked. "I seem to recall you promising me a bonus on that case."

Monk shook his head and chuckled. "At the time I was semiconscious, hanging upside down, and encased in paper mache as part of the killer's sculpture installation at the Palace of Fine Arts. I don't think it's ethical to hold someone to that kind of promise."

"So, I'm just an employee who gets nothing?"

"That's why you should knuckle-down and pass your exam and become my partner. Someday."

"Someday? Until then I get nothing but the occasional paycheck."

"Not nothing," he protested. "Not nothing." I could see him eyeing the plastic roses in my hand.

CHAPTER TWENTY-NINE

Mr. Monk and His Germ Sister

There were so many reasons to be mad. But, more than mad, I was hurt. Buying a car service, which basically meant limousines? How could he have kept this from me? We were best friends. We'd spent hundreds of hours together, and that was just a typical week. He seemed unable to do anything without me. And yet he had managed to buy a company with a fleet of four cars and six drivers.

Of course, now that I think of it, I had been away in New Jersey, and his life hadn't stopped. Even if my daughter, Julie, did pitch in as his temporary assistant, he'd had plenty of time to get into trouble.

But still . . . If I'd bought a car service company, even a small one, I certainly would have told him.

On the plus side, Luther Washington was a sweetheart. He had a true empathy for human foibles, a wicked sense of humor, and extreme patience, all the things you tend to run out of while dealing with my boss. He could also, when push came to shove, turn on a no-guff attitude that Monk somehow responded to.

They had met through cleanliness, of course. Before my last return to San Francisco, Monk had my Subaru towed to a car-detailing shop for a complete antigerm, microbial cleaning, with extra emphasis on the front passenger seat. It was supposed to be a present.

Luther owned the detailing shop, and he and Monk started talking, mostly about the fact that my insurance didn't seem to cover this kind of "required maintenance."

When Luther mentioned his entry into the limousine business, Monk saw this as a perfect opportunity to make an investment and provide himself with a perk. It made a kind of sense, I had to admit, although this didn't mean I was relinquishing my right to be upset.

I drove back to the Myrtle & Thyme, and Luther followed with His Highness majestically centered in the backseat. With Monk now turned over to my custody, Luther drove back to San Francisco and his life.

Monk and I quickly commandeered the lounge, a front room that seemed to be outfitted with half the knickknacks I'd just seen on Main Street. Darlene popped in to offer us tea, which we declined. She didn't mention it, but I could tell she was confused by my choice of companionship.

"Natalie, come back," Monk pleaded. "First, Ellen leaves me, then you. By the way, do you know where Ellen is? She's not at home and not answering her phone." If Darlene was still nearby, listening in, I'm sure she was getting an earful.

"Forget about Ellen for now," I said. "This relationship can only work if you and I are full, equal partners."

"That never bothered you before."

"Well, it does now. I've changed, Adrian. I know how much you hate change. But it's part of life."

"No, it's not. It's part of death."

"Let's not talk about life and death. What we need to talk about is trust. If you want me to help you with your murder, you have to trust me about my suicide."

From off in the kitchen, I could hear a plate dropping to the floor.

The rest of our conversation was a lot more normal. Well, a bit more normal, considering the source. Monk repeated how he couldn't deal with clowns, not without me. And how he was germ brothers with Stottlemeyer and couldn't go back on his word.

Meanwhile, I countered with theories about Miranda—and threw in some punches about how partners shouldn't take company money and spend it on chauffeurs, not without discussing it.

By the end we had come to an understanding.

"Okay," he sighed, exhausted by the effort. "As long as I'm here, I'll check it out."

"No," I insisted. "You have to treat this like a real case. You can't just look at a few things and give me a three percent. You have to promise. Germ brothers." And I held out my hand.

He thought about it. "Can I wipe before shaking and let the disinfectant linger?"

"No. You're not going to wipe and you're not going to run away. We're partners. Take it or leave it."

Monk gulped a lungful, then extended his hand. After the shake, I watched but didn't see him try anything funny. "Good," I said. "Now I'll bring you up to date." As a precaution, I crossed to the lounge door, closed it, and lowered my voice.

There wasn't much to tell. But I reviewed my scanty evidence and ended by showing him the photos: the row of vitamins, the pill on the floor, the monogrammed hand towel.

I could see Monk focusing on the lone pill. "Enlarge!" he ordered the phone, as if it would respond on its own. I zoomed in on the pill as much as I could. "This is from her bathroom, not his?" he asked.

"Yes," I said. "From what I know, they have his and her bathrooms."

"That's Malarone."

I checked the photo. "It's a pill. How can you tell what type?"

"Every prescription pill has a distinct color and shape and markings—to prevent accidents. It's the law. Malarone is pink and round with a GX marking at the top."

I did a Google image search for Malarone. He was right. "Don't tell me you know the markings of every pill in the universe."

"Not the universe. Just North America."

"Okay, it's Malarone. What's Malarone?"

"It's a malaria preventative," Monk said. "Did your cult leader just return from some tropical hellhole?"

"No. As far as I know, she'd been at the Sanctuary for the last few months."

"Make small," Monk shouted, and I returned the photo to its full view. "The rest of the floor looks clean enough," he said thoughtfully, "for a disgusting bathroom."

I could tell this meant something and I wasn't too proud to ask. "What?"

"If only I'd personally seen her jump. I wasn't looking."

"No," I reminded him. "You were too busy lecturing me on cults."

"Which was a fool's errand, wasn't it? I should have been watching."

I had no idea what my annoying genius was thinking, but this time, I knew how to help. "There's a YouTube video," I told him. "It's all there."

One of the many amenities of the Myrtle & Thyme was an aging PC set up in a corner of the lounge, what Darlene had proudly referred to as their business center. I hurried over and woke it from its sleep. Within two minutes, Monk was sitting in a ladder-back chair, bent forward, examining the enlarged view of my least favorite video, now up to more than five million views.

I described the footage earlier—Miranda doing her calm stretch, her walk to the edge, and her jump. Then the shock and confusion. And Damien leading the way to the cliff.

"Stop," Monk ordered.

"Oh, for Pete's sake, Adrian. Do it yourself. It's those two little lines in the bottom left."

"Wipe," he responded, then waited until I took out a few wipes and thoroughly cleaned the mouse and mouse pad.

Somehow, through sheer intelligence and force of will, he managed to stop the video. He also grasped how to move the bottom red line forward and backward. I had no idea what he was looking for. But he did.

"Very clever man. He was counting on the confusion." Monk had stopped the footage at the moment before Miranda's leap. "See that clump of dandelions?"

I shoved my nose up to the monitor and could barely

see it, a yellow pixel or two just to the left of her feet. "Okay . . ."

"Now watch," he said, and moved the red line a minute further along. "See?" He pointed triumphantly. "No more dandelions."

"I don't get it," I said.

"Of course you don't. Here's what happened." My favorite three words in the world.

"Was it murder?" I asked.

"Yes. But don't interrupt."

CHAPTER THIRTY

Mr. Monk and What Happened

It was not a story I wanted to hear.

I don't know what I'd been expecting. Miranda Bigley's suicide had been just so incomprehensible, even after seeing it with my own eyes, that I needed to come up with another explanation.

The motive, as Monk explained, was what we'd always thought: money.

The Best Possible Me empire was a mess, good money chasing bad down a rabbit hole of embezzlement and stupid investments. An audit was coming up and the Bigleys, Miranda and Damien, had to find a way out.

Monk had seen it on the video, the detail that five million viewers had missed. The spot that Damien led the witnesses to, including us, was not exactly the same spot that Miranda had jumped from. In all the confusion and disbelief and the jiggling camera, no one realized her loving husband was drawing their focus to just a portion of the cliff, the sheer face that left no room for escape. No room for doubt.

"The cliff edge is jagged," Monk explained. "You walk twenty feet either direction and it's a different story. Your cult lady must have found a ledge she could jump onto and hide—or found a path leading away from the action. I might not have guessed it myself except for the Malarone she dropped on the bathroom floor."

This Malarone malaria pill, he'd neglected to tell me earlier, is meant to be taken before your trip. For three days before until seven days after.

"It proves that Miranda was preparing to travel," Monk continued. "Someplace far away and disease-ridden. It was her jump to escape."

"Did she accidentally fall?" I asked.

"Not according to what you overheard during your hot-stone ordeal. He met her somewhere and killed her."

I remembered back to that horrible day, two hours after the jump, when Damien borrowed the gardener's truck and sneaked out. He said he needed to "clear his head." What he really needed to do was meet up with Miranda, knock her unconscious, and dump her into the Pacific.

"He was supposed to bring her everything," Monk went on. "Fake passport, money, a disguise. Dead Miranda, lost at sea, would take the blame. Months later, once the Sanctuary was sold and the insurance paid, he would meet up with her and they would both try not to catch malaria. Good luck."

But Damien had concocted a better ending. He would provide the authorities with Miranda's body and live happily ever after with his mistress. With no malaria to worry about; Monk made sure to point that out.

I listened with mixed feelings. It was upsetting to hear that this woman who had been my life coach had planned this kind of crime, with no concern for the millions of fans she would leave behind, confused and depressed.

On the other hand, I understood her desperation. She was faced with total ruin and jail time. What other option did she have? And she didn't kill herself, even though that was what she wanted the world to think, which brought me to another important point.

"I was right," I said, full of righteous vindication. "I knew Miranda Bigley wouldn't kill herself. You never believed me."

"What you had was a feeling. A feeling isn't proof."

"But I back up your feelings. There are plenty of times when Adrian Monk feels that he's right and everyone else is wrong."

"That's different. That's instinct."

"Fine." I wasn't prepared to argue. "Can we prove any of this?"

Monk shrugged. "It's hard when the killer has the victim do most of his work."

That was true. Miranda had performed a great suicide. What little evidence we had was circumstantial. "How about Teresa?" I asked. "She's obviously involved. Maybe we can get her to flip."

"Why would she do that?" Monk said. "We need more evidence. Did you take any other pictures in the bathroom?"

"About the pictures . . ." I guessed it was time for me to come clean. "Adrian, I didn't take them. Ellen did. She's in there. Not still in the bathroom, I hope. In the Sanctuary for the weekend."

His mouth fell open. "You sent her in there to spy?"

"I didn't send her. She volunteered."

"You sent a sweet, innocent woman in there instead of yourself?"

Again, I wasn't going to argue. "She's in no danger. She's a paying guest, along with a couple dozen others. Plus, we have a system." I looked at my watch. "She should be checking in, anytime now." I was lying. She should have called a half hour ago. "I think I'll just call her."

When I pressed one on my speed dial, Ellen's phone went directly to voice mail. She'd turned it off, I thought. Why did she turn it off?

I didn't leave a message. "Not to worry," I told Monk. "She's carrying a backup phone." I pressed number two on my speed dial. But with no voice mail system for it to go into, Ellen's prepaid little phone rang and rang and rang.

"Can I worry now?" Monk asked, already there. "How could you send an innocent woman—"

I cut him off. "Innocent. Got it. Let's go knock on the door."

I retrieved the Glock from my room and slipped it in my bag. Within five minutes, we were in the Subaru, approaching a pair of iron gates with the letters BPM wrought in fancy script, splitting open in the middle of the "P." The "P" was now closed and we were forced to use the intercom.

The receptionist on the other end was as sunny as ever, but said the Sanctuary wasn't admitting visitors. Increased security, she said. She also said that Damien was unavailable to speak with us, even over the intercom. For a moment, I thought about pressing my way in as Officer Teeger of the SPD. But these kinds of quasilegal deceptions can often come back and bite you.

"Is Teresa Garcia available?" I asked. "It's very important."

Something about my voice convinced her we weren't going away. "I'll see if I can find her." And the line went dead.

"We should jump the fence." Monk moaned and wriggled in his seat belt, his voice rising half an octave. "Jump the fence and demand to see Ellen and shoot them if they refuse."

"We?"

"Okay. You."

Monk had just gotten worked up enough to take off his seat belt when a golf cart made its way down the winding drive. It was Teresa. She parked with her cart blocking the gates, got out, and spoke with us through the fence.

"Let me do the talking," I told him. "Seriously."

"Natalie. Hi," she said, looking concerned. "And Mr. Monk." I was surprised that she remembered him from that long, traumatic afternoon after the jump. But then Monk is hard to forget. "Dahlia said it was important. What's the matter?"

"Sorry to disturb," I said. "We need to see a friend. Ellen Morse. It's a family emergency."

"Ellen. Of course. I hope it's nothing too serious."

"She's not answering either one of her phones," Monk blurted out. "Not her regular phone or her backup phone. Why is that?"

"Oh." Teresa seemed taken aback. "We ask our guests to turn off their phones when they arrive. I'm sure that's it."

"Could you ask her to call me?" I said as sweetly as possible.

"Ellen's in the middle of class right now. Perhaps in a couple of hours . . . I'll tell her."

I checked my watch. Having been there twice, I was familiar with the schedule. "Is there a class? I thought this was the hour of solitary meditation."

"No, we changed it," Teresa said warmly but firmly. "It's the affirmative aspiration workshop. Very intense, as you know. When it's over, I can give her a message."

"Yes. Can you please tell her that she's wasting her time and money on this malarkey and she needs to come home?" I don't need to tell you who said that.

I shot Monk a look and jumped in with a smile. "Can you tell her to call me as soon as she can? It's very important."

"Naturally," said Teresa, then backed away toward her cart. "Now, if you'll excuse me, I have a massage. Good to see you, Natalie. I hope you can come back."

I waited until she was up the drive and out of earshot. "Why did you mention the backup phone? Now they know."

"I didn't realize it was a secret."

"Of course it's a secret."

"Then why did you tell me?"

"My fault. Now I know better."

"I have a question. Why didn't you pull out your gun and demanded to get inside?"

"Because I . . . Wait. How did you know I was carrying?"

He pointed to the bag under my arm. "Because when you oiled and cleaned it, you forgot to wipe down the area around the firing chamber."

"Shoot," I said, inspecting the little oval stain decorating the side of my favorite DK messenger bag.

"A Glock 22?" he guessed. And before I could ask how . . . "I know that's what Devlin carries as her personal firearm. You would have asked her for advice. And she would've forgotten to tell you about wiping down the area around the firing chamber."

I sighed with frustration, and not just about the bag. "Okay, Mr. Genius. What now?"

CHAPTER THIRTY-ONE

Mr. Monk and What Happened Next

It took us several minutes to figure out the next step.

Our first thought was to scale the wall, like a couple of middle-aged commandos performing a rescue operation. But we had already forewarned Teresa and Damien, who would assume this would be our next step.

Plus, it didn't look easy. The wall was about twelve feet high, covered in a smooth stucco finish, with no trees or rocks nearby to give us some elevation. There was also, as Monk pointed out, the problem of cameras. Every twenty yards or so, a fish-eyed camera lens stuck out of the stucco near the top. Somewhere inside, in a security office, Teresa or Damien or a member of their team was on the alert, checking a dozen monitors. The welcoming Sanctuary of my first visit, the refuge with the open gates, had been an illusion.

While Monk was in a verbal loop, musing about ladders and catapults and fifty-yard-long tunnels, I was doing what any modern girl would do to solve a problem. I was pressing buttons on my phone.

"Natalie." Monk shook his head in disgust. "The sheriff's office isn't going to help."

"I'm not calling the sheriff," I said. "I'm checking Google Earth."

Monk had always ridiculed me for having so many apps. To him, the idea of a cell phone was still futuristic, something out of Buck Rogers. And the concept that you would use it to do more than make calls was indulgent to the point of crazy. "That's what libraries are for," he would tell me.

"If we can't get over the wall, we'll go around it."

"I am not getting in a boat," he replied. "Boats and I are not friends."

"No boat. On a coastal trail. If Miranda could jump on a ledge and make her way off the property, then we can make our way onto the property."

According to the largest version of the map I could find, there were hints of a foot trail leading from the edge of the property north to a secluded beach. Unless I was mistaken, this was the same beach I'd been on this morning, at the end of the trail below the Myrtle & Thyme.

Monk was odd when it came to bravery. And by odd, I didn't mean his usual, weird, inexplicable behavior. During one nasty murder case, he made me personally check his mail every day for bombs and anthrax. On the other hand, he could occasionally shine, like the time he stepped in front of a bullet meant for me. FYI, the gun jammed and no one got shot.

If only I could find a way to bottle this determination of his and feed it back to him, an eyedropper at a time, when he had to face the horrors of everyday life, like an uneven checkout line at the store.

In this case, Monk rolled up the car window, gritted his

teeth and endured the bumpy dirt road leading down to the deserted beach and all of its sand.

"Do you think this is the place?" I said as we got out of the Subaru. "I mean where he drove to and killed her?"

"Probably," Monk said. "I doubt there's any physical evidence left, but you never know." He was distracted, gazing north toward a narrow, rocky trail that wound its way up toward the craggy cliffs. "Let's do it," he said with a cough and a gulp.

Like I said, inexplicable—except for the fact that Ellen was up there somewhere and probably needed him.

I grabbed the binoculars and my DK messenger bag from the car, and we started up the trail—me in front, of course. You can't expect miracles.

We had gone around several bends, with the trail backtracking on itself, then leading out to a promontory. We lost sight of the deserted beach but were rewarded with an expansive view south to the cliff below the Sanctuary, the waves crashing their spray halfway to the top.

Monk stopped in his tracks, and for a moment, I thought it might be vertigo or sand or the uneven rocks. "It's Damien," he said, and pointed.

Through the spray, I could see a large, beefy man in a dark sweatshirt and sweatpants higher up on another part of the trail. I used the binoculars and saw that he was hefting a piece of driftwood in his right hand. I didn't hand them to Monk because I knew the view might affect his vertigo, not to mention his anxiety.

"He's looking for something," Monk said. Even at this distance, he could tell. "What's he carrying?"

"I don't know," I lied. "But we should try to avoid him."

We lost sight of Damien as the trail backtracked on us again.

Monk's determination was holding up, but I could tell that the height and narrowness of the trail were starting to wear on him. "Do you want to stop for a minute?" I asked.

"If you really need to," he said with obvious relief.

"I do," I said. There was a little cave, more like an alcove, carved out by centuries of wind and rain, about twenty yards ahead. "Why don't we duck in there?"

He couldn't see, but I drew the Glock from my bag right before going into the dark hole. It was one of those feelings you get. And I released the safety.

For Monk, walking into this cave was the lesser of two evils—to be precise, between claustrophobia (#11) and vertigo (#8). But he did his best, going in a full five feet before stopping in his tracks.

"Adrian?"

The voice, surprisingly, wasn't mine. It was coming out of the blackness ahead. "Ellen?"

"Natalie?" She was just a dozen feet in front of us, pressed up against the rock wall. "Thank God." As she stepped out of the dark, we could see she was limping.

I put down my gun and rushed forward. I wanted to hug her, but Monk beat me to it. He didn't even hesitate. "Ellen," he groaned happily, and burrowed himself into her. Then he pulled away. "What happened to you? You're a mess."

It was true. Her white tank top was covered with yellow splotches of dirt. Her black yoga pants were torn at both knees. She was barefoot. Her cheeks were streaked with dirt.

And, although Monk may not have noticed in all his excitement, she was limping. Badly.

"How did you find me?" Ellen asked. "I didn't know what I was going to do."

"What happened?" I asked.

"Do you mind if I sit down?" she said, then hobbled back to an outcropping of rock and lowered herself gently.

"Is it a sprain?" Monk asked. "It looks like a sprain."

"I think so. I can walk on it, barely, so it's not broken."

"I assume you found the right spot on the cliff and you jumped, just to try it out," said Monk, shaking his head. "Why did you do that?"

"I had some encouragement," said Ellen, and lowered her voice to a whisper.

We listened as she went over the details of her adventure: from the climb across to the balcony, to finding the necklace, to the loss of her iPhone, to the leap from the cliff, to the loss of her red backup phone somewhere along the way.

"I didn't realize it was even gone until I crawled in here and tried to call." She sighed. "So much for having a backup."

"At least you got the necklace," Monk said, eyeing the glistening pearls on a nearby rock. Somehow Ellen had managed to keep it with her and in one piece.

"I knew it was important," she said. "I could tell by how desperate he was to get it back."

"It could convict him of murder," Monk said, then gave her the abbreviated version of what he'd already told me, the "here's what happened." As he talked, I could see Ellen going through the same reactions I went through less than an hour before.

Monk continued. "Damien was set to dump her in the ocean. But he got too greedy. He didn't want to risk having the necklace torn lose before the body could be recovered. His plan was to hold on to it, then sell it on the black market."

Monk was right about the conviction part. I don't know how any defense attorney could invent an innocent explanation for how the pearls had gone from around Miranda's neck into her husband's sock drawer.

"So we have him," I said, clapping my hands.

"Or he has us," said Ellen, massaging her ankle. "Damien is still out there, and I can't go much further."

I wasn't too worried about that possibility. True, the killer was large and desperate. But there were three of us. And his weapon was a piece of driftwood, while we had the element of surprise and a brand-new Glock 22.

I had literally just thought of that, honestly, when a noise at the mouth of the cave made me turn.

It was Damien Bigley, pointing my gun at us, with the safety conveniently off, thanks to my negligence. Damn. I really did need to take that firearms course.

"Ellen, you're a tough lady to find." If he was surprised to see the two of us with her, he didn't let it show. "Officer Teeger." He stared at Monk. "And you. You were at the Sanctuary that day."

"The day you killed your wife," Monk said. It wasn't much of an introduction. But no one was interested in exchanging names and shaking hands.

Damien nodded, a sad little smile on his cute George Clooney mouth. "Yes. The ledge under the cliff. The necklace. That would seem the logical conclusion, wouldn't it?"

It's always bad when a killer is holding a gun and being perfectly honest with you. That's been my experience. "I'm going to have to ask for the necklace now," he said.

"You made another mistake," said Monk. He was showing more confidence than I expected. "The throwaway phone."

"I corrected that mistake," said Damien, still holding out his hand for the pearls.

Monk turned to me to explain. "Remember that discrepancy? The one you thought was so important?"

"The phone they found on Miranda's body wasn't hers."

"Correct. Miranda needed an untraceable way to communicate with him in case of emergency. At least she thought she did. Once she left the cliff, any call from her phone would have raised a red flag. But a cheap prepaid phone wouldn't leave that trail."

"You're saying I shouldn't have left it in Miranda's pocket." Damien shrugged. "Maybe. But the phone was returned to me, along with her body. I disposed of it."

"But it was still a mistake," Monk said. "Natalie picked up on it. Didn't you, Natalie? You saw."

"Yes, I did." I had no idea where Monk was going, but I played along.

"Using a prepaid phone is easy. Every cheap criminal and detective uses a disposable phone. You see them all over. An amateur move."

What the hell was he doing? It wasn't like him to goad an armed killer like this. Maybe he was playing for time, I thought. But why? Damien had all the time in the world. No one was coming to our rescue. No one even knew we were here.

"Every dumb poop thinks it's a great idea. Right, Ellen? Every dumb poop."

Damien frowned. "What the hell are you talking about?"

"They're everywhere you look. Little red cell phones."

Okay, I got it now. I didn't see it. But I got it.

"Every poop has a prepaid cell phone lying around."

Got it! I shot Monk a glare, meaning, "Enough." It had taken me just a second to figure out what he wanted me to do with this information. After so many years of facing down bad guys together, we often came up with the same ideas.

"I don't get your point," Damien said. "But if you'll hand me the pearls . . ."

I turned toward the necklace on my right, but not to pick it up. I did it to hide my right hand going into my right pocket.

Monk saw this and smiled. He continued with the distracting patter. "Why don't you just shoot us?" he asked with a casual shirk.

"If I had three guns and three hands, I might," said Damien. "But let's take it one step at a time."

My hand was on my phone now. Monk hadn't been hinting for me to call for help. The idea was ludicrous. No, his comment about poopy people and red cell phones could only mean one thing.

Monk continued with his distraction. "You're going to try to push us off the cliff, aren't you?"

"That's one possibility," Damien acknowledged. "But kind of risky. Whose gun is this, by the way?"

"Mine," I said, raising my left hand. My right was still fumbling in my pocket.

"Thanks," he said. "It makes things a lot easier." Damien was thinking out loud now, with my Glock still trained on Monk. "It'll be a few days before someone else takes this trail. So that gives me time . . ."

I pushed a speed-dial button, waited a second, then gave Monk a slight nod. He nodded back.

Ellen's cherry red clamshell must have been lying near the entrance to the cave, just a few feet behind Damien. I don't know how Monk had seen it, but he had. When it erupted in a tinny, merry "La Cucaracha," Damien's eyes went wide with surprise.

Half a second later he turned to see. That's when we made our move.

I hadn't counted on Monk joining me on this attack. Maybe it was the threat of imminent death or Ellen's vulnerable, injured presence. But with the two of us slamming into Damien's half-turned back, he was knocked off his feet. The gun scuttled across the cave floor.

As the three of us were grappling, Ellen hobbled over and picked it up.

CHAPTER THIRTY-TWO

Mr. Monk's Last Package

The news unfolded in dribs and drabs over the next forty-eight hours.

It began with Damien Bigley's arrest on three counts of attempted murder. Next came the arrest of Teresa Garcia at the San Carlos airport, twelve miles due east of the Sanctuary.

At each one of these press conferences, the county sheriff spoke slowly and modestly. But you could tell how much he was loving it. He mentioned Monk's name only once, as someone who had helped his office in their investigation. He also mentioned my name once, which was a major improvement over the credit I'd received in past cases.

By the time of his third press conference, announcing murder charges in the death of Miranda Bigley, Monk and I were back home, comfortably reinserted into our daily lives.

For the first whole day, Ellen and Monk were holed up at Ellen's house. I had no idea what the living arrangements were there, but I assumed they were hygienic. More than that, I couldn't guess and didn't want to know.

The Best Possible Me Corporation ceased operations on the same day as the sheriff's third press conference. Also on that day, the YouTube video soared to more than ten million views. As for my involvement with BPM, the Miranda CDs quickly found their way into the trash. Nonrecyclable.

It wasn't that I was rejecting her insights. I think she was basically a good person who'd helped millions. Whether she believed in it didn't matter. She had served a purpose in my life, and as Miranda herself would have said, it was time to move on.

By Tuesday afternoon, Monk and I were back at his Pine Street apartment, getting ready for Celine Harriman's seventh birthday celebration.

The plan was that Monk would never have to put on a "facial disguise," as we called the red nose and makeup, or wear a "uniform." That was out of the question and would probably cause a Chernobyl-like meltdown. But he would have to act enough like a clown to get Harriman's permission to enter the garage.

We were rehearsing his patter and were making progress. He could actually say "clown" ten times in a row without stammering. But then came Andrew the mailman, ringing the buzzer with another package.

I'd actually been looking forward to package number four. I just hoped this one wouldn't be too obvious and give the whole thing away.

Monk closed the front door on Andrew and handed it to me. "You open it."

It was like the others, brown paper wrapped, addressed to Mr. A. Monk in the same scratchy handwriting. This one had been postmarked Miami and was about the size of a hardbound dictionary, for those of you who remember dictionaries.

Inside was a child's play kit—for ages eight and up. The name, printed in multicolored balloon letters, was "Insta-Mime" and included, according to the box, "everything you need to turn yourself into a professional-looking mime": white face paint, black and red accent paint, while gloves, and a beret. The box said "mime," but all Monk could see was "clown." As soon as I ripped off the wrapping paper, he fled into the bedroom and slammed the door.

"We have to call off the mission," Monk shouted. "They know what we're up to."

"Who knows?"

"The clown mafia. They're onto us."

Sometimes I wish I was better at fooling people, at drawing out a joke and keeping a straight face and making the most of it. But beyond a certain point, it's just not in me.

"It's not a clown. It's a mime," I shouted through the door. "Just like the book was about clowns and mimes. Just like your brother, Ambrose, used to love mimes when he was a kid. Just like he used to collect Confederate money. Remember? Just like Yuki, his wife, is Japanese and likes to give your brother different kinds of massages."

The good thing about Monk is that it takes him just a second to put things together. He swung open the door and glared at me. "Well, that's just stupid."

"Not so stupid," I said.

Okay. A little bit of background is probably in order.

Monk's brother, Ambrose, is, as I mentioned before, an agoraphobe. For years, he never left his house, which had also been his childhood home, which had also been filled with thirty years' worth of mail, all indexed and cataloged.

The person responsible for bringing some much-needed change into his life was Yuki Nakamura, a twenty-something biker chick with tattoos and a manslaughter conviction in her past. She began by working as Ambrose's assistant. The two—improbably, illogically—fell in love and got married.

Now Ambrose and Yuki were on a prolonged honeymoon, circling the country in an RV, which was acting as Ambrose's temporary home. He might not step outside the RV for an entire year, but at least he'll be able to look out and see the world.

Before they left, I remember talking with Yuki one evening over a few glasses of wine. "We're naturally going to buy things," Yuki said, sounding a bit concerned. "What's the point of traveling if you don't buy things?"

"Sure," I agreed wholeheartedly. "Half of traveling is the shopping. What's the problem?"

"The problem is space. Have you seen that RV? There's no room for anything. We'd have to rent a trailer or tie things to the roof."

"You could just mail them home," I suggested.

"And have them pile up on the front porch?"

"Or you could mail them to me. Or to Mr. Monk." That's what I was calling him back then.

"Good idea," said Yuki.

That was about the extent of the conversation. And that was the inside information I had that Monk didn't. I never really thought of it again, not until after Monk told me about his brother's early fascination with mimes and *The Big Book of Clowns and Mimes* appeared on his doorstep, connecting the dots for me.

"Obviously, that's her handwriting," Monk said, getting all mentally caught up.

"The packages weren't addressed to you. Yuki addressed them to your brother: Mr. A. Monk. She must not have thought about the possible confusion."

"Why didn't she put in a note? Or let one of us know what she was doing?"

"I don't know," I said, only half lying.

"And you figured this out on your own?"

"Yes, Adrian. On my own. You can thank me anytime. Without me, you'd be running to the captain right now, trying to get a task force to track down the clown mafia."

He nodded in full agreement. "You're right. I owe you an apology."

I waited a few seconds. "And?"

"Not now. I'll catch you later."

Instead of apologizing, Monk had me call Yuki, just to confirm and say hello. He couldn't call himself. It's not that he wasn't fond of her; he wasn't. But more than unfond, he was a little intimidated. Not to mention perplexed by how a young, strong rebel could have fallen so completely for his middle-aged brother, whose idea of death-defying adventure was a walk around the block.

I found Yuki and Ambrose in Key West, where they had lucked into a trailer park not far from the center of town. The love birds seemed extremely happy with their long honeymoon, even though Ambrose had never left the RV, not so far. "Oh, I just got another tattoo," Yuki added. "Tell Adrian not to worry. It's someplace he'll never see."

"I'm not sure he wants to hear that, either."

"What don't I want to hear?" Monk asked. "No, don't tell me. Ignorance is bliss."

Yuki confirmed my theory and apologized for not including notes—a real apology, not an IOU. "Things are so hectic every day, I didn't think about reminding you."

Hectic? I thought. What could be hectic about lazily driving around in an RV?

"Sorry, Nat. Gotta go. Ambrose is going crazy with the chickens. He doesn't think a city should allow chickens roaming the streets." She covered the phone but I could still hear. "Honey, no. You can't run them over. It's against the law."

CHAPTER THIRTY-THREE

Mr. Monk Sends in the Clowns

Monk wouldn't be wearing a wire on this one. Not that his track record with wires was all that great. Even the tiniest microphones would make him feel off-balance and tilt him to one side. Plus there was the matter of the annoying wires and the tape itching against his skin. It would be like trying to mic the princess from "The Princess and the Pea."

In this case, the police couldn't be directly involved. That would constitute an illegal search. So when Monk showed up at the house on Sacramento Street, he was on his own, a private citizen invited through the door. His only backup would be a cell phone, a small red clamshell lent to him by Ellen for good luck. If Monk got into trouble, he would have to call.

Stottlemeyer, Devlin, and I were parked in my trusty Subaru across the street, feeling pretty helpless. We hadn't even been able to check out a surveillance van. All three of us had binoculars, although they wouldn't be of much use.

John Harriman had come out to meet Monk on the front porch, wearing a 49ers sweatshirt and a pink paper hat. We caught a glimpse, just before slumping down in our seats. Devlin giggled.

The stockbroker seemed startled. “Smith, where’s your costume?”

“I don’t have a car, so I’m going to have to change here.” Monk pointed to his red-and-white roller suitcase, bought especially for the job. It was filled with costume, shoes, wig, and makeup, all borrowed from the late Dudley Smith. Everything Monk would need to become J. P. Tatters, even though we’d solemnly promised he’d never have to open it.

“Right,” said Harriman with a shake of his head. “I think Alicia mentioned that.” He reopened the front door. “How’s the downstairs powder room?”

As soon as the door was open, the sound of screaming kids wafted down the hallway. One particularly shrill voice dominated. “Daddy! Daddy!”

“Coming, sweetie,” Harriman shouted back.

“Where’s Mommy? Mommy said she’d be here.”

“Mommy is far away. She’ll be home next week.” Harriman raised his voice. “Marina, please settle the children.”

“Yes, Mr. Harriman. I do my best.” Marina was Bulgarian, Monk deduced, between forty and fifty, and, from the timbre of her voice, on the verge of quitting.

“I want Mommy here. It’s my birthday.”

Harriman turned to Monk and whispered with great force, “I need you to take care of these monsters. Now.”

“I need to leave,” Monk said, then corrected himself. “I mean, I need to change outside. Last time, I used the garage.”

“Used the garage?” Harriman studied him with some interest.

"So I can ring the bell and make an entrance," Monk explained. "We don't want to spoil the illusion."

"Where's the clown?" the same shrill voice shouted. "J. P. Tatters. J. P. Tatters."

A dozen other shrill voices took up the chant. "J. P. Tatters. J. P. Tatters." To Monk, they must have sounded like French peasants chanting for the head of Marie Antoinette.

"All right, all right," Harriman said. "Make it fast." Reaching into the Chinese bowl just inside the door, he grabbed a set of keys and used one to unlock the pedestrian door next to the double-bay garage doors.

We watched from the lip of the car windows as Monk walked his rolling bag in. "He's inside," Devlin said. "Good luck, Monk."

"Good luck," Stottlemeyer and I said in unison.

We settled into our car seats, expecting a nail-biting wait of five to ten minutes. Maybe longer. But we were pleasantly surprised when one of the two garage doors shuddered and began to roll up.

"Way to go," Stottlemeyer whispered. And then he looked off to his left. "Damn."

What had grabbed his attention and dampened his spirits was a black Mercedes sedan slowing down and turning into the newly opened bay.

"Who is that?" I asked.

"I'll run the plates," Devlin said, reaching for her phone.

"Don't bother," said the captain. "I caught a glimpse. It's the wife."

And then, as quickly as it had rolled up, the door rolled down.

* * *

Monk's memory of what happened next is a bit sketchy. Blunt-force trauma to the head can do that.

He thinks he'd been in the closed garage for just a minute. He'd barely had time to adjust to the normal grunge and disorder of a typical garage—a hunter green SUV in the one bay, the other one empty—when he heard the gears grind and the second door begin to rise.

Alicia Harriman didn't see him at first. A tall woman, very thin, very blond, and suspiciously free of wrinkles. She emerged from the Mercedes and retrieved a wrapped box with a pink bow from the backseat. Only then, as she was walking around the rear of the car, did she notice the man, stooped over and rolling a red-and-white suitcase toward the pedestrian door.

"You. Stop," she demanded without an ounce of fear. "Who are you?"

Monk stopped and stood. "I'm J. P. Tatters." He realized his mistake the second the words left his mouth.

"No, you're not," said Alicia.

"I am," Monk insisted, and tried to smile. "Technically. The original J. P. Tatters died. I'm his brother. Carrying on the tradition."

"Died?" she asked. Her brow would have furrowed if it could have. "What did he die of?"

"No one knows," Monk improvised. "Some clown disease."

"Wait a minute." Alicia took a step closer. "You're Adrian Monk."

"People say I look like him."

"No, you're that police detective. What are you doing in my garage?"

With all the publicity Monk gets in this city, we've been lucky that more bad guys haven't recognized him. Our luck just ran out.

"I told you, I'm the clown for what's-her-name's party."

'No, you're not. You were snooping. Are the police outside—is that it? I saw a car parked across the street."

"No, no," Monk stammered.

"Is John in trouble?" Alicia whispered, her face clouding with disappointment. "I knew it."

"No, he's not in trouble," Monk lied.

"I'm sorry, Mr. Monk. My husband does stupid things. What is it this time? Insider trading? Did his crazy partner talk him into something?" She seemed genuinely upset.

"No, no," Monk repeated. But his protest was interrupted by a familiarly shrill voice.

"Mommy, is that you?" It was coming closer.

In a second, Monk was at the connecting door to the rest of the house, pushing the little thumb lock. Just in time, too. The doorknob jiggled and turned. "Mommy? Are you home?"

Alicia looked at the door, then at Monk. "Yes, sweetie, I'm home. Surprise!"

A squeal erupted. "Mommy, Mommy. I knew you'd come."

"Happy birthday, sweetie. I'll be there in a minute."

"Why is the door locked?"

"Because I have a surprise for you. A birthday surprise."

"Is it a clown? Is it J. P. Tatters? I love J. P. Tatters. He's so funny."

"Go back to the party, sweetie. I'll be there in a minute."

"Yay . . ." And the squealing voice faded along with her galloping footsteps.

Monk stood staring at the door, trying to figure out how to get out of this mess, when he was hit over the head by what was later determined to be a wooden baseball bat.

His last thoughts before passing out were, "At least I don't have to be a clown. Death is better." Or so he told me.

In the minutes after the garage door rolled down, we sat in the Subaru, discussing our options. Should we just wait it out? After all, Monk, despite all his Monk-ness was an ex–police detective, with my number on his speed dial.

Should we knock on the door politely? Should we draw our weapons and demand to be admitted? Should we have Devlin jimmy the lock to the pedestrian door, which would be an illegal and desperate move, but might save his life? Stottlemeyer suggested we anonymously call in a fire. There was a firehouse a few blocks away. They could be here in no time.

We kept giving Monk an extra minute. Another extra minute. Devlin got out and circled the house, scaling the fence on the right, then coming back over the picket fence on the left. "Nothing," she reported as she got back in. Nothing but the screams of a dozen kids and the pleading voice of the Bulgarian housekeeper.

"Should we call in a domestic disturbance?" she asked.

We were all leaning toward the fire call when the pedestrian door to the garage opened and the staggering figure of J. P. Tatters emerged onto the driveway.

Stottlemeyer gasped. "Oh, my God. What have they done to him?"

It was a horrifying sight: the yellow fright wig, the red nose, the black-painted stubble, the hobo clothes that Monk had insisted on washing and starching and ironing for no logical reason except that he might have foreseen just such a nightmare scenario. The starched tatters, springing out at all angles, could have been the basis for a new series of horror movies.

Stottlemeyer turned to me. "This'll put him back years. Natalie, get Dr. Bell on standby."

No one followed him out of the house. All on his own, he walked uncomfortably, self-consciously to the sidewalk. Then, instead of crossing the street, he made a right turn, picked up a little speed and headed for the corner.

I canceled my call to Dr. Bell, revved the Subaru, put it in gear, and made a quick three-point turn in a neighbor's drive. By the time we turned the corner, the stumbling clown was halfway down the residential block. Luckily it was a one-way street, so driving up beside him wasn't a problem.

Captain Stottlemeyer leaned out the window. "Monk?" But he kept on walking, even faster now. He had already crossed another street and was onto the next block. "Monk!" Why wasn't he stopping? Or speaking? "Monk!"

I looked over from my driving and saw the one thing that Stottlemeyer didn't. "It's not him," I shouted. Sure, this guy was about the same size and same build and covered nearly head to foot in horrible distractions. But I could tell.

The clown must have heard me, because he started running now. It took all of us a second to get over the shock. Then Devlin was out of the car and chasing him down. Half-way along the next block, the clown made a sharp right, heading up a driveway, probably into someone's backyard. Devlin followed.

We sat there, Stottlemeyer and me, trying to make sense of it. It didn't take long for us to realize the only explanation. "Back to the house," Stottlemeyer shouted. "Now!"

I stepped on the gas and almost ran the next stop sign.

I knew I needed to take a right. But the next street was one-way, which meant I had to take Broadway, which was always busy. The next possible right was Octavia, but that put me straight into Lafayette Park, where I had to take a left until Gough. The streets in this city can be so maddening.

By the time I got back in front of the Sacrament Street house, the damage had been done. The garage door was open again and the Mercedes was gone. Stottlemeyer drew his badge and pounded on the front door. "Police."

A beefy Bulgarian woman with brassy blond hair finally answered. "Police?" she said, examining the held-up badge. "Good. Arrest me. For anything. I go peaceful."

We stormed our way past her into the Armageddon that used to be a living room. Crepe paper hung in shreds from the ceiling. So did the head of a shattered donkey piñata. Hard candies littered the floor, along with donkey legs and the detritus of two dozen unwrapped presents.

The perpetrators of this chaos, from the sound of it, were all over the house now, thumping over our heads and running past the doorways like aliens in a high-voltage video game, except that we, the players in the midst of it, weren't equipped with AK-47s.

"Where are the Harrimans?" Stottlemeyer barked.

"They gone," Marina said. It was almost a wail. "Mrs. Harriman come in for two seconds. It makes the kids all crazy. Then they go to garage, mister and missus. I don't know what happens in garage. But they drive off. They drive off and leave me with the crazies."

"Where's the clown?" I asked.

"What clown?" Marina said. "The clown don't come. You think things would be like this with good clown?"

"So no one else came in from the garage? No one?"

"No one. Do you come to arrest me? Please arrest me."

Devlin sprinted through the living room door, her service revolver drawn. She was breathing heavily.

"He got away."

CHAPTER THIRTY-FOUR

Mr. Monk's Vanishing Act

One thing good about Captain Stottlemeyer: He knows crowd control.

Right away he sent Devlin and me to round up the kids, then ordered Marina to start making calls. Within ten minutes, the mothers started coming in their SUVs. Within half an hour, we were down to two resident little monsters: Celine and her slightly older brother, Thaddeus. Stottlemeyer then doled out a hundred dollars from his own wallet and told Marina, politely but firmly, to drive them over to the Swensen's Ice Cream Parlor on Hyde Street. His treat.

"Ice cream?" Marina complained. "No. no. They have too much sugar now. Look at them."

Stottlemeyer didn't have to look. He could hear them through the walls. "This is a police matter, ma'am. Keep them out for an hour. Give them a salad if you want. But personally I'd recommend a double scoop of Sticky Chewy Chocolate."

Once they were safely out the door, the three of us split up and made an illegal search from attic to basement to every corner of the garage. No Monk or hint of Monk.

"Is this a crime scene?" I asked, my heart in my throat.

"Technically, no," said Devlin.

"What do you mean, no? Adrian's been kidnapped."

"We don't know that," said Stottlemeyer.

"Excuse me?" Alicia Harriman had just walked in through the connecting door between the garage and kitchen. That's the trouble with hybrid cars. Half the time, you can't hear them. "Who are you?" she demanded. "Where are my children? Where's the party?"

Trying to explain something like this to someone who obviously knows more than we do . . . that's above my pay grade. I let the captain take the lead, and he made an executive decision.

"I'm Captain Leland Stottlemeyer of the San Francisco police. We got a call from Adrian Monk from this address." He pretended to check his notes. "Mr. Monk is a police consultant. He also works on the side as a clown."

"A detective and a clown?" she asked, cocking her head curiously.

"It's not as rare as you think," said Devlin with a straight face.

"Your husband hired Mr. Monk to entertain at a party at this address," the captain continued. "Would you mind telling us what happened?"

Yes, he was lying. She knew he was lying. But it was still a question that needed an answer.

"He just walked out," Alicia said, raising her hands helplessly. "When I got home, he was in the garage, changing into his costume. He seemed distracted. I think the poor man has emotional problems. Does he have emotional problems?"

Suddenly the captain was on the defensive. "That's not the question, Mrs. Harriman. What happened?"

"I think he has emotional problems. He was babbling something about clowns and murder. Then he just walked out."

"That wasn't him," I said.

"What do you mean?" Alicia asked, her brow attempting to furrow. This woman was smooth. "Of course it was him."

"Where is your husband?" Devlin asked.

"I told him what happened with the clown and he went out looking for him. We were very concerned."

"And where did you go?" asked Stottlemeyer.

"I did the same. I took my car and started scouring the neighborhood. We were being Good Samaritans, Captain, trying to help a man who is obviously disturbed. You would think the police would thank us for this. Instead, I come back and find you in my house and everyone else gone. . . . Where are my children? You haven't answered me."

The captain stuck to the truth on this one. The guests had been sent home. The kids were at an ice-cream parlor, on his nickel, and the housekeeper was ready to run back to Bulgaria.

"Where is he?" I demanded. "Where's Adrian Monk?"

"I don't know," said Alicia, her face hardening. "He came here pretending to be J. P. Tatters, a clown who seems to be deceased. Then he changed into his costume and walked out of the garage. Now, if you'll excuse me, I have my children to take care of and a dozen parents to apologize to."

"That wasn't him," I said. "He would never dress as a clown."

"And yet this was his part-time job."

There really was no response to that, so I didn't try.

Alicia escorted us to the door. "If you have any more questions, I'd advise you to contact our lawyer. I know we'll be contacting him."

The captain and I took a cab to the station, leaving Lieutenant Devlin with my Subaru parked conspicuously across the street. It wasn't bad to have a visible presence, not in a case like this.

"They're obviously in it together," I said, pacing back and forth in the captain's office with the door closed. "And she's the brains. You can tell." I stopped and took a breath. "Are they going to kill him?"

It was something neither one of us wanted to consider. "They're not real killers," said Stottlemeyer, "even though they've killed four times. They're poisoners. There's a difference between that and someone who has to face his victim and get his hands bloody. I think it buys us some time."

"Do they own a gun?"

He had already checked. "No gun permits in their record. But obviously, they can't let him go."

"The question is, where did they take him?"

Stottlemeyer was at his desk, already thumbing through the Harriman file. "It's a weekday, so their office is out of the question. They don't own or rent any other properties in the city, not in their names or their company's name."

"It has to be somewhere fairly close."

"There is one other possibility," he said reluctantly.

I knew where he was going to go. I could tell from his tone and from the way he'd reacted when Alicia Harriman told her story. "It wasn't Monk. I could tell."

"But it's not unreasonable," he argued. "If Monk sucked it up enough to change into a clown, then maybe it got to be too much and he had one of those breaks Dr. Bell talks about."

"A dissociative break," I said.

This was certainly possible. Monk has done strange things when pushed too far, like one time having a gold grill put in his teeth when he was working for a gangsta rap artist. Who knows what he would do if forced into clown attire and makeup? But I knew what I'd seen. "It wasn't him."

"Look, I'm not saying the Harrimans are innocent. But maybe Monk is out there somewhere, catatonic and hunkered down. We have to consider that."

I wasn't about to. And I was angry with him for doubting me. I was just about to say as much when the phone rang. Stottlemeyer instantly picked it up and put it on speaker. "Devlin?"

"John came home." She was calling from the driver's seat of my Subaru. "He was on foot."

"How was he dressed?" asked the captain.

"Same as before. Jeans, sneakers, Forty-niners sweatshirt. Nothing clown-related that I could see."

"Okay. Keep us posted." And he hung up.

"That doesn't prove a thing," I said. "Alicia drove off to meet him. He changed in her car, then walked home. They know we're watching."

"You're positive it wasn't Monk?"

"Captain." I tried to control my temper. "If things were reversed, if that was me in the garage and Monk in the car, would you believe him? Don't answer. You wouldn't even think twice. You would trust Monk."

"You're not Monk."

"You're right. I'm not. I'm Natalie Teeger, the ex-cop who happened to be right about Miranda Bigley's murder when everyone else, including Monk, was dead wrong."

"I get that, but—"

"No buts." I was seething, as angry as I'd ever been. "You trust me or you don't. But every second you waste not looking for wherever they're keeping him is a second off his life. Do you honestly think they're going to let him go?"

Stottlemeyer thought it over. I could tell I'd gotten to him. And then Devlin called. Again, he put her on speaker.

"You're not going to like this," Devlin started.

"Just say it!" That was actually me.

"Natalie?" Devlin was shocked, too. "Okay. John and Alicia just came out and did a little gardening."

"Gardening?"

"Yeah. They're tearing out the rest of the foxgloves. John just took them into the garage."

"Thanks." The captain hung up and stared into my eyes.

"Do you believe me now?"

CHAPTER THIRTY-FIVE

Mr. Monk Is Nowhere

"Natalie, I owe you an apology," said the captain. I didn't say a word, just waited. "And I apologize," he added.

"Accepted."

"I guess I got to looking at you a certain way and I didn't really notice the change."

I understood. If you put any detective next to Monk for all those years, they would have faded into the background.

"Like the Bigley case," he went on. "Prime example. If you hadn't stirred things up, it never would have been solved."

It's funny. You can wait forever to hear the right words, imagining how special the moment will be when people finally acknowledge your contribution. And then when it comes, there's always something marring the moment. In this case it was my kidnapped friend. "Do you think he's locked in a car trunk?"

"Their car? That would mean he's back in their garage, which seems too risky for these guys."

"What about a stolen car or a car rented under a fake name?"

"You would need some preparation for that. And they

didn't have any prep time. The good news is we have a tail. At some point, they'll need to go back and deal with Monk, and Devlin will be there."

"I can relieve her," I volunteered.

"Thanks. But that's our strong suit. Devlin and I will be splitting that in twelve-hour shifts, if it goes that far."

"What do I do?"

"Find where they're hiding Monk?"

"Me?"

"You're a detective. Start living up to your hype."

The captain hadn't said it in a mean way. And he didn't mean that he wouldn't do his part. But if anyone knew how Monk thought, it was me. If anyone knew how he might try to escape or signal his whereabouts, it was me. If there ever was a time when I had to step up and prove myself, it was now.

I drove Devlin's car to the Sacramento Street stakeout and switched it out for the Subaru. Then I drove it back to my Noe Valley cocoon, fortified myself with a half glass of wine, and made a very difficult call.

"Hey, Ellen." I knew she'd been waiting to hear from me. "I'm afraid everything didn't go as planned."

Ellen was as understanding as could be. It didn't hurt that she had just been on the other end of just such an undercover operation—one where everything had turned out all right, except for one badly sprained ankle. It gave her an unwarranted sense of optimism. "You guys have been in tighter spots, right?"

"Of course." Only this time Monk was in the spot alone with a pair of serial killers.

"I suppose the police just can't go in and arrest them and demand answers," she half suggested.

"Not since that pesky Fourth Amendment."

We talked for twenty more minutes, both of us spouting words of reassurance. But my mind was elsewhere.

If Monk was alive and conscious, he would be trying to contact us. I couldn't count on him using the red cell phone. I was sure they'd already found it.

I flashed back to my own experiences with him in similar situations: like the time we were chained to a bathtub and drew attention by sending smoke signals up through the chimney; or the time we were locked in a vault, running out of air, and called for help by hacking into the wiring for the electronic display outside the bank.

"Think like the person you want to be," Ellen said, bringing me back into the conversation. "Remember? That's what Miranda said. You can do this. Just try to think like Adrian."

I spoke to Stottlemeyer twice more that evening, asking for little pieces of information, sharing a stupid theory or two, and checking to see if John and Alicia had made a move. They hadn't. Both were still at the Sacramento Street house.

That night I barely dozed off. I was relieved that the Harrimans hadn't even tried to leave, but worried for Monk. Had he been without food and water? Were they planning to starve him? No, they weren't. They were in their garage, making poison. Somehow that didn't make me feel better.

The next morning, around sunrise, I made a pot of strong coffee, which only succeeded in making me more jittery. Then I took my phone from the recharger, got in my car, and began to aimlessly cruise the streets of the city. For a Thursday morning, the traffic was pretty light.

I stuck to the central part of town, the three or four miles surrounding the Pacific Heights home. Somewhere in this sea of a few thousand buildings, Adrian Monk was waiting for me to find him. I don't know what kind of inspiration I was expecting, but it wasn't hitting me. Once, while crossing Ellis Street, I saw a red balloon floating away on the light morning breeze, a fugitive perhaps from a birthday party, one that I hoped was going a little better than Celine Harriman's.

I don't know how long I did this. Less than an hour. Then I stopped for gas, just to stop and have something to do. Stepping away from the pump, I called Stottlemeyer again. He was still on duty, expecting Devlin to relieve him at any moment.

"Any ideas?" he asked, yawning into his end of the line.

"Is there a shed behind the Harrimans' house?" I asked.

"No shed," he said. "Just a tiny yard, typical for that neighborhood."

The pump had just clicked, but I didn't want to go back, not with my cell phone open. Call it an urban legend if you want, but a gas-pump explosion was the last thing I needed that morning.

"How about any relatives in the city, someone away on vacation?"

"No relatives," said Stottlemeyer. "And we checked out the Bulgarian housekeeper. She lives in a two-bedroom apartment with her family of six."

I was leaning against the Pump 'n' Go trash bin, with a clear view down Van Ness Avenue, the sun just rising above the buildings. Another red balloon floated gently by. Or could it have been the same red balloon? No, that didn't make sense.

"Hold on," Stottlemeyer said. The line went silent. "Garage door's opening up. The green SUV. They're on the move, both of them."

"Follow them," I shouted.

"Thank you, Natalie. I'll do that." And the captain hung up.

I didn't know what to do now, except worry and stare at my phone. I moved my car away from the pumps, just to be polite, and left it idling by the front of the Pump 'n' Go convenience store.

It must have been a full fifteen minutes before Stottlemeyer called back. "We lost them."

My heart sank. "What do you mean, you lost them?"

"They parked at their office building, in the garage. I parked a level up. Devlin got there just in time and she followed them into the lobby, just ahead of me. By the time we showed our badges and got past security, they were gone."

"Did they go up to their office?"

Stottlemeyer sighed. "We called their office. His assistant said they weren't in. The building apparently has two entrances. Devlin's on the street now, trying to track them down but it doesn't look good." He paused and sighed again. "Natalie, I'm sorry."

"That's okay," I said, not meaning it.

"John was carrying a backpack," he added.

"A backpack?" My mind raced to the obvious, and I wasn't happy. After half a day and a night alone, wherever he was, Monk would be desperate for food and water. Showing up and poisoning him would not be impossible. "They're going to kill him now," I shouted into the phone.

"Not if we can help it. Call if you have any breakthroughs."

I let the captain get back to his problem and I got back to mine.

I don't know how long I was standing there, my back against the trash bin, when I caught sight of yet another red balloon floating down Van Ness. This was a different one. For one thing, it wasn't flying off. It was floating lower than the others, bumping its way amid the power lines and streetlamps. Another fugitive from the same party? And then it struck me. I had seen the first red balloon less than an hour after sunrise. Who would be having a party at that hour?

There was also something odd about the string on the balloon, more like a kite's tail than a string and probably what was weighing it down. I grabbed my binoculars from the backseat and focused as best I could.

It wasn't a string or a tail, not in the normal sense. It was either gray or brown, maybe two inches wide and less than two feet long. It wasn't made of Mylar or anything else festive. It was basically just a strip of cloth—a long, tattered piece of cloth. And then it hit me.

I knew where Monk was.

CHAPTER THIRTY-SIX

Mr. Monk and the Balloons

The realization came suddenly and completely.

There might have been other explanations for the appearance of balloons with tattered tails—three balloons that I was aware of in the space of an hour and a half. But as a cop, you're taught not to trust coincidences, especially on the morning when I was scouring this forty-block area for some communication from Monk

It made sense. A place with access to red balloons, a helium tank, tattered strips of cloth, a window or vent, all at some location the Harrimans knew would be empty and safe. Monk might have even written a message on the cloth, using the AG-7 astronaut pen he always carried in his jacket. But I didn't need a message. I knew.

Stottlemeyer wasn't answering his cell. So I left a quick message, then drove, trying to remember which one-way streets would take me the four or five blocks I needed to go. I had never been there before, but I had learned the address and a lot of other details from Lieutenant Devlin.

I parked in front of a hydrant on Willow Street, between the Vietnamese restaurant and the fitness center and grabbed my bag from the passenger seat. Like Devlin said, it was a narrow one-story building that had once been an alley. Right away I could see that the wooden door had been jimmied, the old wooden doorjamb pried back enough to disengage the flimsy lock.

Poor Monk, I thought. Did the Harrimans appreciate their cruelty, not only subjecting him to a kidnapping and the threat of an agonizing death, but to do it in the abandoned clown lair of J. P. Tatters, the one place he dreaded above all others?

Okay, there were several places Monk dreaded above all others. But you get the idea.

For a few seconds, I thought about waiting. Stottlemeyer would be getting my message any minute now and be racing on over. But then again, so would the Harrimans with their backpack, if they weren't here already.

Gently, I forced the lock, eased open the door, then eased it shut behind me. The useless lock clicked into place.

The interior was black and silent. Good news. No, not quite black or silent, I gauged as my eyes started to adjust. There were soft, scraping, hissing sounds coming from the back left corner. And a small horizontal window at eye level, also in the back left corner.

I switched on a ceiling light by the door, a bare bulb that threw its glare only halfway through the space. "Adrian?" Making my way back through the shadows, I could see on both sides the collections of noses and wigs, seltzer bottles and bright oversized shoes. It gave me the creeps, and I actually like clowns. "Adrian?"

Between the lightbulb and the window, there was enough light for me to see the whole ridiculous, fascinating picture.

A duct-tape gag hung loosely from his shirt and handcuffs connected his wrists around a vertical pipe. Throughout his eighteen hours of captivity, he had managed to reach out and drag in his supplies. I know eighteen hours sounds like a long time, but I was still impressed by what he'd been able to do, especially given the dirt and the handcuffs and the imminent threat of clowns.

As I had guessed, there was the helium tank with its hose. Also a box of red balloons from a nearby shelf and pair of J. P. Tatters' tattered slacks from a hanging rack.

The window, the only window in the tiny building, had been built for ventilation and opened onto an air shaft, facing someone else's brick wall two feet away. It was an impossible escape route, but Monk had seen it as his only means of rescue. He had figured out how to attach a message to a balloon, hold it outside the air shaft, fill it with helium, and let it go, like a shipwrecked sailor sending off a message in a bottle.

I caught him just as he was trying to tie off an inflated balloon. The surprise of seeing me made him let go, and the balloon sputtered and deflated and fell. "Natalie." He sounded annoyed. "Now I have to start again."

"No, Adrian. I'm here. You don't have to send any more."

"But I only did nine." He voice was hoarse, probably from the hours of shouting and the lack of water. "Help me make it ten."

"No." I turned off the tank valve. "That's okay."

"Do you have anything to drink?" He tried to clear his throat. "I would prefer Fiji Water in an unopened bottle. Thirty-eight degrees."

"Soon. Very soon." Then I took him by the shoulders and looked him in the eyes. He was too weak to squirm. His wrists were cut and bloody from the handcuffs. "They're going to be here soon. I'm going to hide, but I need you to focus."

"Who's going to be here?"

"The bad guys. You need to get them talking."

"Natalie, no. You can't leave."

"I'm not leaving. I'm just going to hide in a corner."

"Can I hide in a corner?"

"No. You have to stay here and make them talk—about Dudley Smith or the Cemedrin murders. We can't let them lie their way out of it again."

As I was talking, I took my phone out of my bag and began to scroll through the screens.

"Do you have an app for Fiji Water? Any temperature."

"Sorry." I found what I was looking for, the Voice Memo app. I just hoped it would record long enough to do us some good.

As soon as I heard them prying at the door, I pressed "record," slipped it behind a purple fright wig on a shelf, and headed for a disorganized pile of boxes marked "props." If worse came to worst, I could fight them off with a rubber chicken.

I knelt behind the boxes, pushing one aside to give me a sliver of a view. For a hopeful second, I thought it might be Stottlemeyer and Devlin coming to the rescue. But I knew the sound of their footsteps. These were different.

It took them a few seconds. Perhaps they'd been momentarily concerned about the light being on. Then John and Alicia Harriman walked into my line of sight. They stopped, openmouthed, as perplexed by Monk's ingenuity as I had been impressed.

"What are you doing?" asked Alicia. She said it disapprovingly, like he wasn't supposed to try to escape.

"You can't squeeze out that window," John said.

"I wasn't squeezing out," Monk said, his eyes wandering to the purple fright wig. "I was sending a message in a balloon about how you kidnapped me and are going to kill me."

The Harrimans didn't seem fazed by his convoluted balloon scheme. But murder? They glanced at each other, then back at Monk. "Kill you?" Alicia said with more disapproval. "No, no. We just want to talk."

"We should have left water," said John. "I'm so sorry." Despite the situation, explaining themselves to a handcuffed man in an abandoned office, they treated it as perfectly normal. "Are you thirsty?" John rummaged through his backpack and came out with a water bottle with a blue snap cap.

I could tell Monk was desperate. He would have salivated, if he'd had any liquid left in him. He stared at it. "Is that the same poison you used on Dudley Smith?"

"Who?" John shook his head. "The clown? I never met him."

"We didn't even know he'd died until you told us," said Alicia, in a statement that could probably pass a polygraph.

Monk kept staring at the bottle. "Or is that what you used in the Cemedrin murders back in oh-nine?"

That did it. That revelation managed to break through their composure.

"He's just guessing," Alicia said out of the corner of her mouth.

"That's quite a guess," said John.

"You poisoned the money without even knowing who it would kill. Of course, it wasn't the first time you'd sent poison out into world."

"It seemed like a clean way to deal with a problem," Alicia admitted almost nonchalantly. "I'm afraid this one's going to be messier." I'm sure Monk didn't like the sound of that, the messy part and the death part.

"How did Dudley know?" John asked, genuinely curious. "I assume it was something in the garage."

"I kept telling you to clean that garage," said Alicia.

"Garages are insidious," Monk agreed.

In the stillness of the shadowy room, the beep, the signal from my phone that the Voice Memo was shutting off, was louder than I'd ever heard it.

Monk glanced toward the wig. Alicia followed his glance and knew. "I thought you took away his phone."

'I did," said John.

"Obviously you didn't." The wig and the phone were out of reach for Monk, making it easy for Alicia to grab it and bring it back to her husband.

"That's not his phone," John said.

She shook her head. "You always refuse to take responsibility. Of course, it's his phone. Whose phone would it be?"

"Not his." John stiffened and began to look around. "His phone was a little red thing."

Alicia seemed ready to dismiss her husband's excuses. But then she looked at Monk, who is a terrible liar, even when he's not saying anything. This time Monk really tried. He was looking everywhere but the boxes, his eyes darting this way and that around the room, then skipping the boxes like they were made of snakes. Alicia figured it out.

Slowly, silently, she came toward me and the boxes. Along the way, she picked up a giant umbrella, bright pink, with tassels hanging from the tips. Her eyes locked on the sliver and I stepped back into the darkness. In time, I hoped.

When the pink umbrella pushed aside the box and sent it crashing to the floor, I was almost ready.

I had already grabbed the Glock 22 from my bag, released the safety, and was pulling it up to aim. I stepped to one side, keeping both of the Harrimans in my line of fire.

"Officer Natalie Teeger, SPD." Even as I said it, I promised myself never to use this little lie again. "You're under arrest. Put your hands in the air. Both of you."

Alicia was closer to me and the threat of the gun, and she did as she was told. John was maybe forty feet away. My fear was that he might ignore me and reach for a weapon. And in a way, he did.

For a moment, he stood there, frozen. Then, with a flick of his right thumb, he popped open the blue tip of the water bottle and started to raise it to his lips.

"Don't," I shouted. "Put it down."

He smiled. "What are you going to do, shoot me?"

That was a good question. Was I ready to shoot a human being and have that on my PI record, not to mention in my nightmares? Or was I more willing to watch a cold-blooded killer drink the poison he'd been meaning to force on my friend? A kind of just deserts.

"It's very painful and messy," Monk advised him. "Seizures. Cramps. You should have seen Smith after. His clothes. His bed. A god-awful sight. It's seared in my mind."

Monk wasn't describing Smith's death throes, but the fact that Smith had been wearing a stained T-shirt and ratty jeans and was lying on a rumpled bed covered with dirty money. His heartfelt description made Harriman pause.

"Mr. Harriman, don't," I urged. "Backup is on the way with an ambulance. Even if you do it, you'll survive. It'll be excruciatingly painful but you'll survive."

The threat of pain trumped the appeal of death. I had a feeling he might be like that. Despite four murders, they were amateurs and had probably never seen a dead body. For them it was all about the easy way out. And for right now, staying alive seemed easier.

He lowered the bottle. I told him to drop it and kick it over. He did, and I breathed a sigh. "Now stand together," I ordered. "Now." They did, and I breathed another sigh.

By the time Stottlemeyer and Devlin broke in, guns drawn, ready to save the day, I had everything under control.

"Monk. Natalie. Are you guys all right?" The captain took control of the suspects while the lieutenant did a sweep of the rest of the building.

"We're fine, Captain. Thanks."

I was tempted to throw him a snarky smile and say, "What took you so long?" But I resisted. They had actually saved the day many times in the past. I didn't want to say or do anything to discourage this behavior.

CHAPTER THIRTY-SEVEN

Mr. Monk and the New Deal

A tabloid magazine has heard a rumor that Justina, a popular singer, has been injured in a domestic altercation with her boyfriend, and it wants visual proof. The magazine hires you to take her picture.

You find Justina inside a clothing store, see a bruise on her cheek, and ask for an interview. Justina says, "Not now," and begins to leave. You physically block her exit from the store and take several pictures. Which of the following is true?

(a) You are free to take her picture as long as you don't block her exit for an "unreasonable" amount of time.

(b) By asking for an interview, you misrepresented yourself and are subject to a fine of $3,000 and/or suspension of your PI license.

(c) No charges or suit can be filed, since celebrities are public figures and have no expectation of privacy in a public place.

(d) You are liable for damages from a civil suit. You are also are subject to a fine of not less than $5,000.

The answer was d, according to the California Antipaparazzi Law of 2012, which prohibits "an assault or false imprisonment committed with the intent to capture any type of visual image, sound recording . . ." Blah, blah, blah. I also couldn't use my car to block her car.

I aced this question and the rest of them and was out of the Hayward facility twenty minutes before "pencils down." They don't tell you your score at the end, just pass or fail. But I'll bet I left with the highest score of the day. After two tries and hundreds of hours of study, the license was mine.

My motivation for racing through the test on that Tuesday morning was not to show off—okay, that was part of it—but to get back to San Francisco in time for the ceremony.

Captain Stottlemeyer had received three commendations throughout his career, so he pretended number four wasn't any big deal. But you could tell from the way he stood on the platform in front of city hall that it was.

For Lieutenant Amy Devlin, this was a first. Like her boss, she pretended not to care. But I can tell when someone's just spent two hours at the stylist. Her short black hair had suddenly grown red highlights and her prized Edward Scissorhands look had been noticeably softened at the edges.

Monk and I sat on the platform for the ceremony. Each of us rated a special mention from both the mayor and the police commissioner for our part in bringing the Cemedrin killers to justice—"for their invaluable consultation services to the department," as the commissioner so blandly put it.

For me, the best part of the afternoon wasn't the official shout-out. It was the view from the platform.

Ginny Costello's family—her parents and two sisters—

were seated in the front row. Little Craig Tuppering's parents were right beside them. A row behind them, Harold Luckenby's three grown children sat solemnly, their own families at their side. All wore black for the occasion, although I had to think this was a good day for them, finally getting some answers about these senseless murders and seeing justice done.

I can't say for certain, but I think the best part for Monk must have been the presence of special agents Grooms and Cardea. They were also seated on the platform, but in the back row and off to the side. The mayor mentioned their names in passing, as investigators who had worked tirelessly over the years to solve these heartless crimes. But I think everyone realized that this was just code for "not being able to get the job done."

I counted four times when Monk, pretending to have a crick in his neck or the sun in his eyes, craned himself sideways to catch a glimpse of the stone-faced agents. On two occasions, I also found myself with a crick in my neck.

In the original plan for the ceremony, Monk and I were scheduled to receive letters of commendation from the FBI. The San Francisco field office had fought this, of course, with Grooms pointing out the jurisdictional irregularities of the investigation, among other things. The compromise was that Monk and I would receive the letters through the mail and not at the ceremony.

We were off the platform by three and back at my mini-Victorian by three thirty, where Ellen and my daughter had organized a little party.

Julie had made the trip from Berkeley with a carful of

classmates, including Maxwell, her too hot/too cold boyfriend. For the first little while, Julie mingled, congratulating Amy and Leland, as she called them, and catching them up on her college adventures. Then she gravitated back to her friends, especially Maxwell. That was normal, but it made me a little sad. She had her own world now.

Maxwell seemed nice. But it's strange when you've heard so many personal details about someone before meeting them. You form very specific opinions and suddenly have to deal with the reality of whoever they really are.

I could see from the way he glanced sideways at me that he was slightly in awe. His girlfriend's mother had actually caught the Cemedrin killers and had held them at gunpoint. For me, the sideways glance was better than an FBI letter of commendation, although I was still planning to have that framed.

Monk is not a public person, to say the least. The ceremony had probably taken as much out of him as eighteen hours of captivity. But since Ellen had planned the party, he felt he had to come. The two of them stood in a corner of my kitchen, separating themselves from the crowd and talking like teenagers. Still, I wasn't surprised to look up one moment and find him missing in action.

"Did Luther pick him up?" I asked Ellen, who by now was standing alone, out on my front porch.

"Luther picked him up," she confirmed.

An hour later, the party was still going when the hostess herself sneaked out and wandered over to the Pine Street apartment.

I found Monk in the middle of his sofa, his lightbulb-cleaning kit on the coffee table, picking up where we'd left off a few weeks ago when we'd been interrupted by the mysterious arrival of Confederate bills. Or he could already be starting on the next cleaning cycle. I didn't ask.

"Ellen was in an odd mood," he said without looking up from the compact fluorescent three-way in his hands. The compact fluorescents were always a challenge.

"What do you mean, odd?"

"She seemed happy. She even thanked me, for some reason."

"A woman thanking you," I mused. "That is odd."

"Extremely. She kept talking about having time now to make the right decisions in her life and not to feel boxed in by money worries. I pretended to know what she was talking about. It was easier."

I felt this was as good a time as any to break the news. "She was probably talking about the reward money we're going to get."

He finally stopped polishing and looked up. "What reward?"

"Miranda Bigley's insurance. They don't have to pay out the policies, now that we proved fraud."

I was making it sound simpler than it was. It had been a lot of work in the past week—contacting the three insurance companies, informing them of our role in uncovering the Bigleys' fraud, getting statements from the San Mateo County Sheriff's Office to back me up, and reminding the companies repeatedly of their own whistle-blower guidelines.

Insurance companies don't like paying out anything,

even when you've just saved them millions. But they wound up seeing it my way.

"So I'm getting a reward?" His face lit up, brighter than a freshly cleaned bulb.

"No, Adrian, you're not. *We* are getting half a reward, which is going into the general fund for Monk and Teeger, Consulting Detectives, a Limited Liability Corporation."

"But I'm getting the other half."

"No," I said firmly. "The other half goes to Ellen Morse."

He didn't like other people standing and talking while he sat—something about heads not being at the same level—so I sat across from him and gently explained my agreement with Ellen.

Ellen had believed in me when no one else had. She had agreed to help and footed the bill for her visit to the Sanctuary. She was the one who had found the pearls and gotten them out of Damien Bigley's sock drawer. . . . "Plus I promised her she'd get half."

"But I solved the case," he whined. "Don't I get a say?"

"Actually, you don't. I'm the one with the private investigator's license and the legal right to start a business. They're making out the checks to our corporation and I'm the head of the corporation."

This was all technically true. According to the state of California, if Monk wanted to be in the PI business with me, he would have to be my employee. Not that it would make a big difference in the real world. But it just might give me the extra bit of leverage I needed to get treated like a real partner.

"Don't worry, Adrian. When the checks come, I'll give you a nice bonus. As long as you promise not to buy any more limousine companies."

"You'll give me a bonus? Wait a minute. I hired you. You're my employee."

"Times change."

"Don't remind me."

Monk returned to his lightbulbs, feverishly attacking another compact fluorescent three-way. I could tell he was stewing and thinking, trying his best to adjust to this grim, new reality.

He had just switched over to the row of eighty-watt interior floods when he spoke again. "Don't you want to stay and help me clean the bulbs? I know how much you like that."

Who in the world could enjoy sitting inside on a beautiful late afternoon and cleaning lightbulbs? When there was a party to go back to? A party full of friends who loved and admired you and wanted to be with you?

"You're right. I do. It's my favorite thing."

"Good."

I got up from my chair and he scooted down on the sofa. He passed me a linen polishing rag and we quickly formed our own little obsessive assembly line.

Again we fell into silence. This time it felt much more comfortable. Like old times.

"You know, now that we're legally in business together, you can call me Mr. Monk. I won't mind."

"Sorry, Adrian."